W9-BRJ-469

Despite his threats a few moments before, she had sensed no real animosity in him. She'd been treated well since arriving at the Aerie. Her dream of a home, with people who cared about her, perhaps a family of her own, rose unbidden to her mind, and with it came a familiar lump in her throat. She was tired, she thought, to let that longing overwhelm her now. She folded her arms under her breasts and kept her eyes on the flames. She heard Toran move from the door to stand behind her. She tensed as his hands came to rest on her shoulders. He turned her gently, but irresistibly, to face him.

"What should I do with so beautiful, so valuable, a prize?" he murmured, almost to himself.

His deep blue gaze ensnared Aileana as completely as his hands. She knew she should be outraged at being called a prize. He'd done it before, on the way here. Did he truly see her that way? She refused to be chattel any longer, she told herself, and would not allow him to treat her so. But she found she could not summon her ire. One of his hands left her shoulder and he lightly touched her cheek, then slowly slid his fingers down her throat to her collarbone. There, he hesitated, and Aileana held her breath until he moved the hand back to her shoulder.

His simple touch sent shivers dancing and nearly undid her.

Praise for *HIGHLAND HEALER*

Winner (as *Warrior*) of the 2011 Marlene,
Paranormal Category

"A captivating hero and heroine and a deft plot make this a must-read historical romance."

~Rebecca York

~*~

"Lose yourself in this lush, romantic adventure by a new and gifted author."

~Kathryn Johnson, author of the award-winning
The Gentleman Poet

~*~

"Start reading and the rest of your day is shot. Definitely a winner!"

~Chassie West

~*~

"A unique story with just the right mix of romance and action—a truly enjoyable historical."

~Elizabeth Ashtree

~*~

"Being of Scottish descent, I greatly enjoyed the graceful interweaving of Scottish history and sense of place with the heartwarming love story."

~Nancy Baggett

To Dolores,
Enjoy!

Highland Healer

by

Willa Blair

Cheers,
Willa Blair

This is a work of fiction. Names, characters, places, and incidents are either the product of the author's imagination or are used fictitiously, and any resemblance to actual persons living or dead, business establishments, events, or locales, is entirely coincidental.

Highland Healer

COPYRIGHT © 2013 by Linda Williams

All rights reserved. No part of this book may be used or reproduced in any manner whatsoever without written permission of the author or The Wild Rose Press, Inc. except in the case of brief quotations embodied in critical articles or reviews.
Contact Information: info@thewildrosepress.com

Cover Art by *Tina Lynn Stout*

The Wild Rose Press, Inc.
PO Box 708
Adams Basin, NY 14410-0708
Visit us at www.thewildrosepress.com

Publishing History
First Faery Rose Edition, 2013
Print ISBN 978-1-61217-678-9
Digital ISBN 978-1-61217-679-6

Published in the United States of America

Dedication

To Ruth Glick (Rebecca York) and the rest of her awe-inspiring critique group: Chassie West,
Toby Devens, Elizabeth Ashtree,
Kathryn Johnson (Mary Hart Perry),
Nancy Baggett, Cronshi Englander,
Binnie Syril Braunstein, Connie Hay,
and Joyce Braga.
You've freely shared your wisdom, experience and humor. Thanks for your inspiration, encouragement, and occasional kick in the pants when I needed it!

~

And to Eileen Buckholz, who opened the door
all those years ago and dared me to walk through it.

~

And especially to my heroic husband.
Though he dedicated his life to his country,
he gave his heart to me.
Through all the years we've been together,
he has believed in my talent and supported my dream.
Most of all, this book is for you.

Acknowledgements

To misquote John Donne, no book is an island. Hours of research and soul searching by the author go into every one, along with ideas, techniques, and critique from others. This book is no exception.

The list of people I need to thank, in addition to the awe-inspiring authors mentioned in the dedication, includes the members of the Washington Romance Writers, the RWA Online, and the San Antonio Romance Authors chapters of RWA for inspiration, classes, speakers, and support.

I especially want to thank my fabulous TWRP Editor, Sarah Hansen, and my Beta reader, Dr. Lisa Benton-Short. You both saved me from myself throughout this book with your insights and eye for detail.

More thanks are due to my local color and dialect consultant, Lisa's husband, Dr. John Rennie Short. Any mistakes are entirely mine. Thanks, too, to the maternal member of the family, Bonnie Benton, who read the book after Lisa and has cheered me on ever since.

And finally, thanks to Tina Lynn Stout for cover art that blew me away. She listened to what I wanted, then gave me even more than I dared hope for.

Chapter One

Scottish Highlands, 1516

They brought the man into the tent on a makeshift stretcher, bound and unconscious. A hunting plaid of muted earth tones draped over his broad chest and across one muscular shoulder, where it fastened to his tunic with a simple brass pin. Quartz crystals decorated the open ends of a braided gold torc at his throat. That fact alone, that jewelry remained on his person, told Aileana that he was being accorded special treatment, not robbed like the common soldiers fallen on the field of battle. He would be a warrior, probably a laird, of the clan that Colbridge fought today.

She nodded for the stretcher bearers, two of Colbridge's strongest men, to put their burden down on the long table she used for her surgery. As her assistant Ranald limped in behind them, she saw guards standing just outside the tent's entrance and wondered how strenuously her new patient had objected to his captivity.

Ranald stood by the entry but his gaze stayed on the man on the table until the stretcher bearers left. "He's a chief."

Those few words explained both the man's presence here and his appearance. A valuable prize indeed, deliberately captured rather than killed. No small feat in the heat of hand-to-hand combat where killing came easy. Capture was not. Impressed, Aileana bent to determine the extent of his injuries.

"Make sure he lives," Ranald cautioned. "Colbridge brought this one to us during the battle."

Aileana straightened up and frowned in surprise toward the entry, but Ranald had already left her alone with her patient. She turned her attention back to the man on her table. He was another victim of Colbridge's ambitions. Like her. And like her, one with no chance of escape.

His soft linen tunic and leather breeches were of better quality than she'd seen on the other captives. Blood matted his shoulder-length dark hair and streaked both the side of his face and one strong arm revealed by a torn sleeve. She needed to remove the tunic and the torc around his neck to be certain his wounds were clean. But she did not want to turn him yet and possibly worsen other hurts she could not yet see. The strap that secured a sword's sheath lay buckled across his chest. The weapon itself was missing. Aileana supposed that one of Colbridge's men had claimed it, or even Colbridge himself.

Carefully, she undid that clasp and the one at his belt, and let the heavy leather and the end of the plaid fall aside to dangle off of the table out of the way. Next went the simple pin at his shoulder. Only then did she notice the pattern of his plaid. It appeared similar to the one most of the rest of the captives wore, but not exactly the same. She did not know enough about Highland clans to know what that meant. She laid it aside. With regret, she took her looted French scissors Colbridge had given her from the pocket of her dress and began cutting the tunic from the man's upper body.

After each snip of the blades, she lightly touched each area she revealed and let an awareness form in her mind and within her body, focusing on the soundness of each part beneath his summer-bronzed skin and firm flesh. She laid one palm against his chest, feeling the strength of the heart that beat within, the rise and fall of his breathing. She slid her hand down his ribs onto his belly. Strong muscles there, and no harm done. She moved to his arm next, relieved to find the cut moderate. His arm would be sore from a grazing blow by the flat of a blade that had left a gash, and be lucky to be no worse for the battle. It took little of her Gift to mend such a shallow wound. The Healing tingled as her fingers traced the edges of the cut. He would recover to fight again if the head wound had not addled his brain—and if Colbridge let him live.

She moved to his head and took a deep breath, gathering her strength for what could be a very difficult mending. He had escaped death so far, but the blow to his head might have destroyed his mind. Or only part of it. Her fingers clenched. The empty ones were the worst. But the need was strong in her to repair and restore—to heal. She could not stop now any more than she could stop breathing.

She slowly placed her hands along both sides of his face, then drew them up over his forehead into his hair, listening. The force of will that she encountered nearly sent her reeling. Relieved, she gently cradled his head and slid her hands to the back of his neck. Other than a shallow cut at the back of his scalp from the blow that had knocked him out, she could sense no deeper bleeding that would threaten his life or his mind. She mended the broken skin with a few gentle touches, glad that he had taken no further harm. He would awaken soon, with a massive headache. She would soothe that away when he could speak to her and she confirmed that his mind was whole.

She stood back and for the first time really looked at the man. What she saw took her breath away. Strong of limb and clean-lined, he boasted the massive shoulders and arms of a warrior. Despite the bindings that held them together palm to palm, she could see that his hands were large and calloused, probably from wielding one of the heavy longswords—claymores they called them here—as well as other hard work. Fine, dark hair swirled lightly across his heavily muscled chest and trailed down his flat belly to disappear beneath the leather trews that covered narrow hips and muscular thighs. A strong pulse beat in the brown column of his throat. And his face, under the blood and grime of battle, boasted even features: the nose unbroken, lips full, and eyelashes long and dark where they rested on high cheekbones.

As she regarded him, she fought the urge to caress his face with her fingertips. Tiny laugh lines around his eyes and mouth betrayed the only trace of the person within. For a moment, she allowed herself to imagine his smile. Her Talent did not help her with that. Though she often wished it would show her the past or the future, it persisted in showing her only the now and the needs of her patients, no more. Until he awoke, she would not know the color of his eyes, nor the temper of the spirit that dwelled within his massive body. She moved to her chair and sat down to wait.

****

4

Toran became aware of his surroundings slowly. First came the pounding in his head, painful evidence that he was not dead after all. He should be glad, he supposed, and would be when the infernal hammering stopped. Then he realized that his hands and feet were bound. He was a prisoner? How the devil had he allowed that to happen? His nostrils flared and he fought to remain still in case someone watched. Try as he might, he could not remember. His head hurt too much to concentrate. Instead, he kept his eyes closed, and listened intently for any sound that would give away the presence of a guard. The faint whisper of soft breathing told him someone else waited nearby. Distant shouts and clangs pierced the silence. Did a battle still rage?

What had happened to the two men who'd come with him to meet with the MacAnalen laird? Had they escaped, or were they dead on the field of battle?

He carefully tested the strength of his bonds and found them damnably sufficient to restrain him, at least for now. Focusing inside himself to gingerly catalog other aches, he tried to recall the last moments of the battle that brought him here. The usual residue of physical violence remained in the arms, shoulders, back, and legs, all of which were old companions, and none of which brought back any particular memories of the fight. Suddenly, he noticed cool air on his skin, skin that should not have been bare to any breeze. For a brief moment, he hoped he was wrong about being a prisoner. If he'd been stripped and left for dead on the battlefield...but nay. If that were true he wouldn't be bound.

A soft cough startled him and his eyes flew open.

He was surprised to see rough-spun cloth peaking over him, blocking the anticipated view of the sky. He turned his head slowly against the pain to survey the rest of his surroundings and saw a lass dozing in a chair set against the wall of the tent.

Only a lass to guard him? Was he injured worse than he kenned, then? Nay, none of the all too familiar pain that came with serious wounds plagued him, thankfully, except the damnable throbbing that threatened to split his skull. So he gathered his strength and pushed up to sitting. The tatters of his shirt fell away from his back, leaving him bare from the waist up. Dizzy fairies whirled in a mad dance before his eyes, then settled and disappeared as he pulled in a deep breath and bit back a curse.

He turned carefully and looked around the tent. One entry, flap askew just enough to show a sliver of trees, sky, and movement when anyone walked past, but not to allow anyone outside to see within. He sat on a table crisscrossed by his plaid, and by his belt and his claymore strap, which must have been unbuckled to allow his shirt to be cut from his body. He groped frantically at his throat as another thought occurred to him. A relieved breath gusted from his lips. The Lathan torc remained around his neck. That his claymore was missing failed to surprise him. He reached into his boot. His dirk…ach, gone, too. Damn. Injured, without weapons, and in a strange camp. He'd seen better days.

The only other furniture was the chair occupied by the bonny lass. Even in his present condition, he could appreciate her beauty. Auburn hair fell in a thick braid over her shoulder onto the nicely curved breast of her deep green dress. Slumped in her doze, he could not be sure, but she seemed tall and slender. Her face was fair, with smooth skin and full lips. Toran wondered why she alone attended him, why there were no guards in the tent, and why he was restrained so lightly by leather cords instead of chains. In time, he could weaken and break bonds such as these. Did they think him so enfeebled by battle wounds that a mere lass could hold him? He didn't ken whether to be insulted or embarrassed. But the question remained. What had happened to him and why didn't he remember? Why was he here and not dead on the battlefield?

He needed to get a look outside. If he could move quietly enough so as not to wake the lass, he could peer out the tent flap. His boots were lashed together with enough slack between them to hobble him, but not to prevent him from walking in some limited fashion. He considered trying to remove them, but the bindings around his ankles were too tight, and even if he got the boots off, he didn't want to lose them. He wouldn't get far on bare feet, so he'd have to find a way to cut the cord between them. First things first. He started to stand, teeth clenched against the throbbing pain that movement caused. But the table creaked as he gained his feet. The lass stirred, then blinked, and with dismay plain on her face, noted his position, half on, half off the table.

"Oh! You shouldn't be awake," she said, smoothing her dress as she stood and moving quickly to the tent's entry flap and peering out. Did she mean to leave or call the guards? He didn't want her to do either.

"Wait," he said, wincing. "I won't hurt ye. I want to look outside." He hoped his warning would allay any fears she might have. He kept his gaze on the entry as he stood the rest of the way up and hobbled carefully forward. He didn't want to seem threatening by staring at her, though she was worth gazing upon. As he approached, she stepped back. He pulled the flap a finger's width aside and peered out. Aye, he was held in the invader's camp, and things had not gone well for the MacAnalens. Judging by the few wearing MacAnalen colors that he could see, they, too, were bound in leathers, and talking to others beyond Toran's line of sight. And those were the guards, he supposed, facing this tent, sitting by a small fire. He could see plenty of men around similar fires within view. Too many. And a few more practicing at arms. Even a brief glance was enough to show him that he'd not walk out of here easily on his own. He hoped that a lot of MacAnalens survived. The more there were, the better the distraction whenever his own men arrived to free him, and the better all their odds of getting away.

He sighed and turned back to the lass, who stood quietly by as he peered out of the tent. As he faced her, she backed up a step, but only one. It puzzled him that being left alone with a strange man seemed to cause her so little concern for her own safety. She was no match for him, even with him injured, bound, and weaponless, but she neither called for help, nor tried to escape the confines of the tent. Instead, he saw with pleasure, she stood tall and proud.

If she was meant as a serving wench for an important prisoner, he might yet enjoy this captivity.

"Now that your curiosity is satisfied, you should not be on your feet," she said as she pulled him away from the entry toward the table. He nearly stumbled in the fetters, but her grip held firm, and he stayed upright. At the table, she urged him gently to sit, and then more forcefully said, *"Lie down."* He moved to obey before he could consider objecting. Her voice held a tone of command that he found he could not ignore. He lay back, puzzled. As he did, the pounding in his temples reached a new crescendo, preventing rational thought. He tried to stifle the groan, but it escaped. "Damn," he growled, lifting his bound wrists to his throbbing forhead.

"Ah, your head," she said, moving to the top of the table and leaning over him to push his arms down. With that nearness, her scent floated over him, softly pleasing, and something more...much more. His groin tightened in response. "This will help," she said and straightened, taking her scent with her.

He could not see what she did, but her fingertips whispered across the skin of his forehead to ruffle his hair, and the pounding receded.

"You took quite a blow," she said quietly. "'Tis a good thing you have a thick skull."

He could hear amusement in her voice, but felt none of his own, only relief. The pain continued to recede as her hands stroked gently over his forehead and down the sides of his face. Tension he was not aware of holding ebbed, and he sighed deeply.

"Who are ye?" he asked, feeling more and more at ease and drowsy as she continued, the pain blessedly fading away. "How can ye do that?"

"I should be asking the questions, don't you think?" Her voice projected calm reason, as if she was discussing nothing of importance. But she delivered her next question with more emphasis. *"Who are you?"*

"I am called Toran," he heard himself say, biting his tongue before he said the rest of his name. What was she doing to him?

"And you do not belong to this clan Colbridge fought today, do you?" she asked. "Your tartan is different than the ones the other prisoners wear."

Damn. Confusion and dismay washed over him and he reached for an answer that would satisfy the lass. He was in great danger here, bound and without his weapons in an enemy camp, but it would be worse if she found who he really was and told her leader. He'd fought with the MacAnalens, so the invaders probably believed he belonged with them, at least until she of the sharp eyes and soft hands noted the small differences in the tartan he wore.

"Aye," he improvised. "My clan is related."

"And you're a chief?" she asked, seeming to accept his evasion. She continued to stroke his neck and shoulders, her fingers brushing over his torc, and Toran's strange lassitude deepened, but not enough to halt his tongue.

"Aye," Toran admitted after struggling not to speak, his voice sounding curiously distant to his ears. He tried to clench his jaw shut, but found that he couldn't do it with her hands so warmly soothing on his skin. "Clan Lathan," slipped out before he was even aware he was about to speak. He groaned his dismay and tried to clamp his lips between his teeth, but numbness stole his ability to compress them. Was she a witch, then, he mused dreamily, to pull answers from him even when he did not wish to give them?

"Ah, well then; that is why Colbridge wanted you," he heard her murmur to herself as he slipped into a warm, blessedly pain-free sleep.

****

Gar Colbridge stood on the edge of the field of battle and looked around him with grim satisfaction. In the waning sunlight, the bodies of his enemies lay strewn like so much chaff across the landscape. A few of his men and some of the camp women picked through them, stripping useable clothing and searching for weapons and other valuables. Those, he knew, would be few and far between in this poor countryside.

"A good day, all in all," his master-of-arms remarked, dropping his reins and dismounting next to his commander's horse.

"Aye," Colbridge answered, giving a nod to the sturdily built man beside him who had, under his guidance, molded a ragtag band of reivers into a passably capable fighting force. "We've achieved what we meant to do this day, and reaped a bonus, too...the MacAnalen chief, alive."

He relished the moment, in the heat of the battle, when he'd recognized the clan leader. He had noticed the man's torc a moment before striking and turned his blow to disable rather than kill. Odd that none of the laird's men were nearby to defend him, but luck, it appeared, was in Colbridge's favor this day. The tides of battle must have swirled them away, leaving him the element of surprise.

A clan leader, even an inexperienced one, as most were these days, would be a valuable source of information about his own holdings, and those of his neighbors. Colbridge congratulated himself on his forbearance. "Aileana's tending him," he continued. "Once he's awake and talking, I'll have what I need from him, and then be done with him. Scotland lost many lairds at Flodden three years ago; one more won't matter."

He noticed a man roaming alone among the bodies, stooping now and again to examine one but taking nothing.

"Who's that? Ah, of course, Aileana's man, Ranald. He'll be looking for live ones, then, as if there are any worth keeping."

The wounded clansmen did not have the value of their laird, but some of them made acceptable additions to his army. Once their clan was broken, they had little choice but to join him or die. Many were so grateful for life and health after suffering grievous wounds that they took little convincing, especially the ones only Aileana could heal. Her abilities saved many when their wounds were beyond the care of the lesser healers.

She had talent, that one, and the Sight. While he had never yet been seriously injured in battle, with her considerable skills on his side, he believed that his conquest could not be stopped by the blows he might take in the future. That made him fearless, and feared. Word of his prowess traveled ahead of his army, so that a few clans surrendered rather than fight, and gained his protection. Not all. Not the MacAnalens today. They paid the price of defiance. Their dead lay before him. The rest were prisoners whose fate would be decided by the choices they made. Their women, children, and old ones huddled in their village, begging for mercy. He would give it. He had more important matters to attend to than his new subjects.

His companion's expression turned grim. "There were observers on the ridge early this day," he said.

Colbridge nodded with satisfaction. When the observers reported back, their unknown laird would have an advantage, but only briefly. "They'll know we're here, and in what strength," he said. He grabbed the reins and pulled his horse's head down, preparing to mount. "They hung back to assess the enemy rather than rushing in to defend another's turf. Just as I would have done." He considered his next moves and swung onto his horse. The observers would carry word of his prowess to the neighboring clans and villages. That was good, if they chose the wise course and surrendered to him. If not, well, he must find the observers' clan and destroy their ability to fight, or they'd be a viper at his back when he turned south.

"Get the men together," he ordered. "Send out scouting parties now and again at first light. Find the ones who watched, assess their strengths, and report back." His underling started to object, but Colbridge shouted over him, "We have no time to waste picking over the bodies of peat cutters and crofters. Go!"

His sense of satisfaction returned as he watched the man hurry to obey. A lightning strike and all would be over here in the north for the year. He would spend the winter at his keep in the south. It would be done.

Chapter Two

Toran came awake to the sound of men moving around outside the tent. Damn, whatever the healer had done to him had put him to sleep. He needed to stay awake if he was going to get out of here.

He listened intently, barely breathing, until the footsteps moved away. Just the guards changing, then?

Nay. He breathed a sigh of relief as he heard horses moving away from camp. A patrol going out. For one bad moment, he'd feared that they'd come for him. It was still black as pitch but it must be getting on toward morning. Their leader would not leave him here indefinitely.

He glanced around the tent. The interior was barely visible, but he could tell that the healer's chair was empty. Nor did she stand by the doorway. Where had she gone? Did she have somewhere else to sleep?

No matter. This was just the opportunity he needed. He sat up carefully, determined not to make any noise that would draw a guard. He stretched his bound hands over his head to wake up his arm and shoulder muscles, then began to twist and pull at the leather binding his hands together. If he could loosen the bonds, get even one had free, he'd have the use of his hands and arms and have a fighting chance. Though whether he could get free of a camp full of armed men, he had no idea. But if he could get these bonds off while it was still dark, he might manage to escape into the forest and make his way back to the Aerie. Or meet his people coming to look for him.

He worked for what seemed like hours, ignoring the pain and the dampness. The tough old leather was tearing the skin of his wrists and the abrasions bled. But if his blood softened the leather, it might stretch faster. He kept tugging, stopping every once in a while to rest his wrists and worry at the leather with his teeth. It was slow going. Painful. And bloody. But it was the best chance he had unless the healer came back with whatever she'd used to cut away his shirt.

Twice he was forced to stop and lie back as footsteps neared the tent he was in, but they passed on. He kept at it until warm wetness started to run down his arm. Even with the added slip of his own blood and saliva, he could not pull a hand through the loops. His wrists were raw and the bindings were still too tight. He had to stop before he did so much damage that he'd be unable to use his hands at all.

Resigned, he rested. Surely the healer would be back to check on her patient. Perhaps this time she'd bring a blade. He could wait for her to arrive.

****

Dawn had brightened the mists an hour earlier, and Aileana heard men on horseback leaving the camp soon after. Rather than get up, she claimed the luxury of dozing a while longer, taking advantage of the relative quiet that followed their departure.

At rest in her solitary blankets, she recalled Toran's efforts to resist her questions, something no one before had been able to do. That worried her. Worse, she'd been a fool, dozing off instead of keeping watch over him. There was no question in her mind that even bound, he was fully capable of injuring or killing her before she could say a word to him or could scream for the guards. But he had not harmed her.

Instead, he'd focused on learning more about his enemy, as any warrior would do. She'd held herself still, but had fought back tears as he'd peered out of the tent for the first time and seen what he was up against. No escape. She used to dream of it, of finding a crofter who would shelter her, or disappearing into woods too thick for Coldbridge's men to pursue her, anything that would lead to returning to what remained of her village. However, after the first summer passed and winter threatened, she became resigned to her fate. As Toran would.

He appealed to her in a way that was new to her, pleasurable yet also a little frightening. As a healer, and a daughter and granddaughter of healers, she knew what happened between a man and a woman, but she'd never experienced it herself. She turned and punched the bag of rags that served as her pillow, trying to achieve some comfort. And, if she were to be honest, trying to distract herself from the memory of his handsome face, his strong body that so pleased her eye, his... Oh, damn. This was hopeless. She might as well get up.

It would be wise to check on her patient before he awoke. There would be less temptation that way, on her side and his, assuming that a handsome laird such as he would have any interest in a simple lass from a small village such as she. All the more reason to control her wild imaginings, check on her patient, and see him taken out with the other prisoners. Then she could soon forget him. Breakfast would have to wait until she finished doing all that.

As expected, Toran still slept when Aileana slipped softly into the Healer's tent and paused by the entrance. He lay on his side, facing the doorway. The deep blue eyes she'd admired yesterday were closed, his head pillowed on his bound hands. Her newfound resolve crumbled as she watched his chest move with his breath, and she wondered what it would be like to remove his bonds and feel his arms wrap protectively around her. Except to take her arm and hurry her along, no one ever touched her. Not even Ranald dared more than that.

Aileana shuddered to think what Ranald would make of her interest in her present patient if he knew. Ranald was the son of her father's first wife. Despite being only a handful of years her senior, silver glittered in the dark hair at his temples, giving him an appearance of experience and wisdom. Since he had been fostered away after his mother died, Aileana rarely saw him while she was growing up in the village. She'd been shocked to find him attached to Colbridge's army. His battles were fought before she encountered him, including the one that nearly cost him his leg. To keep himself alive and of value, he'd been using the simple treatment skills he'd learned from her mother during his rare visits to his father. She'd recognized him immediately, and they had protected each other since. She made it clear he was useful to her and he made it clear she was off limits. In fact, it had been Ranald who had started the tale that her Healing was tied to her maidenhood. He would be concerned about her interest in this patient, this Toran, Laird Lathan. Ranald would think her a silly girl, indeed, to risk everything that had kept her safe so far.

Aileana moved silently to Toran's side and raised her hands over him, intending to monitor the beat of his heart and the depth of his breathing.

Instead, he rolled to sitting, jerked her off her feet and hauled her against his bare chest within the circle of his bound arms. "Look what I've caught," he murmured. "The healer. What are ye doing here alone? Where are the guards?"

"Outside," she gasped, answering his last question first, since it only required one word and she didn't have breath for more at that moment. "I've come to...to see how you fare," Aileana stammered, still breathing heavily from the surprise and the exertion of struggling within the circle of his impossible strength. She'd wished for his arms around her, and here she found herself. She wrenched her attention back to the very real man in front of her. She kept her voice low, not wanting the guard to overhear, rush in, and attack. Not yet, anyway. If need be, she could scream. "I did not mean to wake you, only to see if you were recovered."

"And ye would know that merely by watching me sleep?"

Aileana could see he was wide awake now, and studying her intently as he held her. That regard gave her pause. How to answer him? She was a Healer, not a witch, but an ignorant Highlander might not know the difference, even if that ignorant Highlander was a laird. She'd heard they burned and drowned witches in the south. She had no intention of meeting either fate.

"By your breathing, and repose," she finally answered. "If you were still in pain, you might have slept fitfully, or not at all. But I see that you are rested and well recovered."

"Recovered?" One eyebrow lifted, as if he didn't recall being wounded, and didn't know what she meant. That gave her a bit of confidence that he wasn't completely resistant to her will.

"I believe I am," he continued, studying her face. He gave her a small smile. "I suppose ye want me to put ye down." His regard never wavered, but his tone softened and his vise-like grip on her relaxed as he leaned forward and set her on her feet.

"Aye." She'd replied with the only proper thing to say. Although, her body reveled in the sensation of his arms around her, and she wasn't sure she wanted to be released. Had she lost her mind? She chided herself again for her foolish fantasies. It was one thing to imagine herself in the arms of the man as he slept, and quite another to consider it when he was wide-awake and looking at her in that...way. Oh, but he tempted her beyond reason, with his deep blue eyes drinking her in; his full lips, now slightly parted as if he contemplated kissing her senseless. Senseless she was to even be imagining it.

He lifted his arms, releasing her, but as she stepped back, he reached out and cupped her face with warm fingers. She gasped at the sudden sensations that gentle touch evoked, so different from the effortless strength he had used to lift and restrain her. The heat from his fingers on her face nearly burned her, yet chills skittered down her neck, across her shoulders, and she fought the urge to lift her fingers to his lips in turn.

"Ye're a bonny lass..." he whispered.

Her shiver of anticipation surprised her, and she

firmly stifled it. Instead of giving in to the yearning to feel his warm skin under her fingers, she stepped back out of his reach.

"Don't...you can't...touch me," she breathed, still fighting the power of her desire to hold the warmth of his face in her palm.

"But lass, I already did," he said, looking her up and down and grinning, but making no move toward her.

A small, mirthless chuckle escaped Aileana. Aye, he had. It had all happened so fast, and she'd been so lost in her own sensations that she'd protested too late.

From the dubious safety of her position a step away from him, she studied him. He seemed well enough to go out with the other prisoners. He could not languish here in the Healer's tent. She might soon have others to care for. Then she noticed the skin of his wrists around his bindings. Red, raw, oozing blood in a few places. He'd tried his bonds, but hadn't succeeded in breaking them. Not yet.

"That must hurt," she said, stepping forward to take his wrists in her hands.

He didn't answer, merely shook his head, eyeing her.

"Not much," he finally relented, shrugging his big shoulders. Should she leave the wounds alone, and let the pain deter him from straining further against his bonds? Or heal his wounds and hope he'd have better sense? No, of course he would not. He would continue to try to escape. As, she supposed, he thought he should.

Her hands moved almost of their own accord, and her healing energy flowed into the skin she touched.

After only a moment he jerked away, long before she finished. "What are ye doin'?" he demanded.

She let him go. It was foolish, even dangerous, to try to continue. Wide-awake, he could sense something happening where she touched him. Her compulsion to heal would get her killed yet.

"Ye did something to take away the ache and make me sleep." He rubbed his forehead, eyes closed, frowning, as he tried to remember. His words froze her in place, and she knew she must divert him, or he might just stop wondering *who* and begin to wonder *what* he was dealing with. His next statement frightened her even more. "And while ye did, ye asked who I am, and I told ye, though it pained me to do it."

Remembering the Healing was one thing, but he should not be able to remember her laying the compulsion to speak upon him! "Your pain resulted from a blow by the flat of a blade to your thick skull," she replied tersely, more worried than she dared show. She struggled not to cross her arms defensively across her chest.

There was danger in this man, many kinds of danger. How could he resist her will, while ensnaring hers so that she took chances like this? What was she thinking? The sooner she got away from him, the better. "It's your good luck that your head's still attached to your neck," she continued in the same curt tone, still trying to divert him from his memory of the day before. If she could distract him, perhaps it would fade away, as it should have before he awoke, and she would be able to convince him it had been a dream.

He did seem distracted, Aileana thought as he frowned and fingered the torc at his throat.

He stood then and moved carefully around her, hobbled by the fetters, but giving her room enough so as not to feel threatened. He shuffled to the tent's entry and peered out through the narrow slit. "How long have I been here?" he asked.

Aileana breathed a sigh of relief as he changed his focus from her to his situation. "You were injured yesterday in the battle with the local clan."

"Yesterday," he said, and sounded relieved, as if he feared he'd been here longer. "Yesterday, ye stood by as I looked outside. Why did ye not run from the tent or scream for the guards?"

"Because I deemed it better to allow you to satisfy your curiosity, so you would know you are outnumbered and cannot escape."

"Ye must have a name. What are ye called? And why are ye here with this army?" He turned away from the entry to pin her in place with his gaze.

There was no help for it. She'd taken his identity; now he wanted hers.

"Aileana. Aileana Shaw. Or Healer."

"Ach, from the low country, are ye?"

"Aye. Colbridge destroyed my village. My family died. A woman alone, I had nowhere else to go. So I'm the Healer." She should have said "his healer" but she knew if she phrased it that way, any chance of Toran trusting her would disappear. She wanted him to trust her. But why?

"How long ago did that happen?"

"Summer, two years gone."

"The summer after the massacre at Flodden Field, aye?"

Aileana shook her head. "Flodden Field?"

"Surely ye heard of it? James IV died along with most of his nobles and lairds at the hands of the Sassenach…the English. 'Tis why there's a bairn on the Scottish throne."

"Oh, aye. I've heard Colbridge say that the Highland clans have been ripe for the picking with none left but women and children. That must be why."

Quiet settled into the tent, but the peace was illusory. Aileana had seen the result of the events Toran described. Wherever Colbridge went, Highlanders joined with him or died. So far, he had taken many lives, warriors and innocents alike. She feared the struggle would leave them all too weak to repel the English who harried the borders from the south.

The wind had begun to shift out of the north, a bad sign. This summer, Colbridge's army had cut a swath into the Highland mountains, but winter threatened in the chilly mists and the mellowing color in the leaves. Colbridge was running out of time to return to the Lowlands for the winter.

Nothing good ever came of haste in war.

Toran straightened and moved away from the entry, taking small, careful steps that had to be difficult for a man his size. But it was that or trip over the leather cord between his feet. He moved around the table, inspecting the paltry furnishings in the tent—the table and chair. And her. She saw him eye the tatters of his shirt on the table. He must be looking for the tool that she'd used to cut his linen.

"Colbridge?" he said as he picked up his crumpled plaid and tossed it over one shoulder. Bound, he could not wrap his belt around himself without lying back down on the table. Aileana moved to assist him.

"He leads this army," Aileana answered as she buckled his belt over the ends of his plaid. Her breath caught as her knuckles brushed against the heat of his belly. For a moment, he froze, then he exhaled and picked up the claymore strap, staring at the dangling sheath as if expecting his sword to appear within it.

"So, Healer," he said, calmly, making a simple statement of fact, "it was yer task to question me while I lay half asleep and less likely to govern my tongue."

Aileana blanched. She'd had no business asking him his name, but her curiosity often got the best of her, just as it was doing now. If Colbridge knew she'd been talking to his prisoner, he'd be furious.

"Nay," she admitted, head down. "I only wondered. You seemed…different."

"Different?" He bunched the leather strap in his hand and dropped the whole thing back on the table, as if dismissing it when it failed to produce his weapon.

"Aye," she murmured, not daring to say what about him was really different—his ability to attract and ensnare her. "Your tartan…"

Toran began his hobbled pacing again, making a circle around the table and her, getting better at moving, his bonds affecting his balance not at all. "How many men does he have? How big is this camp?" He stopped in front of her, not touching her, but effectively trapping her between the table and his large, intimidating self. He held his hands out toward her, as if asking her silently, so as not to be overheard, to cut his bonds with the knife or scissors that he thought she must have. But she'd left them in her sleeping tent. She could do nothing to help him. But would she, if she had them? Did she dare defy Colbridge so openly?

She shook her head and held out empty hands in silent response to his unspoken entreaty, then answered his spoken one. "I don't know. The number changes every time he fights."

He dropped his arms and stepped back, but she doubted he would give up so easily. With a shrug, he ran his bound hands down her skirt until he located the pocket low on her right hip. She held herself still as he searched even though heat lightning shot from every place he touched. She knew the pocket was empty. Now he did, too. She suspected that he regretted it no more than she did.

She loathed Colbridge for his brutality toward his prisoners and his men, but she stayed with him because she had nowhere else to go. And because she believed that she was safer under his protection than she could ever be on her own. But she also depended on more than Colbridge's orders to his men to leave her alone for her safety. Out of his sight, they could be tempted to try anything. So she allowed the misunderstanding be taken as truth: that her Healer's talent depended on her remaining untouched. Colbridge and his men believed that once taken, she would lose the healing powers that they depended on to restore them to health and strength if they were injured in battle. Those who thought to try her quickly learned their lesson, usually at the hands of their comrades-in-arms who believed that having her skills available outweighed any momentary lusts, or any fears that she might truly be a witch.

Aileana took a deep breath. It was a mistake. With Toran so close, his scent surrounded her, filled her lungs, and the longing within her intensified. She struggled to focus on what she needed to say to him.

"And the MacAnalens?" he continued, as if nothing had happened, and she had not just denied him some measure of freedom. "The clan he fought yesterday. They're prisoners?"

"Aye," she answered, seeing no harm in telling him that news. "If they join with Colbridge, they'll live." But that was not enough information. He needed to know. "He'll kill any who refuse."

That set him on his heels. Frowning, he began to pace again. "Where is Colbridge?"

"I don't know." She fought back the tears that threatened to spill as she realized that the same choice would likely not be offered to a laird, no matter his clan, whose presence might undermine Colbridge's authority. She barely had time to digest that disturbing idea, when he continued.

"Ye were able to make me answer ye, though I fought against it," he said, a hard, undeniable statement of fact. He allowed her no chance to revise his recollection. "What else did ye make me do?" As he rounded the table behind her, he stopped pacing and settled one hip on the edge of the table. "What else did ye do to me?"

She had to lie. She refused to look at him as she said, "Nothing save soothe your headache." She prayed he would not ask her how she'd accomplished these things.

"Ye're his healer. Why should I believe ye?"

Her earlier phrasing mattered little, it seemed. This laird was too clever by far. "Because I've told you all I can." She hoped he would accept that and stop interrogating her.

"Or all ye should?"

"All I can," she repeated, suddenly wondering why she risked telling him anything at all. She owed this man nothing. She was attracted to him, true, but it was also true that Colbridge would not be pleased if he found out about this conversation. She risked much, and for what?

Toran fell silent after that, thinking, glancing toward the entry, then back at her, then back to the entry, as if concocting some plan to escape. That, she knew, was not possible. Too many of Colbridge's men camped nearby, a guard outside the tent and others not far away.

"And what's to be done with me?" He stood and splayed his hands on the table, leaning toward her across its suddenly much too narrow top. He locked his gaze on her, and refused to let her look away.

"I don't know." She answered truthfully if not completely, disturbed by the odd mixture of vulnerability and confidence she saw in his eyes. "That's up to Colbridge." Colbridge would surely want to get all the information that he could from this prisoner, but it was not Aileana's place to discuss that. She feared that with Toran's innate strength of will, it would go hard for him. Colbridge would not be denied any information that he wanted. She had seen the results of his efforts to break a prisoner who wouldn't talk. Toran would be back for more of her care, with wounds much more serious than she had treated yesterday, before Colbridge finished with him. And when Colbridge did finish with him...no, she would not think about that.

Saddened by Toran's prospects, she moved away, trying to put distance between herself and the fate she saw before him. She paused in the doorway of the tent, out of his long reach. From there, she could duck outside where the guards would see her and come to her aid if he tried to restrain her again. She no longer trusted that she could control him with her Voice. "Now that you're feeling better," she told him, "the guards will put you with the other prisoners."

When he didn't react, she took pity on him and added, "I'll send food and drink before they do." With that, she ducked through the entry, the urge to run warring with the urge to stay and give the doomed man the one thing he'd not quite asked for: herself.

****

Cool morning mist pooled in the valleys and steamed off the burns of Colbridge's new holding. The fog hid most of the landscape, but he followed a path, little more than a cattle track, as it wandered upward over a ridge and into the hills. Trees grew in dense clumps in the deepest glens, but thinned out quickly at higher elevations, leaving no cover save the mist. The call of a golden eagle on the hunt pierced the stillness.

The scene was eerie enough to make him wary and he ordered his men to silence, suddenly fearing that the fog could hide an entire army. They rode slowly and cautiously on their way back to camp, alert to any sound their horses did not make. The level of concentration that he demanded was beginning to take its toll on men not yet rested from the contest the day before. A badger returning late to its burrow crossed their path and growled a challenge that startled the horses. Soon after, they came to a small burn in a ravine and he called a halt.

"Water the horses and stretch your legs." Colbridge

swung off his mount and reached into his pack for some of the bread and cheese he carried. "Keep your eyes and ears open. We're getting closer to camp, but scouts from other clans could be anywhere."

Leather creaked as the men dismounted. Relieved of their burdens, the horses sank their noses in the cold water.

"Dorton, head downstream on foot. Carey upstream. Keep an ear out and signal if anything moves."

"Aye." Dorton hooked a thumb at Carey. "We're off." He picked up his horse's reins and led it off at a steady pace into the fog. Carey soon disappeared in the opposite direction.

Colbridge allowed himself to take his ease. With two scouts flanking the main party, one or the other would make it back to give warning if needed. He began to regret not waiting for the sun to rise far enough to burn the mist away. In the clear, they would be able to see from ridge to ridge and spot riders while still well away. Of course, his own group would be more visible, too, but he was confident that they could overcome any challengers they could see.

The observers on the ridge had been identified and the route to their holding described, under some duress, by one of the surviving MacAnalens. It always pleased Colbridge to demonstrate his dominance over these Highland savages. As for the observers, he'd let them dither for a few days before giving them the choice to join him or die.

Settling his back against a rock a few steps from his horse, he studied his men while he ate. They looked tired but alert, and he saw more than one watching the mist while they rested. He heard little conversation and that at a whisper. He had turned this rabble into seasoned warriors. Pride suffused him at this accomplishment, small though it stood against his greater goals. He had subdued every challenger. He deserved to be laird of all the Highland clans and he would be. It mattered little whether the title was bestowed upon him by the regent or by that infant on the throne to the south. After all his victories, they would have to acknowledge him.

He heard the thunder of rapidly approaching hoofbeats—many of them. He surged to his feet, dropping the remains of his meal. This was not a single rider, Dorton or Carey, returning. This had to be trouble.

As the first stranger on horseback broke through the mist, he cried, "Up, men, up!" and swung into his saddle. He wrestled his mount around to face the oncoming horses. His men moved quickly to their mounts, but just as quickly, five more men on horseback charged out of the haze after the first, swords drawn and swinging.

Despite the surprise, Colbridge's pulse ignited with sheer exultation. He lived for battle, for victory. This small band would be no challenge to his men, who had defeated an entire clan the day before. It mattered not if his forward scouts were already taken or would circle back to join the fray. He would prevail.

Shouts and ringing blades on blades broke the silence of the mist. Horses screamed and hoofbeats drummed on the rocky ground. He thrust and parried, drawing blood from an adversary whose horse carried him away into the melee. He whirled in his saddle as some sixth sense warned him of a foe at his back. A large Highlander swung his blade, and Colbridge jerked his mount to the side. The impact slammed into his shoulder and back, and then his attacker was set upon by another of his men, and disappeared into the mist.

Suddenly, it seemed that men and horses moved in surreal silence. Blades bounced off blades without ringing. Mouths opened in soundless screams. Colbridge didn't notice the blood streaming down his arm until he saw his sword drop from nerveless fingers. He retained enough presence of mind to know his danger. Abandoning his men to the fight, he rode as hard as he could back toward his camp. He felt his horse increase its pace and he held on, his vision wavering.

Aileana would fix this.

Chapter Three

"Aileana!" Ranald's urgent call brought the Healer running from her sleeping tent where she'd returned with her breakfast after sending food to Toran. The camp had gone dead still and silent. When she saw who Ranald led toward her Healer's tent, she knew the reason. Colbridge, covered in blood, slumped, cursing, over the neck of his lathered and blowing horse.

"Get him down," she ordered the men who stood frozen in place by the spectacle. She ran to the Healer's tent, intending to lay Colbridge out there, but remembered Toran as she reached the door flap.

Entering quickly, she was relieved to see him on his feet facing her, claymore sheath in hand. He nodded, clearly aware of the commotion.

"Go with the guard." At least she would not have to waste time getting him out of the way. "Andrew!" As the guard entered, she gestured to Toran. "Take him to the other prisoners and keep him there. Colbridge needs my help in here."

She was not so distracted that she did not see the musing look Toran gave her as he moved carefully to the door, mindful of the leather cord that hobbled his movement. It took only a moment, but the size and sheer presence of the Lathan laird gave her pause. Too late, she realized that her comment would allow him to recognize his captor. Keen wit glinted in those eyes, assessing her and the situation around him. But he left the tent quietly enough. Aileana followed him outside.

There Colbridge stood slumped, supported by two of his warriors. He was pale but conscious enough to eye the prisoner as he passed by under guard. "MacAnalen!" Aileana heard him mutter. "You'll pay for this."

A look of surprise crossed Toran's face and he cut his gaze to Aileana, then quickly looked away. Andrew prodded him to keep moving. In that moment, she realized that Colbridge did not know whom he held prisoner.

Then Colbridge wilted between the men supporting him, and Aileana had no time to ponder that startling fact, or to wonder what Toran might imagine to be her reason for not betraying him to her chief.

"Bring him in," she told the men and reentered the tent. Ranald followed, and the men supporting her patient came right behind him. "On the table." She cleared away the tray and cup, all that remained of the Highlander's breakfast, and worked to gain the calm that she required to do what she must. Too many distracting thoughts would keep her from the focus she needed. The men laid their burden down, and she waved them out. Ranald stayed, watching her.

"How was he injured?" She raised her hands and began her assessment, knowing Ranald would not remain for long.

"He went out this morning to survey his new territory. So far, he's the only one returned." Ranald said volumes in a few quiet words. Never before had Colbridge been a casualty. That might mean that they'd met an overwhelming force, which could now be on the way here. Or they'd met a scouting party who were simply much better fighters than the MacAnalens had been yesterday. Either way, it did not bode well if they meant to finish this campaign and leave these mountains before winter set in. And with their leader down, his army might fall apart and none of them survive the day.

Aileana met Ranald's impassive stare with one of her own and then turned back to Colbridge. She suspected she knew what went on behind Ranald's expressionless eyes. Colbridge lay pale as death. Blood soaked the tunic and leathers meant to protect his upper body, and pooled on the table beneath him. The metallic tang of it filled the tent. If she let him die, Aileana fretted, what would be the consequence? Another pretender? More battles and more death? Was he really any worse than any other who might follow him? His methods were more brutal than necessary to achieve his ends, but he'd come so close to having everything he'd fought for—including, she hoped, peace.

Yet she knew what likely lay in store for Toran Lathan if Colbridge survived this day. Could she condemn the laird who so captivated her to die slowly, in agony, at this man's hands? Or did her contempt for Colbridge influence what she thought he'd do? And what did she really know about Toran...Laird Lathan? Perhaps he was as bad as Colbridge, or worse. He wore the body of a hardened warrior. He'd fought; he'd very likely killed, for his clan. Did that make him any better than the man on her table? How could she know which was the right path to take?

Then she recalled the calm certainty in her

mother's voice as she'd told her daughter and apprentice, "Our place is to care for the wounded and the ill, no more than that."

Aileana took a deep breath and shook off her doubts. She had no choice. She placed her hands a breath above the slope of Colbridge's shoulder. Her Talent told her much more about the injury than her eyes alone.

"He's lost a lot of blood. His collarbone is broken," she told Ranald, her voice even, betraying none of her concerns, "but he'll live. Get the leathers off him while I stop the bleeding and check for other wounds."

Ranald scowled and opened his mouth to speak. Aileana frowned and shook her head, demanding his silence, and his compliance. His teeth clenched on what he intended to say and with none of his usual care quickly stripped Colbridge's upper body. Then he turned Colbridge's limp form to bare the ugly gash that split the top of his shoulder and ran in a deep slice along his back to the shoulder blade. She'd seen worse, but this would tax her energy. She'd sensed no other injuries, so went back to the shoulder.

Ranald stepped back as she began. On his way out of the tent, he turned and announced, "I'll have food and drink waiting for you when you finish." Then he left.

She sighed and tried to put Ranald out of her mind so she could set to work closing the wound, knitting bone, muscle, and tendon. Ranald's comment reminded her of the many times he'd provided for her when she was too exhausted to see to her own needs after a difficult healing session. Was he trying to make amends? Or trying in a subtle way to tell her that he would support her if she changed her mind and let Colbridge die?

In the time that passed while she worked, no attack came. Despite her concentration, she heard several men from Colbridge's scouting party calling out as they straggled into camp. The sounds seemed distant and faint, and she quickly forgot them as she focused on the minute repairs that severed blood vessels and nerves required. At last, Aileana finished. Exhausted, she left her patient to recuperate on his own, and ducked out of the tent.

She found Ranald on a bench he'd placed near the entry. He held a tray filled with bread and cheese. Two tankards of mead waited beside him, untouched. Without a word, he handed her one tankard and she drained it quickly. Collapsing beside him, she consumed the food and the second tankard. Finally she could speak. "He'll be fine, but he'll sleep the rest of this day and night. In the morning, he'll need broth and mead before other food to help him replace the blood and strength he's lost."

"I know, Aileana," Ranald said quietly. She was aware that he chided her gently because of her fatigue. They'd been through this many times. Ranald knew what to do.

But she saw his tension in the stiff way he sat and stared off into space, and knew that he disapproved of her saving Colbridge. She doubted that she approved, either. But she had followed her mother's teachings and done as she had been trained to do. She dared not stray from that path. There was little else left to her. No home, no parents, no real friends. Just her God-given Talent and her training, to be used to the best of her ability. She did not wish to decide who should live and who should not. After she did all she could do, whether her patient lived or died was in God's hands, as it should be.

"And what of the rest of the scouting party?" Aileana asked.

"Half made it back and have been cared for," Ranald answered simply. "They reported that they drove off the raiders. Escaped them is more likely."

Grateful for the news that there were no other urgent needs for her Talent, she raised a hand in weary salute, stood, and crossed back to her sleeping tent with nothing on her mind but getting the rest she required after an intense healing session.

But oblivion eluded her as she remembered the scene between Colbridge and the laird called Toran. Colbridge held the chief of an unknown clan already in his clutches, but knew it not. That Aileana did know gave her an unaccustomed sense of power.

While she enjoyed some small status as the Healer, she lived at Colbridge's beck and call. Her Talent was her protection. No one accosted her, but no one accepted her, either. Here she had neither friend nor foe, only wary companions among the other healers. Even Ranald kept a circumspect distance.

What would her life be like, she mused, if Toran, who could captivate her with a look or a gentle touch, made her his own? Could he give her the home she missed? Was the attraction between them something real or something borne of her longing for a different way of life, a different use for her Talent? This would bear thinking about. While she did, Toran's secret was safe with her.

****

A chill breeze laden with the remnants of morning mist swirled in the shade under the tree where guards had tied Toran. Some of the leaves overhead were still green, but most were tinged with rust and gold. Autumn had begun to paint them with bright hues, but Toran suspected jealous winter snow waited, not far off, to strip the branches bare with cold and wash the colors away. Shirtless, Toran hunkered down and tried to keep warm.

The survivors of the MacAnalen fighting force, hands and feet securely bound with leather strips, sat or stretched out on the ground, leaving a clear space around each. Two guards walked slowly among the prisoners, then joined other soldiers at a nearby fire to warm up. Toran kept an eye on them, knowing they or others like them would be back. It was fortunate that the tartans of the two clans were so similar. Except for the torc that had probably saved his life, Toran blended in with the other captives.

Toran's men were missing, which worried and saddened him. Had they fallen in the conflict or gotten away to carry the warning to the Aerie? Nor was the MacAnalen laird anywhere in sight, and Toran feared he'd met his fate on the field of battle. The leader of these invaders, Colbridge, had threatened Toran on his way from the healer's tent, and clearly mistook him for the laird of this clan. Toran couldn't decide whether that gave him some advantage or not. But he was disturbed by the fact that the invader needed the services of the healer a day after routing them. Did the battle still rage closer to the Aerie, and were Toran's men caught up in it as they searched for him?

If he weren't bound, he'd kick himself for ignoring Donal's warnings. He should not have been out of the Aerie, not after the news had come of the rabble headed their way. But the meeting had been set with the local lairds a month past and no one expected an invader to arrive so quickly. It was just bad luck that Toran had stayed behind after the meeting to consult another day with the young MacAnalen, which was why he'd wound up fighting alongside his hosts. Damn fool stunt, that's what Donal would call it, especially since it had gotten him captured for his troubles. It could have gotten him killed.

The captives around him carried on subdued conversations among themselves. Several greeted him quietly after the guards who'd tied him to a tree left the area. A few complained that as their closest neighbors and advocates of the peacemaking talks, the Lathans should have supported them in the battle. Angus MacAnalen, one of the MacAnalen chieftans, who sat nearby Toran, quickly silenced them.

"Stop yer foolish blather," he warned them. "If our runners had gotten through, the Lathans would have fought with us." He slanted a look at Toran.

"Aye," Toran agreed, keeping his voice low, "and now that I'm overdue, my men will come looking for me. We'll all get out of here then." Angus and his men could count on the Lathans for support when the need arose. Despite the old lairds' feuding before Flodden, their clans had long been linked by fostering and marriage.

That got a chorus of nods and soft "ayes" until Angus again motioned them to silence by opening one bound hand and closing it into a fist, not wanting to draw the guards' attention.

"How long before yer clan arrives, do ye think?" Angus quietly asked Toran.

"Not long," Toran replied. "If my men got away, they could have reached the Aerie during the night and be on their way back now. Perhaps the invaders' leader was injured by Lathan scouts on their way here."

"Injured?"

"Aye, he went into the Healer's tent with a sword cut to the shoulder. He'll be out of action for a while, perhaps permanently."

"That's good news," Angus replied. "Cut off the head and the body dies. We may yet get out of this with our skins whole."

Toran studied his surroundings, noting the size and strength of the invading force encamped here. He tried to ignore the chill that crept down his naked back with every breeze. What he saw surprised him. The army was not a large one, nor was it well supplied, so far from home. But it was large enough to take on Highland clans, crofts, and villages decimated by the loss of their most experienced fighting men three years ago. And here it camped, within hailing distance of Toran's home. But the Aerie would be a much more difficult challenge for this rabble.

The type of restraints they used spoke volumes, too, as the MacAnalens were bound as Toran was, hands in front. "Angus, why have yer men no' untied each other?" Toran asked. "We must break free. According to the Healer, those who don't join with this Colbridge are put to the sword."

"We wondered why they left us here. They must be waiting for their leader to decide what to do with us,"

Angus mused, then shrugged and continued. "They don't want to bind our hands behind our backs because they'd have to feed us, or untie us to take care of necessities." He gestured at the space between his men. "That's one thing the guards do enforce. If we get too close to each other, they move us farther apart. As long as they see enough ground between us, they stay by the fire."

"Best yer men start working their bonds loose while the guards are over there, then," Toran whispered. "Donal won't bring in more than a scouting party until he kens what he's up against. There won't be enough men to cut everyone loose and fight off Colbridge's guards, too."

"Aye," Angus agreed. He passed the order to the men around him in a low voice and told them to tell the others. "When the guards come this way, stop what ye're doing," he warned. "Have a care, lads. That lot will stay by the fire most of the time, but others may not."

Toran was gratified to see that the MacAnalen captives retained the sense to be careful. If a few could get free, they could help free the others when the time came. Toran kept his gaze moving around the camp as he carefully flexed and stretched the leather binding his hands. His efforts in the Healer's tent that caused the abrasions on his wrists had resulted in a small measure of space, but not enough to slip his hands through the loops, and not enough to break the bindings. He kept working, stilling only when the guards moved their way, and beginning again as soon as the guards turned their backs.

Eventually, another low rumble of conversation

caught his attention. He turned to see what interested the men and saw the Healer cross the camp. The skirt of her green kirtle swirled around long legs as she strode, then draped over a pleasantly rounded backside as she bent to enter a small tent.

Toran's pulse kicked up at the sight of her. What was it about that Healer that drew him so?

"There's a lovely lass," one of the men said, leering after her and distracting Toran from his troublesome thoughts. "Had we won the field yesterday, there might have been a better use for these fetters on her." He tugged on the leathers binding him to the tree. "Just let me get free of here and..."

"And what?" one of his fellow prisoners jeered. "That's the Healer, ye fool. She has the Sight and can make yer puny manhood wane even smaller than it already is. If ye cross her, even the wee fairy maidens willna have a use for it."

"Aye," a third man laughed. "If she hears ye prattlin' on this way, ye might begin ta feel a certain shrinking, even now."

The first man got a worried look on his face, then growled as the men around him laughed. "Go on w'ye," he barked.

Someone hissed, "Now look what ye've done— here come the guards."

Indeed, the two guards who'd made a round earlier were joined by another of the invaders. They stayed together, but looked the bound men over, one at a time, as they moved among them.

Toran recognized the tactic, meant to intimidate and to quell the rising spirits of the prisoners. "Keep quiet, do you hear?" one of the guards finally demanded, kicking the nearest prisoner before the three turned and walked back to their bonfire.

"With their chief under the care of the Healer," Angus whispered to Toran, "it seems they lack the stones for more confrontation than that."

"What do ye ken about the Healer?" Toran asked.

"We've heard she's a captive, too," Angus began, "but the benefits of her skills award her the freedom of the camp." Angus hesitated, then at Toran's nod, went on, "The men may have the right of it," he said, clearly troubled by the subject. "Some of our men were seen to take grievous wounds in the battle, yet they sit among us, whole and healthy, just hours after they were taken near death to her tent, with no memory of their injuries. Had only one claimed to see this, I'd lay it to the confusion of the battle, but there are several."

Toran's thoughts whirled as he wondered just what had happened to him to require her attention. Had he also been near death? This...Talent...Toran wondered what to make of it. But he did ken one thing: it would not be wise to leave her here. She'd learned too much about him. But even more important, it would be wisest to deprive the enemy of her skills and bring them to his clan. For that reason alone he should take her—or kill her. Toran put that thought firmly aside. That she was a prisoner here, just as he and the MacAnalens were, meant that she deserved to be freed with them. That he wanted her past all reason was perhaps the poorest of motives, but the one which drove his thoughts, and would also drive his actions, he decided, should the opportunity present itself.

"Angus, I have a plan, but I require the assistance of one of yer men."

"Aye?"

"We can't leave the Healer here to aid the invader. I'll take her with me back to the Aerie, but one of yer men must feign illness to draw her among us once Donal arrives."

"Perhaps something he ate?" Angus suggested.

"Aye, causing a great deal of belly pain. That might do the job. He must appear to be ill enough to fetch her, not one of the other healers."

"I think I know just the man," Angus said, chuckling. "Brodric is always telling tall tales. This should suit his talents very well."

Angus leaned toward the man next to him and gestured to another nearby. Ah, the man who'd warned that the Healer could cause serious shrinking. Toran watched the whispered conversation as Angus told his man what they wanted. A grin split Brodric's face. He clearly relished the challenge. Angus turned back to Toran.

"Brodric is ready whenever Donal arrives."

Laughter drifted over from the bonfire, and Toran wished that some of the heat it generated would, as well. Glad he was to be wearing breeches instead of a kilt. At least his manhood suffered no immediate danger of shrinking from the cold. He rested his arms on his knees, and dropped his chin, making his upper body as compact as possible for a man as large as himself. It would be a long day, and an even longer night, even if he wrapped his plaid about him.

But the position had the added advantage of allowing him to worry at his bonds with his teeth while appearing to simply rest his head on his hands. He'd made some progress when riders leaving camp had awakened him at dawn, but the damage he'd done to his wrists was greater than the damage done to the leather before the Healer arrived.

As for what she'd done when she'd seen the condition of his wrists, Toran didn't understand what he'd been feeling then, but even the brief touch he'd allowed her had helped heal the worst of the damage inflicted by the leather. In hindsight, he should have let her finish the job. He'd be in better shape, and he might have a better understanding of what exactly she could do.

Or perhaps not. If she used magic, her methods would be past his kenning. But if she truly used magic, surely it was benign or even good magic used to heal and help, despite the warlike setting. Perhaps her life depended on providing aid the invader by keeping his troops sound. If so, why was he, a captive, given to her to heal? Ah, the torc. If they thought he ruled as laird here, they would think he kenned a great deal about the lay of the land and the capabilities of nearby clans. Indeed. The invader wanted to learn more about the area.

Several hours passed. The guards handed out a midday meal. While they ate, Toran questioned the men around him about the battle the day before and the invaders who now held them.

"No one has seen the MacAnalen since the battle," Angus told him, grief plain on his handsome face. "He's the only brother left to me and I fear he's among the dead. The men are calm for now, but their rage over their losses will not be denied much longer. When your men come, the fighting could start again."

"Nay," Toran advised, "there are not enough of us

to take them all. We need to get away so that we can return to fight on our own terms. Where are they keeping their horses?"

"On the other side of camp," Angus replied. I saw a line of them tied out in the trees when I was brought here."

"All together? That's convenient, and sloppy. It will be easier to cut them loose. Steal those ye can. Scatter the rest. If ye make for the hills, ye can hide out where ye can re-arm and strike at a time of yer choosing. We'll stand with ye o'course. But it may be as ye said. With their leader out of action, or dead, this army may disperse on its own, saving us all the trouble."

"Ye speak sense. We'll be glad of the chance to chase them south into the arms of the Sassenach."

"And if they won't go, we'll take care of them, together."

Angus, thoughtful, nodded before speaking again. "Most of these guards pay little attention to us, preferring to stay by the fire. We could let the men farthest from them start to slip into the woods when they get free of their bonds."

"Nay," Toran answered. "The risk is too great. If they're seen, the guards will stay closer and more alert. Better the guards are lax in their duties. Donal will have time to cut several loose to help the others before we're noticed. And my men will be armed and able to defend us."

"Aye, that's sensible," Angus agreed, still tugging and twisting his bonds to stretch and loosen them.

Toran approved of the young MacAnalen lieutenant. If the MacAnalen was truly among the dead,

Angus would be a suitable successor to lead his clan, though that must be confirmed by what remained of his people—if they could win free from the muddle they were in now.

Toran's thoughts returned to his own situation and that of his home half a day's ride away. The fact that the invader chief languished here meant he had not been able to carry the battle on to the Aerie in Toran's absence. That would be ironic indeed, to waste his effort attacking its walls, when he already held its laird, and did not know it.

****

Though he fought to stay alert, Toran was nearly dozing from fatigue when the sudden flicker of shadows in the trees at the edge of the encampment caught his attention. Under half-closed eyelids, he began to study the perimeter of the camp, watching for the tiniest hint of movement in the weak sunlight of early afternoon.

Nothing happened. He began to think it had been only a stray breeze, when the leather thong binding him to the tree suddenly went slack. Donal's familiar low whistle sounded behind him in the brush. Toran carefully studied the guards at their fire. They were paying no attention to the cluster of prisoners. The rest of the camp seemed quiet. It was time to go.

"Angus," he hissed. "Tell Brodric to start."

Angus straightened up and glanced around. "Donal?"

"Aye." Donal's whisper came from the brush at their backs.

Toran motioned for silence as a guard started in their direction. But after only a few paces, the man

47

turned back to the fire, called by his compatriots to answer a question. Toran exhaled.

"Donal, send one of the men to cut the lines to their horses and lead them quietly into the trees," Toran ordered. "Angus's men will retrieve them. And stay put where ye are until I signal."

"Already done, Lathan," Donal responded dryly. In other circumstances, Toran would have chuckled. But there was too much at stake now.

"Always a step ahead of me, are ye?"

"Who trained ye, lad?" Donal answered simply.

At that moment, Brodric, only a dozen feet away from Toran, began to moan then doubled over, feigning agony. Others in the group called for a healer. Toran leaned back against the tree he was supposed to be tied to. One of the male healers approached with the same three guards.

"Here, now. What's this?" the man demanded. He bent to examine his moaning patient, and Brodric's cries of pain escalated. The healer sent one of the guards away and Toran's pulse quickened. Angus slanted him a look, then went back to watching their drama play out. The healer continued his examination for another moment, then sat back on his heels, waiting, while Brodric writhed and moaned.

Soon she approached. The Healer. Toran's senses went on immediate alert. He studied her as she hurried up, noting how the sunlight brightened the red in her hair, how gracefully she moved, even in haste. Even the guards by the fire turned to watch her pass, Toran noted. That worried him until most of them turned back to the fire, used to her presence.

As she passed under the trees, she flipped her

heavy braid over her shoulder and down her back before kneeling by the groaning man. Toran's palms itched with the desire to unbraid that wealth of hair and fill his hands with it. Mayhap he'd have the opportunity, once they returned to the Aerie. That thought cheered him as much as the knowledge that Donal waited behind him for the right moment to make his move.

Toran watched for long minutes as she ran her hands lightly over the torso of her patient, pausing as if to listen, before continuing her odd regimen of stroking, then pausing again, occasionally looking puzzled. It was a strange thing to see, but Brodric quieted as if she was having some effect, and she coaxed him to uncurl. Two guards, bored with the process, left. The male healer followed on their heels to the fire. Only one guard remained with the prisoners.

Toran nodded. Better and better.

Brodric sat up suddenly, red-cheeked and smiling. He reached out to grasp the Healer's hand. If he was playacting, Toran thought, he excelled at it. He seemed genuinely relieved of pain. The Healer quickly pulled her hand away, frowned, and stepped out of his reach, but closer to Toran. "My pardon, lady," he said. "I only meant to thank ye."

She nodded and spoke to him, so quietly that Toran had to strain to hear her. "No one touches the Healer, man. Rest well." She turned to step away.

Toran gestured urgently for Donal to move, and the snap of a twig broke the stillness. The undergrowth around the prisoners suddenly sprouted six armed men. Donal's gruff greeting sounded sweet as he darted around the tree to cut Toran's hands and feet free. So did the sight of the men he'd feared killed in the fight yesterday. They'd gotten away and brought help. One of them, Callum, silenced the guard behind Aileana, then moved to cut Angus's bonds.

"Get moving, lad," Donal hissed. "We've only these few to break ye out and hie to the hills, not an army to take on this whole damned camp."

But the Healer still stood only a few feet away, wide-eyed, frozen in place by the abrupt appearance of dirk-wielding strangers. The opportunity was just the one Toran had planned for. He gained his feet, then scooped her up, clamping one hand over her mouth to stifle any scream before she attracted the attention of the guards and roused the rest of the camp.

"Quiet," he warned her. "Ye ken what will happen if we don't get out of here. Colbridge will kill us all." Still stunned, she nodded.

Some of Angus's men slipped their bonds from their wrists and bent to untie their feet. "Donal," he hissed, "cut Angus and the rest of his men loose. Arm them as best ye can and silence the guards."

"Aye," Donal answered, motioning to the Lathan men. "Kyle's waiting in the trees with the mounts. Take the lass and go."

"Nay, I'll hand her to Kyle and bring back more weapons." With that, he ran into the trees as hard and fast as he could with the burden of the dazed woman in his arms.

"Toran," he heard Kyle call softly, "this way!" He dodged small saplings and ran into Kyle, already mounted and holding two other horses—Donal's and his. More horses waited just beyond Kyle in the trees. Toran was happy to see extra swords in scabbards tied onto several of them.

"What have ye there, Laird?" Kyle asked.

Finally, to Toran's amusement, the woman found her voice.

"Put me down! What do you think you're doing? I'm a Healer. You can't take me hostage!"

"Aye, lass, I can," Toran countered. "And I have." With that, he set the Healer on her feet, grabbed her arm, and moved with her to the horses.

"I'm glad to see Banner made it home," Toran said, freeing one hand to stroke the big horse along its neck.

"'Tis how we knew ye were in trouble and not just delayed by a wen..." Kyle stuttered and then cut a glance to the woman with Toran. "Uh, until Callum and Brian got back, that is."

"Give me yer spare sword and dirk," Toran commanded, ignoring Kyle's gaffe and gesturing for him to dismount. "Keep her here until I return. Tie her to a tree if ye must," he said, giving Aileana his sternest frown, then warned Kyle, "But don't let her touch ye."

Kyle nodded and handed over his weapons. Aileana, he was glad to see, stood stock still, watching them.

He glanced around as the sound of fighting filtered through the trees, then turned back to Aileana. "Stay with Kyle." He took a few steps back toward the fighting, and then turned back. "He won't harm ye," Toran promised her with a mirthless grin, "unless ye give him reason to."

Aileana's eyes widened. He decided the message had been delivered clearly enough.

A shout behind him in camp alerted him that their escape been discovered. Toran ran back in time to see his men and several of Angus's doing battle with the guards. Toran moved fast. He stooped quickly to cut another of Angus's men free and gave him the dirk he'd used. Then he ran toward the clump of combatants. He got there just the last guard fell. But help from the rest of the camp was starting to arrive a few at a time. They were quickly dispatched by the combined force against them. Toran glanced around. All of the MacAnalens were free of their bonds. Some, weaponless, were already moving into the woods. Several picked up the fallen guards' weapons and waited with the Lathans. Shouts echoed around the camp and Toran knew more men would arrive soon. They had to get out now or take the chance of being overwhelmed and killed or captured again.

Toran exchanged nods with Donal and Angus MacAnalen who signaled to the remaining prisoners.

They ran.

Angus paced Toran stride for stride. "Take yer men and go," Toran ordered. "Split up. Make for the cave on Penwyms Hill. 'Tis hard to find if ye don't ken it's there. My men will take care of any who pursue ye ahorse." Toran gave Angus the sword he carried. Angus passed it to Brodric on his other side.

"What about ye?" Angus asked.

"I ride for the Aerie with our prize," Toran told him. "I'll send out scouts to find and supply ye as soon as I have her secured," he promised.

"Aye," Angus agreed, then raised his sword and shouted, "MacAnalens to me!"

Toran returned to find Kyle and Aileana where he had left them. They were eyeing each other cautiously, but Toran was pleased to see that Kyle had not found it necessary to tie her up.

"Kyle, let's go. Healer, with me," he commanded.

The rest of Donal's party arrived then and mounted up. Aileana chose that moment to begin protesting, backing away from Toran and shaking her head. Out of patience, Toran scooped her up and tossed her onto Banner, then swung up behind her. Toran pulled her upright before him and wrapped one strong arm around her waist.

"Donal," Toran called, "I need a sword." One was quickly passed to him. He slid it into Banner's scabbard. "Take the men and ride escort for Angus," he continued. "He may need help with stragglers from the camp. I'll take our lass on toward the Aerie."

"Aye," Donal answered. "We'll find ye. Just make sure none of that lot do," he said, hitching his thumb over his shoulder toward the invader camp.

"They willna," Toran agreed and kicked his horse into motion. Kyle's mount stayed on Banner's heels. The rest of Toran's men would follow as soon as they ensured the MacAnalens' escape by harrying any invaders who managed to round up a mount. Gripping the reins one-handed, he increased their pace until they raced through the trees, ducking branches and flying down slopes, then climbing quickly to the next hill crest. Aileana struggled now and again, and Toran allowed it until Banner nearly stumbled on a downslope.

Toran gripped her waist more tightly as she squirmed. Whether her agitation was from discomfort or an attempt to escape, he didn't ken, but it mattered not. "Have a care, lass," he warned her. "I dinna wish to drop ye on yer pretty head. A fall from horseback will likely spoil my plans for ye."

"Plans?" she gasped. "What plans? How dare you! Let me go!"

"Why, lass? Do ye wish to stay with Colbridge?" Toran tensed, unwilling to accept the possibility that she could choose captivity with the marauding army over the freedom he offered her.

"He has protected me."

"So far, perhaps." Toran slowed Banner just long enough to capture Aileana's chin with his hand and force her to look up at him. It took real effort to ignore the softness of her breasts against his arm. "But ye were never safe there, lass. Ye saw how sloppy his guard became when we wasna able to keep his eye on them. With him gone, ye'd be prey to all."

"Nay!"

"Lass, even some of the prisoners had ideas ye'd no' appreciate, could they but get their hands on ye."

At Aileana's gasp, Toran returned his hand to her waist and kicked Banner into a gallop.

"Ye'll bide well with me," he promised as she digested that bit of news.

"I can take care of myself!"

Toran admired her heart as much as he decried her logic. She was actually arguing with him as they rode headlong through the woods, gaining speed as they went. But words would not free the beautiful Healer now. She was his.

Chapter Four

Aileana was quickly reminded that it was of no use to struggle against the strength of the Lathan laird. Despite his warnings to the contrary, she was in little danger of being dropped. He held her securely against his hard torso, one strong arm an iron band under her breasts. That he controlled his spirited mount with only one hand and the power of his thighs proved testament to his strength and skill, for they rode hard and fast.

Despite the security of his grip, Aileana huddled deeper into Toran's embrace and held on to his arm for dear, sweet life. As they flew faster and faster, she could not even summon her Voice to order him to stop, or to slow to a pace that would seem less fraught with chances for mishap. But being thrown from the horse, or dashed into trees or rocks, was one thing. She feared even more that Toran was right. If they were caught, Colbridge's men would kill the lot of them. Even she could not count on being spared, since she now appeared to be a runaway. If Colbridge decided against her, he wouldn't care if she had been carried off against her will. He wouldn't believe her. And what he and his men might do to her before they killed her was not to be imagined.

Toran's grip on her never loosened as they bolted between the trees. They ducked overhanging branches. They bounded down the sides of gullies and flew over ridges until it seemed that they would race into the setting sun itself. Aileana clung to the strong arm wrapped around her. She alternated between squeezing her eyes closed and opening them because not seeing where they went frightened her even more than the sight of branches whipping by. One moment she was holding her breath and the next gasping with fear at an uneven jolt or when Toran's weight shifted as he folded over her and ducked oncoming obstacles.

Kyle followed them at a distance. Aileana might have thought him gone except for the pounding of his horse's hooves behind them. He pulled even once or twice and exchanged a nod with Toran, then dropped back again. She supposed he served as rear guard and kept watch for pursuit.

Finally, Toran slowed his mount to a walk, cooling it down. He eased his vise-like grip, allowing Aileana her first deep breath in an hour. Pine sap and leaf mold odors filled her nose, sharp above the musk of hard-ridden horse and the heady scent that was uniquely Toran's own. She heard nothing but the sigh of the wind, birds chirping in the trees, and the steady beat of Toran's heart against her ear. Leather creaked as he shifted in the saddle to look behind them. Before long, Kyle rode up and stayed along side them for a few paces until he got his breath. "All clear," he reported.

"Good. Ride back to Donal; make sure they're away safely," Toran ordered.

Kyle raised a hand in salute, turned his mount and headed back the way they had come.

While the men talked, Aileana had tried and failed to unclench her cramping hands from Toran's arm. Seeming to sense her difficulty, he stopped their horse completely, draped the reins over its neck, and wrapped his other arm around her. Gently, he pried her fingers free.

"Why did you stop?" she asked, half turning in his arms to see him. The frown on his face did nothing to ease her fears.

Then Aileana looked down and saw blood where her nails had pierced his skin. Embarrassment washed through her. How could she have clung so desperately to him without even knowing it?

"I'm so sorry," she said softly, keeping her gaze cast down to the small wounds she'd caused.

Instead of admonishing her, Toran took one of her hands in his two large ones and carefully began to rub and knead her cramping fingers. Pain she had not been aware of finally penetrated, and as quickly, began to dissolve away under his care. Aileana realized that it was not unlike what she herself did when she healed, though he lacked her Talent.

"Ach, lass, calm yerself," he admonished, and the deep rumble of his voice vibrated not only in her ear, but in her back where she leaned against him. "There's naught to fear. I didna drop ye, now did I? And I'll get ye to the Aerie ahead of Colbridge's men."

Leaning against his skin was like leaning toward a blazing hearth warding off the chill of the gathering gloaming. His voice and his hands were so soothing that Aileana could almost believe him. No one had tried to comfort her in a very long time and the simple kindness of this man's caring touch filled a need she hadn't known she had. But she also worried that his kindness might reflect more than simple caring. What if he was trying to lull her into accepting him, allowing him to use her as he pleased?

He released her hand and picked up the other, treating it to the same gentle stroking pressure. Despite her misgivings, she could barely hold back a moan from the pleasure of his touch, until she saw again the blood on his arm and was reminded both that she was his hostage, and that they were not safe.

"How much farther must we go?"

Toran pulled her hand up and dropped a light kiss on the back, sending a thrill up her arm to somewhere deep in her chest. She clamped down on the feeling, refusing to be taken in. Then he released her hand and pointed at the high ground still ahead of them in the distance. "We've still a way to go, but just over that ridge and the next, ye'll look upon it." He picked up the reins and flicked them, urging the horse into a walk.

Aileana flexed her fingers, already missing the soothing warmth of his hands, telling herself sternly to forget the velvety feel of his lips on her skin. But her hands were lax and supple again. She laid them atop his arm, covering the bloody punctures she'd made, and called on her Talent. Toran stilled behind her. She knew he was aware of the soreness diminishing when he tensed. Finally, she lifted her hands and brushed away the bits of dried blood that remained under them, revealing newly healed pink scars.

"Good God, lass, that's a rare skill ye have," Toran breathed behind her as he raised his arm and saw her handiwork. "Is it witchery that ye do? To see it…what ye started to do to my wrists in the tent…and now this…"

His question shocked her, and she berated herself for her audacity. She should have let him bleed rather than give him more evidence against her. Then she sat up straighter. No. She would not be labeled that way. She was no witch, but an orphan, a prisoner, and a healer. If he did not see her as herself by now, nothing she said would change his mind. Her anger made her bold. "That was just a small thing," she boasted, "and simple to do." Let him make of it what he will.

Silence greeted her announcement. They continued at a walk for a while. Aileana wondered what Toran was thinking. She longed to touch him and get a sense of what he felt, but her boldness fled with her annoyance and she didn't dare. Had she said too much? Had her defiant tone provoked him in some way? He did not move, except to avoid low-hanging branches. Finally, he flicked the reins again and increased their pace up the hillside.

"I'm thinking that ye're a rare prize, and one I'm wagering I'll be glad to keep. Let's get ye home to the Aerie. Ye'll be safe there. Colbridge willna be able to reach ye once ye bide inside its walls."

Walls? Aileana's heart lurched to her throat. Once Toran got her in there, would she be able to get out? Would it be just another prison for "such a rare prize" as she? One even more impossible to escape than Colbridge's camp?

And how would Toran use such a rare prize? She no longer had Ranald to assist her and care for her after her healing sessions drained her.

Or could she believe Toran? "Let's get ye home to the Aerie," he'd said. Could she find a home there? she worried, wishing suddenly that she was back in Colbridge's camp, where she knew her role and her place.

"What is it like, this Aerie of yours?" Aileana asked.

"Ye'll see soon enough," Toran deep voice rumbled behind her "'Tis a home like any other, filled with kin and friends, bairns and beasts."

Aileana heard the pride in his voice as he described something so commonplace to him, yet so foreign to her. Sadness she usually kept at bay welled up, and she fought it back. She would not get homesick now. Her parents were long dead, her life in the village gone forever. She would not cry in the arms of this stranger. She would do as she had done for the last two years— she would do everything necessary to survive.

They rode on, stopping occasionally to rest the horse and relieve themselves. During the first such stop, Aileana considered slipping away into the forest, but suspected that Toran's tracking skills might equal his fighting and riding abilities. Nor could she outrun his horse. She considered using her Voice to order him to release her, but here in this vast wilderness, she doubted her ability to survive more than a few days. She had no idea where the next village might be.

Kyle caught up with them once, reporting that Donal and their men followed after relieving some of their pursuers of their mounts. But they were slowed by some of their and the MacAnalen wounded.

"How bad?" Toran asked.

"A few scratches and bumps," Kyle reported with a grin. "Naught to keep them from the Aerie and auld Senga's ministrations."

"Take me back to them," Aileana argued. "I can help."

"Nay," Toran said, and his tone brooked no further

discussion.

Aileana pursed her lips, but managed to keep her silence. Did he so fear her abilities that he would deny her help for his men?

Then Toran added, "They'll catch up to us soon enough," and her anger evaporated into relief. Toran was just trying to keep her safe. "Kyle, ride back and hurry them along. I don't want any of Colbridge's men nipping at their heels. And stay with them. Another good sword arm will come in handy if they do meet trouble."

Kyle balked. "Are ye sure that's wise, Laird?"

"Aye." Toran glanced ahead of them and noted the lowering sun in the western sky. "We're hours away from their camp, and we've been on Lathan land for a while now. If they havena caught us yet, they willna between here and the Aerie."

Without another word, Kyle turned his horse and headed back the way he'd come. Toran urged their mount to a quicker pace, and settled Aileana firmly against him.

After hours of hard riding, Aileana's back ached and her backside felt numb to the toes. She remembered wishing that she'd been left behind in Colbridge's camp. She didn't want that, not really. At least there she could move about as she pleased. Even her earlier enjoyment of Toran's arm about her was beginning to wear thin. She wondered how he still controlled his monstrous steed. Surely he must be as tired and numb as she.

Suddenly lights danced amid the wind-blown leaves of the trees ahead of them. Her breath seized and she straightened, pointing. "What is that?"

Toran slowed the horse to a walk and let his arm drop from below her breasts. With some satisfaction, she saw him shake it a bit, easing the circulation back into it, before he spoke. So, she wasn't the only one suffering.

"What ye see are the lights of the Aerie. We're nearly there."

As they rode closer, the trees thinned out. She gaped at the fortress that stood revealed. Steep-sided and tall, it loomed proud and alone on its high tor, keeping watch over the valley at its feet. The last rays of sunlight glinted on diamond-paned glass windows set near the top of a tall tower. Torches burned along the merlons, limning the top of the defensive works with flickering gold and sparking off of metal pikes that lined the crenellations.

Her heart began to pound as they left the trees and descended into the narrow glen. The closer they got, the higher the tor and the castle atop it loomed. She crossed her arms in front of her. Despite the chill wind, her palms were sweating. This edifice could indeed be defended against Colbridge. And the man who held her in his arms with such casual strength claimed to be the laird of all that light and soaring height. Her home had been a small village of farmers and herders, tied to a manor house, not to a castle with lords and ladies. Tears pricked her eyes as she realized she might never be accepted by people who lived in such a place.

And what would he do with her once he got her there? Shivering, she remembered that castles had dungeons. Surely, he couldn't mean to throw her in the dungeon, could he?

Then she recalled how Toran had described it. A

home like any other. Longing warred with anxiety and fatigue. Longing won.

"Let's go, then," she said, and heard Toran's chuckle behind her—with amusement or sinister promise, she couldn't tell. He wrapped an arm around her as he flicked the reins. The horse broke into a trot, headed home.

****

The evening activities in the Great Hall of the Aerie were usually just a congenial gathering of the men of the clan over their mead and ale, complete with boasts of conquests, be they battles or ladies, or discussions of current concerns. Tonight, the Hall was quiet, and the men sat at leisure staring into the fire, or carrying on low-voiced conversations. Toran took the subdued mood to be a reflection of their concern for the MacAnalens. Or his clan's relief at his safe return. He found both ideas acceptable, until he noted Donal's frowns in his direction as they ate a late meal.

"What ails ye, mon?" Toran finally asked. "Have I grown two heads, then?"

"Nay, Lathan, but I sometimes despair of the one ye do have."

"Why is that, I wonder?" Toran said and gave Donal a grin, finding himself not to be so worn that he could not goad his long-time advisor. "Is it not handsome enough to please the ladies for miles around?" Coira liked him well enough. But why did he not seem to please the beautiful Healer? Toran's grin fled his face. Damn, he ached to hold her again, as he had on the long ride to the Aerie. Her body had been lush and warm against him, her breasts heavy on the arm he'd wrapped securely around her ribs. Her body had been so tightly pressed between his thighs that even her tiniest movement had been sweet torture.

"Did yer head please the invader who captured ye?" Donal said, challenging him, yanking him back to the here and now. "He left it on yer shoulders, I see." Donal leaned forward, glaring. "What did ye think to do, then, lad? Take on the whole invading army by yerself? Ye damn near scared the life out of me."

"Nay, Donal," Toran said, irritation growing along with embarrassment over Donal's loudly expressed concern for his welfare. "But once the fighting started, I could scarce leave them to it, now could I," he said, then sipped his mead, watchful of both his and Donal's tempers. "I was there trying to make sure the feud our fathers fought died with them at Flodden. What do ye think the MacAnalens would ha' done if they'd seen me riding away just as they came under attack?"

"Aye," Kyle interjected.

Donal gave him a quelling look, and Kyle went back to serious drinking. Toran hid a smile.

"During the battle," Toran continued, "I saw a lad too young to defend himself about to be overrun. I simply meant to give him time to slip away. I could not let him come to harm, now could I?" Toran's expression was all innocence. He knew full well that Donal held charge over training the lads in the Aerie in the skills a warrior required for defense as well as for offense.

"Well done, then," Donal remarked, taking a swallow from his tankard. Apparently this motive met with his approval.

"Not so well," Toran continued, "for a moment later, the battle o'ertook me. I fought off the two who threatened the bairn." Toran paused, trying to clear his foggy memory. "I took a blow from behind before I kenned it." Toran fingered the torc at his throat. "I suspect the sight of this saved me. Likely whoever took me down mistook me for one of the MacAnalen lairds."

"Ye always did have the luck," another voice chimed in.

Toran glanced around to see who was listening to his well-deserved comeuppance. Ah, Parlan, the blacksmith, and several others, their attention rapt on the byplay between their laird and Donal. So, let them learn from his mistake. He certainly had. And the MacAnalens had suffered for it. Had he thought to send one of his men when he saw their peril...but no. He shook his head. It would not have helped. The Aerie lay too far away to get there and back with reinforcements before night fell or the fight ended. They'd done as well as anyone could, bringing Donal and the others to free him and the MacAnalens.

The best he could do for Angus now was being done. His scouts headed out to the hills around the invader camp. They carried weapons and supplies to help Angus protect his people until the invaders were gone, or until Toran could bring them safely into the Aerie.

"Mayhap they were surprised and engaged too quickly," Kyle ventured. "Or their ghillies were slain before they could reach us. 'Tis good that our men made it back to raise the alarm, though seeing Banner riderless gave us a bad moment."

Toran shrugged. "Whatever the reason, the battle went against them. And I spent the night enjoying the hospitality of the Healer's tent."

"The lass ye carried home?" Kyle asked, with mead-soaked admiration. "She's a rare beauty, and one I wouldn't mind trying."

A sharp spasm of jealousy pierced Toran, but he hid his frown behind a quick swallow from his tankard.

"Aye, she's a gifted healer, though I had little beside wounded pride and a pounding head to attend to." Toran fixed Kyle and the others with a stern glare before he continued. "She's a guest here, and not for the likes o' ye," he growled. "Nor me, either," he muttered under his breath as he raised his tankard to his mouth, remembering how she'd fought him. But then, she'd responded to his kindness by healing the punctures in his arm. What did it mean?

Donal's smirk told Toran that he'd overheard, but Kyle looked suitably chastened, so Toran went on with his tale and related what he'd learned from the MacAnalen captives before Donal and his men showed up to rescue their laird.

"The rest ye ken, except for the fact that the army's leader took a bad cut to the shoulder and back this morning and rested in the Healer's tent when ye arrived."

Donal frowned. "Aye, that must ha' been the scouting party we fought on the way to ye." He slammed his tankard down and rose to his feet, hands planted on the tabletop. "Damn it, we had the bastard and let him live twice, is that what ye're telling me? Once when we wounded him and again when we left him alive in the camp?"

"Ye didna ken who he was," Toran said, excusing Donal, waving him back to his seat. "And I thought it more prudent to leave while we could than to risk recapture while trying to get to him in the camp."

But Donal would have none of that, not Toran's excuses, nor his own. He was the same way on the training field. Toran expected no less from him.

"Nay, it can't be. I'm certain I delivered a killing blow," he said, his face stony, his voice subdued, as he sat, Then he straightened, his eyes gleaming with purpose. "Laird, I'll go back in the mornin' and finish him off."

"Nay," Toran replied, quickly, knowing Donal when he got his mind made up. Colbridge had been near to death, at least until the Healer got involved. "He'll be too well guarded. Anyway, I expect we'll have another chance," Toran warned. "If he survives his injuries, he'll no' ignore an insult such as we gave him. The Aerie will be where he goes next, to take revenge on the ones who dared to free his prisoners and take his healer from his own compound."

"A winter camped on the glen will take care of most of them for us," Donal said, nodding slowly as he considered the matter. "The rest will be foolish enough to challenge our walls and we'll pick them off at our leisure."

"Indeed we shall," Toran agreed. "We'd best be prepared to do so. Increase the watch on the walls, and make sure the gates are secured after the riders bring in the folk from the outlying farms. If Colbridge and his men should arrive before they get back, I want to know it."

"Aye, Laird Lathan," Donal said, acknowledging the order. "I'll see to it, meself."

Toran stood. "And if Angus MacAnalen shows up, no matter when, bring him to me immediately." He drained the last drops in his tankard and set it on the table. "Get some rest," he commanded. "We'll be busy tomorrow, with or without invaders at our walls."

****

Candles lit the chamber where Aileana had been taken. A modest fire glowed in the hearth, adding a faintly smoky scent to the air. The large bed beckoned with crisp linen sheeting, a seductive pile of furs and woolen shawls. But Aileana fretted over what might be expected of her here. Toran had not claimed her as his prize during any of their stops on the way from Colbridge's camp. Did he instead expect her to welcome his advances in the comfort of the big bed?

A small window glazed with the diamond-shaped panes of glass like the one that she'd seen catching the waning sunlight as they'd arrived opened onto a view of the outer bailey. Far below, men were calmly brushing horses and preparing to bed them down for the night. She would not escape that way. Beyond the walls of the Aerie, in the last dim glow of evening, she could see the ridge lines of the hills they'd ridden over this day.

She closed the window against the chill air and the view that reminded her where she had just come from. Colbridge's camp. Hours away, and yet still with her. Ranald would be sitting vigil over Colbridge. Did he yet know she was gone? If he did, he would be concerned about her. Would he worry that the skills of the rest of the healers might not be enough to ensure their leaders' well-being? Or would he still be intent on the unspoken question he had posed to Aileana before she had proceeded with her Healing? Would he finish Colbridge off and blame the earlier wound? She couldn't guess.

The rest of the camp, she supposed, would be regrouping from the unexpected raid and release of the MacAnalen prisoners. And when...if...Colbridge awoke and discovered what had transpired while he lay in the healing sleep she had imposed, there would be hell to pay. Of that, she had no doubt. She hoped Ranald kept his distance until Colbridge vented his fury and returned to some semblance of reason.

She turned to pace in front of the hearth, considering this drastic change in her circumstances. After two years of captivity, seasons of travel with Colbridge's army, waiting to be overrun and killed at the start of each campaign, and dealing with the aftermath of battles, she couldn't help but welcome the comfortable security of this room. But had she merely exchanged one kind of captivity for another? It was too soon to tell. She rested her arms on the top of the high-backed chair and stared into the fire, tired, but too restless to sit just yet. She eyed the tools set by the hearth and wondered if she would have to try to defend herself with them against Toran's impossible strength.

If this was indeed captivity, it was certainly of a more enjoyable kind. Male servants had brought a tub as soon as she'd arrived and filled it from buckets of hot water. A graying serving woman named Elspie had shooed them out, then taken Aileana's clothing away to be cleaned while she bathed. After washing in icy streams for nearly as long as she could remember, Aileana had been unable to prevent herself from luxuriating in the tub, letting its heat soothe muscles sore from the long ride. When Elspie returned a short time later with a tray of food, the tantalizing scents of a hearty soup and warm bread had filled the chamber. Hunger and Elspie's mother-hennish demands that she get out of the water and eat had roused Aileana from her doze in the still-warm tub. Then the busy Elspie had left her alone again. Now clean, well fed, and wrapped in a soft, thick robe, she surrendered to fatigue and moved around the chair to take a seat in front of the fire, refusing the bed until she could be certain she'd not be molested there.

A light tap on the door startled her, and announced Elspie's return, arms laden with under shifts, and kirtles of many colors. "Here, now," the woman said by way of greeting, "the laird bid me find ye aught to wear. Some of these should fit ye right enough." She deposited the pile on the bed and began to sort them and hold them up for Aileana's inspection. "This is a lovely green, lass. 'Twould set off yer hair." She picked up another gown. "Or a blue. See, it's edged in white. And there's a brown with lovely carved buttons."

"No," Aileana objected, though in truth, she needed a dress. The one she'd had on today was fraying at the seams, and she'd washed blood out of it too many times to count. Her other kirtle and the few other things she owned had been left behind in her sleeping tent and were probably now the property of one of the few camp followers who had dared to journey this far north with the army. "Where are my clothes? Who do these belong to? Surely they don't want to give them away?"

"'Tis no matter," Elspie assured her, holding up a kirtle made of rust-colored wool. "That lass is long gone from the keep. Thank the saints! She'll not miss these. And anyway…"

"The green," Aileana said, interrupting her prattle.

The pile of clothes Elspie sorted through was too much. Added to the chamber, the bath, the food, well, she feared how she might be asked to repay this generosity. But she'd accept one dress. She needed it.

Aileana had worn green since her talent had come on her. Usually her mother's hand-me-downs, as green stood for life and marked the healer's apprentice as well as the healer. She'd continued the tradition even to refusing new clothes from Colbridge's conquests, as a way to remember her mother, and as protection. She would not owe Colbridge for anything that was not absolutely necessary. So who had these belonged to, and why was Elspie glad that she was gone from the Aerie? Aileana wondered, regretting now that she'd cut Elspie's comment short. A former lover of the laird's perhaps, dismissed from his presence without her belongings?

"Then the green it shall be," Elspie agreed, shaking out the dress to rid it of wrinkles. She produced a clean linen undershift from the pile on the bed and handed it to Aileana. "Here, lass, put this on first, and we'll try the green afore ye go to yer rest. Moina can alter it tonight for ye to wear on the morrow."

"Aye," Aileana acquiesed and dropped the warm robe onto the chair. Cold air chilled one side of her body, while heat from the fire warmed the other. She stepped closer to the fire and lifted her arms to slip the shift over her head. The green dress went on over it.

"'Tis near ta right," Elspie muttered as she fussed with the cloth. "A bit in here, a bit out there. Let down the hem. Verra well. Ye can take it off and put on the night rail I brought ye. Ye must be worn out, poor lass. Moina will have this ready for ye tomorrow, and perhaps a few others, too."

Grateful to be done, and reassured by Elspie's comments that she would not be accosted, at least for tonight, Aileana changed into a soft linen gown as Elspie gathered up the pile of dresses on the bed. "Please, only the green," Aileana told her. "I'll need no others."

"But lass, ye'll need several dresses. 'Tis no trouble for Moina. How the girl loves to ply the needle! She'll be up half the night and happy for the chance. Nay, lass, dinna fash yerself. In the morning ye'll have these and no argument. And if the laird approves, tomorrow will see a visit from the cobbler as well, mark my words."

Too worn out to argue, Aileana did not contradict her, but rather bid her good night, mindful of long-unused courtesies common in the company of women. She'd been so many years with only Ranald for anything approaching companionship, and sometimes the company of the other male healers when they worked together. But Colbridge moved so relentlessly from one conquest to another that there had been no opportunity to pass time with women in the villages doing the womanly things Aileana recalled from her childhood. She'd been safer that way, she now supposed, but it was also a lonely way to live.

"Sleep well, lass," Elspie said, then opened the door to leave and revealed the massive form of Toran, fist upraised, poised to knock.

Chapter Five

Toran had wandered the keep, deep in thought, recalling his conversation with Donal. What if Donal was right and he'd landed a killing blow on Colbridge? The man had been pale as death when Toran encountered him. What had Aileana done to him after she'd summarily ordered Toran out of her tent and into the negligent care of the guards? And if Colbridge still lived, how quickly would he be able to come after Aileana? Those thoughts kept him occupied until he realized where he'd arrived. Instead of standing outside his own chamber, he had followed his thoughts to the Healer's door. So. Now that he was here, he might as well see to her comfort. It was possible that he owed her that and more, in payment for what she may have done for him. He raised a fist to knock just as the door swung open. Elspie, arms full of colorful dresses, stood on the threshold. Her eyes widened as she stared up at her laird.

His gaze lifted into the room beyond. The sight that greeted him stunned him into immobility. Aileana stood near the hearth wearing a thin night shift made nearly transparent by the glow of the fire behind her. Heat to match the blaze that lit her luscious form flared up from his loins to his eyes. Her unbound hair cascaded down her back to frame her slender waist and rib cage. As she turned her back to him, he caught the silhouette of her full, firm breasts, and the shadows of their rosy tips. His mouth went dry.

"What are you doing here?" she demanded over her shoulder, clearly startled and not at all pleased to see him. "Get out."

Her imperious attitude diverted Toran from enjoying the sight of her. Elspie coughed, drawing Toran's attention downward. She looked appalled as she stared up at her laird, though it was not clear if it was the Healer's tone, or Toran's presence, that scandalized her. Either way, her censure, and the Healer's demand, irritated him and his answer came out sharper than he'd intended.

Keeping his gaze on Elspie, he barked, "'Tis my keep." Then he glared at Aileana. "Ye're my prisoner—or my guest." The anxiety on Aileana's face should have stopped him, but it failed to do so as his temper gained mastery over him. "Ye choose how ye're to be treated. Ordering the laird about will, like as not, get ye treated as a prisoner."

With that, he stepped into the room around the usually unflappable Elspie, whose eyebrows now arced up to her salt-and-pepper hairline. He gestured her out, and closed the door softly, menacingly, behind him, leaving the Healer gaping at him over her shoulder.

"Cover yerself," he commanded, noting the tempting swell of her backside and grabbing onto his control with both hands, "unless ye want me to make something more…or rather, less, of yer current attire. Something more appropriate to the treatment of a female prisoner."

To Toran's sneaking amusement, the Healer's mouth opened and closed, twice, before she could get a sound out. "At least," she began, then apparently thought better of her temper and started over. "Could you at least turn your back?" That was better. He would not be ordered around in his own keep. Satisfied, Toran turned to face the door and exhaled his annoyance with a breath.

"While ye dress, ye can tell me whether Colbridge survived his wounds, and why he's gone to war with the Highland clans."

Behind him, he could hear the soft rustle of a robe sliding over the night shift, hiding that beautiful body. Disappointment settled over him as the robe settled over her.

"You can turn around," the Healer told him, and he turned to see her finish pulling soft slippers onto her feet. Toran was struck again by her beauty and grace as she sat down at the dressing table and calmly began plaiting her hair. The urge to gather those tresses in both hands and bury his face in them overwhelmed him. He nearly stepped forward to put thought into action when the Healer began speaking, stopping him in his tracks.

"He lives. Or he did when last I saw him. And I know little more about him than I told you this morning," she said quickly while she worked. Her eyes never left the fire. "Colbridge owned, long ago, a minor hold on the border. He has taken advantage of the lack of clan leadership since the massacre at Flodden. I heard him once call a clan he'd beaten easy pickings because its surviving laird was a seven-year-old boy. He gathered broken men together with him and headed north. He destroyed my village two summers past."

She glanced toward Toran, then looked away. "My

family did not survive. When my mother discovered my father's body among the dead in the field, she could not go on. She killed herself with his dirk." She paused before quickly resuming her braiding. Toran noticed that her hands trembled ever so slightly.

"One of Colbridge's closest lieutenants was injured. They brought him to me when they found out I remained the only living Healer in the area. The Talent had come on me four years before. I was born to it," she said, "like my mother, and hers before her. When Colbridge moved on, I had no choice. He took me with him. I've been under his protection ever since, and the men have come to respect and depend on me, so they do not accost me. I was in no danger in the camp you took me from."

A fierce sense of elation, tinged with relief, shook Toran as he digested that news. She was untouched. Incredible. He couldn't take his eyes off of her as she finished with the heavy braid and secured the end with ribbon. She tugged the braid over her shoulder to drape down the back of her robe, then folded her hands in her lap, but kept her head erect.

Toran suffered a moment's regret for what the girl had been through, but only a moment, for those trials had brought the woman before him into his hands. He recalled the headlong ride from Colbridge's camp, and how, despite being consumed with controlling the horse and avoiding pursuit, he'd been aware of her body pressed against the arm he'd wrapped around her waist and the tightness in his groin where he held her in front of him. It had taken all his skill, if not quite all his concentration, to get them safely to the Aerie. Having seen her sweet form in the firelight, Toran did not know if he would again have the power to hold her in his arms and concentrate on the ride, no matter the danger.

As he watched her wait for his next question, he also recalled the warmth of her hand on his arm where her nails had pierced the skin. Absently, Toran rubbed the area. Only faint pink lines remained. How had she done that? What had she done in the tent as he lay senseless from the blow to his head? What did she mean when she said talent had come on her? Wasn't healing all potions and poultices and herbs from the garden?

By main force, he brought his wandering thoughts back to the present and the information he needed tonight.

"How did Colbridge surprise the MacAnalens, and prevent them from summoning aid?"

"I am not privy to his tactics," she replied evenly and shrugged. "I know he sends out advance scouts. Perhaps they surrounded the village and prevented the escape of any runner." Finally, she turned her head, met and held his gaze.

"Perhaps," was all Toran could manage to answer while the meadow green of her eyes held him mesmerized.

"My assistants and I are always well away from the battle," she continued, looking away. "Colbridge's wounded are carried to us for care."

"Which ye seem to do verra well." With her eyes averted, Toran found his voice and his focus returned to him. He studied the proud and defiant lass before him and waited, in silence, for her to go on. But it seemed she knew that tactic, and was prepared to wait him out. He smiled to himself as he leaned against the door and crossed his arms over his chest. "How is it that a man still lives who seemed near to dead this morning of a blow that would kill any other?"

"I healed him." She barely breathed her simple answer.

"Like ye healed my arm where yer nails pierced the skin?"

"Aye."

Toran pushed away from the door and stood straight, hands clenched at his side. "And like ye healed my battle wounds?" he demanded.

"Aye." Aileana's voice didn't waver. Though he saw her tense as he stood, she did not flinch at his tone. *Stop being such an ass,* he told himself, *or ye'll scare her into silence.* He leaned back against the door.

"And where is Colbridge next taking his campaign?"

"Here, I'd imagine. Especially now that I am here." Her flat, even tone made it clear that she believed that to be a simple statement of fact.

Toran shook his head in wonderment. Before he could say anything, she continued, "He will discover where I've been taken and will want me back, as much as he will want to capture the Aerie."

"Ye place great value on yerself, to equal the Aerie."

"Not I. Colbridge."

"Ah, of course. He values ye as I do my home and my people because...?"

"Because I can keep him alive. And his men," she said, returning her gaze to him. "Without me, the success of his campaign is no longer assured."

Satisfaction surged through Toran, warming him

78

from the inside out. Without this Healer, Colbridge would be at a disadvantage—real or imagined, it mattered not. He would be weakened. He would know that he had walked away from a battle wound for the last time.

****

Aileana studied the big man leaning so casually against her door. He'd been formidable, stretched out on the table in her Healer's tent. On his feet, healthy, fully in his power and in his own keep, formidable was too weak a word. He fascinated her. His genial arrogance annoyed her; his size, strength and powerful position frightened her, but still, she found him compelling.

She'd distracted herself by braiding her hair, keeping her eyes away from the bed, and looking anywhere but at him as he questioned her. Now, she had no further diversion, and no excuse to look anywhere else, nor did she want to.

In the flickering firelight he seemed taller and broader than any real man could be. The metal and crystal of his torc gleamed at his powerful throat, half covered by the fall of his thick, dark hair. But she knew just how real he was. She had touched him. She had healed his hurts. She knew the beat of his heart, the rise and fall of his massive chest, the length of his lashes when they rested on his high cheekbones. She'd depended on the strength of his arm securing her against his hard torso as he rode headlong through the hills, and blushed at the forbidden hardness of his manhood pressing against her hip.

The idea of this beautiful, powerful man becoming hers thrilled her, but scared her witless, too. How could she hope for a fantasy like that to become true? She couldn't, not with any man, and especially not with him. Her position here was too precarious. Not knowing what else to do to save her composure, she stood and moved to the fire, to stare into the flames and burn Toran's image from her eyes.

"What do you intend to do with me?" she asked at last, afraid and hopeful at the same time. It was too much like the last question he'd asked her this morning: "And what's to be done with me?" She recalled the dismay that had filled her at his question, and her certainty that Colbridge would torture him for information, then kill him. But only after she'd healed him again and again, and only after he'd given up his secrets to his tormentor.

So now it was her turn to wonder. Despite his threats a few moments before, she had sensed no real animosity in him. She'd been treated well since arriving at the Aerie. Her dream of a home, with people who cared about her, perhaps a family of her own, rose unbidden to her mind, and with it came a familiar lump in her throat. She was tired, she thought, to let that longing overwhelm her now. She folded her arms under her breasts and kept her eyes on the flames. She heard Toran move from the door to stand behind her. She tensed as his hands came to rest on her shoulders. He turned her gently, but irresistibly, to face him.

"What should I do with so beautiful, so valuable, a prize?" he murmured, almost to himself.

His deep blue gaze ensnared Aileana as completely as his hands. She knew she should be outraged at being called a prize. He'd done it before, on the way here. Did he truly see her that way? She refused to be chattel any longer, and would not allow him to treat her so. But she found she could not summon her ire. One of his hands left her shoulder and he lightly touched her cheek, then slowly slid his fingers down her throat to her collarbone. There, he hesitated, and Aileana held her breath until he moved the hand back to her shoulder.

His simple touch sent shivers dancing and nearly undid her. That frightened her enough to break the spell he wove. "Please, don't," she asked. "Let me go. The Healer is not to be touched."

"Aye, I heard ye tell Brodric MacAnalen the same thing. Did ye learn that from Colbridge?" Toran asked, slowly stroking along her collarbone with his thumb. "Or is that what he told his men, to keep them from...hurting ye?"

Aileana shook her head. She could try to force him away, but she felt less and less able to summon the energy as his touch ensnared her.

"Have ye spent the last two years without any human feeling? Without a simple handclasp between friends?" Toran's tone dropped along with the hand that he slid slowly down her arm and back to her shoulder. "Without the embrace of a lover?"

Unfamiliar, liquid sensations trickled into her very core from the places where Toran's warm fingertips touched her. The heat radiating from him nearly matched the heat from the hearth at her back. As Aileana melted into his gentle seduction, she let her head fall back in enjoyment. Toran's breath warmed her cheek as he slowly lowered his mouth. His lips were soft as they skimmed lightly over hers, questioning, not quite demanding. He dipped his head and his tongue left a trail of damp fire along her throat, then moved back to breach her defenses and probe her mouth, leaving behind a faint peaty taste. Of whisky? His teeth nipped gently at her lower lip, and his mouth caressed the small pain away. Her body's answering eruption of need finally burned away the haze of desire building in her. No. This could not be happening.

Shocked at her body's willingness to succumb to his seduction, Aileana turned her face away from his gentle assault, summoned her Talent and found her Voice. *"Let me go,"* she commanded, as tears welled in her eyes. Never had she desired a man's touch like this. Never. But she had no choice. She had to remain untouched. As long as this man believed her talent depended on it, she would be safe.

To her relief, he obeyed, though his slight frown betrayed his puzzlement. His hands dropped to his sides and she stepped back, putting some distance between them. "It's late. You must leave." She gestured toward the door, not daring to risk her Voice again, trying not to look again at the man who breached her defenses with such ease. But she could not control her willful eyes.

The dazed expression on Toran's handsome face evaporated, to be replaced with one more neutral, yet not without lingering warmth. "Aye, I must." Aileana froze as he glanced toward the bed, then back at her. But he made no move toward her, and she found she could breathe again when he murmured almost to himself, "'Tis been a trying day and ye're tired. Sleep well, lass."

Toran turned and strode to the door, but paused before grasping the handle. He seemed fully in command of himself, with a trace of his usual arrogance restored, when he told her, "I'll have a man outside, of course." Or perhaps it was merely simple courtesy she saw there, as he continued. "If ye should need anything, ask and he'll see it provided—and keep ye safe through the night. Have no fears, lass. No one will disturb ye." With that, he opened the door and left her, closing the heavy oaken barrier softly but firmly behind him.

She heard him call for a guard, and soon thereafter the low rumble of male voices penetrated her door as he issued orders. Then silence descended. So, she would be guarded. Treated as a guest and a prisoner, it seemed, until Toran decided her fate. Aileana wiped her eyes and slid the robe off her shoulders, still flushed with the power of his touch. So small a thing, but it had unnerved her more than years of blood and grime and gore. She slipped into the luxury of a real bed, mindful of the temptation it represented. Comfort, stability...and the embrace of a lover. Perhaps there was more danger here than she'd imagined.

****

As he strode away from the Healer's chamber, Toran puzzled over what had just happened between them. Something she'd said, or done, hovered on the edge of recollection. Whatever it was, she'd done it before, damn it. He recognized the fog plaguing his mind. He'd been this confused in her tent after talking to her. This muzziness was why he'd decided to post a guard outside her door. He hadn't lied to her. Having Davie there should give her a sense of safety until morning, and he could call for anything she needed. But it had also occurred to Toran that he didn't want her wandering the keep at will during the night. She'd done something to him, something he didn't understand. He shook his head in exasperation as he opened the door to his spacious chambers. Whatever it was would occur to him eventually, he thought, dismissing the concern for now. Tomorrow would come all too soon, and he needed to get some rest before it did.

The fire in the large hearth warmed his room and cast dancing shadows on the walls. This had been the laird's chamber for as long as the Aerie had stood. The big bed had been crafted by his great-grandfather. The tapestries on the walls were the work of several generations of clan ladies plying their needles, and depicted different seasons of life in the Aerie. The lairds had allowed no reminders of battle in their private chamber. Toran continued the tradition. Here was where he came for solitude and peace, and both would benefit him after the events of the last few days. He suspected that there would be little enough of either in the coming weeks.

If Aileana was right and Colbridge still lived, then he would march on the Aerie, and when he learned that he could not overrun such a stronghold by main force, he would lay siege with his ragtag army. That would gain him naught but a long, hard winter camped on the glen, slowly freezing or starving to death while the Lathan clan bided well, warm and fed in its fortress. Toran was confident in his defenses, and the history of the Aerie gave him no reason to doubt the safety of his clan behind its walls.

He unbuckled his belt and unwound the plaid that he habitually wore at home from his body, then kicked off his boots. Dressed only in his shirt, twin to the one the Healer had cut to rags, he added more peat to the fire. The Healer…at that thought, he stripped off the tunic and stood naked, letting the firelight illuminate the new scars on his upper arm and forearm, still pink and shiny from Aileana's healing, that mixed in with old white scars from battles long past. Toran had taken wounds severe enough to know that these new injuries should not yet be healed, not even such minor wounds as the ones Aileana had made on his forearm. Baffled, he twisted and turned, examining every inch of skin that he could see for more of Aileana's handiwork. Nothing. There were no other new scars anywhere visible to him. He flexed his shoulders and arms, trying to sense the tightness of any new scars on his back and shoulders. Again, nothing. He ran his hands over his buttocks and the back of his thighs. Nothing tender, nothing scarred that hadn't been there two days ago. His fingers found a new ridge on his scalp. That brought back the memory of the headache and Aileana's soothing hands. Perhaps he did owe her something. Then he stretched out on the bed to watch the flames dance, letting his mind wander.

The Healer. Aileana. What was it about her that drew him so? And what powers did she have that left him so befuddled, so willing to do as she wished? Even now, he ached to bury his hands in the mass of her hair. Her skin, where he'd touched her, tantalized him, heated and soft. The memory of it sent fevered blood surging through his body. And the sweetness of her mouth…Toran shook his head, trying to dislodge all thought of her from his mind.

He had been playing with fire, there in her chamber. He could not have her. He knew better. He would not force himself on any unwilling woman, and she was not yet willing, despite her response to his kiss, his caress. Yet she tempted him; she had tempted him from the first moment he'd awakened and seen her dozing in her chair, sitting vigil over his unconscious body. She was beyond his ability to resist, but resist her he must if he meant to win her.

He needed her.

Since he'd first seen her, thoughts of other women had fled. He was no stranger to teasing the lasses, nor to pleasing them. Daracha had initiated him into his manhood many years ago. A few others, then Fia, his childhood friend, who had left the clan after he'd refused to consider taking her to wife. He regretted her anguish. Lately Coira, who would not take kindly to being set aside. But until he resolved this burning need for Aileana, until he resolved her place in the clan, there would be no other for him.

Something more than the hospitality owed a guest, or the care owed a captive, held him in check. Must he keep her untouched so as to use her as a bargaining chip with Colbridge should the circumstance arise? Or to preserve her Talent for his clan? He had never heard of such a thing, but he could not risk it until he knew more. This damnable ignorance kept him from the bliss he'd come so close to tasting...everything he so fiercely wanted from her, with her.

Bargaining chip...fah! Toran knew he was deceiving himself. He could not imagine the circumstance under which he would willingly give her back. Aileana was a puzzle he had to solve before her presence here drove him to madness. No, not before he solved the puzzle of the Healer...and of the woman...nor after, would he give her up.

He wanted her, of that he had no doubt. But it wasn't just upholding his clan's traditions that restrained him. She was different. Something about her made him consider her future and the clan's. Rather than ravishing her, loosening her braid and thrusting his burning hands into her wealth of hair, he had tried to content himself with a gentle touch, a few soft words. He'd known he couldn't take her, not then, perhaps not ever, but once he'd seen her in the firelight, he'd had to taste, to touch, to know, what he might never have.

He was a damned fool.

With a muttered curse, he heaved himself off the bed and pulled on his shirt, trews, and boots. He picked up the woolen plaid, then dropped it. The cold of the night air would cool the fever in his blood. He would inspect the guard on the ramparts, check on the horses, even wander Senga's garden, anything but stay where he was. He slammed the door on the way out. There was no peace to be found in his chamber tonight.

Chapter Six

Ranald paced the floor of the Healer's tent, waiting for Colbridge to wake up from the restorative sleep Aileana had laid on him. Night had fallen long since. Day was still far off, and Ranald feared that once he delivered his news, he'd not see it, nor the light of any other day, ever again.

The raiders had taken Aileana.

Colbridge had killed men for lesser tidings than that.

Delivering the news of the loss of the MacAnalen would be perilous enough to the messenger, but Aileana! Ranald feared he was counting his last hours.

Was she safe—or even alive? No, he could not think that. She had to be alive and well. Surely he would know, down in his bones, if she were gone from this world to the next.

Colbridge stirred on the table and groaned. Ranald stiffened, not daring to take the next step. His blood turned to ice in his veins. He held his breath as Colbridge sighed and settled. Long minutes passed before Ranald allowed his muscles to unclench. How despicable for a seasoned warrior to quake like a child before a raging parent. Even though it had been two years since he'd been fit enough to fight, he knew better than to exhaust himself this way. He resumed pacing, slowly, carefully, silently, around the interior of the tent to the entrance. He lifted the covering flap aside and looked out into the night.

The notion tempted him, but he could not just walk out of camp. Colbridge's guards would stop him before he got beyond the firelight. And where would he go? His own clan was broken, destroyed by Colbridge's forces in the battle that had nearly cost Ranald his leg, and his life. If not for the work Aileana had done on his bad leg after she'd recognized him, he might be dead, or so lame as to have no way to support himself. Truth be told, he did not want to leave her. He could no longer imagine his life anywhere but at her side, working with her. No, he could not leave, not without knowing her fate.

Though he'd never dared tell her, he'd stayed with Colbridge to be with her and watch over her. He owed her so much, and she needed him to help her, to be her eyes and hands on the battlefield once the fighting ended. And to protect her. He felt certain Aileana did not know that he stood guard outside her tent on the nights the men celebrated their most recent victories. Let them have their camp followers, or the women of the villages they destroyed. He had kept the few away from Aileana who had dared consider her their prey, or who were drunk enough not to care about the consequences. His presence served to remind them what they stood to lose if they violated the Healer—to be left with only the rough surgery and bandages of the other healers to save their lives.

She had to be found. He needed to plan, to think of a way to avoid his otherwise certain fate when he broke the news to Colbridge. Ranald dropped the flap and turned back to regard the man on the table. He had to persuade him that there existed a way for Ranald to play a part in finding Aileana, in getting her back. If he could no longer fight, surely he could do something. But what? He didn't know who had taken her and the MacAnalen. Likely she'd been carried off to this Aerie that he'd heard the men talking about. No other strongholds existed close by, and who else would be so daring?

Their raid was surely a message to Colbridge. To persist in his conquest would be foolish against a clan so bold as to steal into an armed camp and retrieve the captured laird and a woman, and to free the rest of the prisoners. Most important to least important, in their barbarian eyes, Ranald supposed, a sign that they could act against an armed camp without heed to its defenses, and take whatever they liked. They could not know what treasure they'd stolen when they spirited Aileana away.

Colbridge suddenly snorted, and sat up, blinking. "What...where..." he mumbled, then looked around the tent, still groggy from his rest. He rubbed his face with one hand, and that seemed to wake him up even more.

Ranald stood, silent, determination overriding his fear, waiting to be acknowledged. "Ah, now I remember," Colbridge continued, talking now to Ranald. "I was injured. Aileana did her magic, did she?"

"She did, sir."

Colbridge shrugged his shoulder, then lifted his hand over his head and brought it back down. "It all seems right enough. So, then, how long did I sleep? Where are the men? What news?"

Ranald steeled himself. "You slept the day away.

'Tis past midnight, and the camp is quiet—now."

Colbridge did not miss the hesitation or the inflection in Ranald's voice.

"Now? What do you mean, now?"

Might as well get it said while Colbridge was still bleary and had no weapon to hand, Ranald thought. That might save him.

"There was a disturbance midday. Raiders came for the MacAnalen. They took him, and..."

"What! They came right into my camp and took my prize prisoner? Where were my men? How could this happen!"

"That's not all they took." Ranald rushed to get the words out before Colbridge's temper got worse. "They took Aileana and set the other prisoners free." Ranald held his breath, waiting for the eruption that would signal his doom.

Colbridge's sputtering stilled as Ranald's words sank in. Ranald watched his eyes narrow as he absorbed their meaning. "They took the Healer? And the MacAnalen? Out of an armed camp? And freed the rest of the prisoners, too?" Colbridge's voice grew louder and higher with each sentence as he repeated Ranald's news, disbelief plain on his face. Suddenly his teeth clenched and his face flushed scarlet. "Where are the guards? Bring them to me! I'll have their heads!" he shouted as he stood up, then swayed and grabbed the table edge for support.

Ranald reached to steady him and had his hand batted away for his trouble.

"No!" Colbridge gasped, and straightened up. "How can I prevail without her? Men are going to be wounded and die. I need her!" Suddenly, he grabbed

Ranald around the neck, and growled, "Where ever she is, you're going to help me get her back, do you understand?"

"Of course," Ranald rasped, fighting to be still, trying not to provoke Colbridge further. Despite his weakened condition, Colbridge was entirely capable of crushing a man's throat with one hand.

As suddenly as he'd attacked, Colbridge loosed Ranald and turned for the entry. "Bring me the guard captains!" he shouted, slapping the tent flap aside. With that, he staggered out of the tent and into the firelit night.

It was Ranald's turn to sag against the table. He still lived while Colbridge shouted for the guards. He knew he'd had a narrow escape. He'd be wisest to stay out of Colbridge's way until he'd slaked his temper in the hapless guards' blood and cooled off. But Ranald had to do something to find Aileana, to discover who had taken her and where, anything it took. He hadn't spent years training as a warrior to cower in this tent now. It was time to resume fighting. And if he could not get her back, perhaps he could join her, alive or dead.

Ranald followed Colbridge into the night.

****

The day dawned bright and cloudless. Aileana took it as a good omen that the mists made no defense against the cheery sunshine, and that blue skies replaced the gray damp of yesterday's dawn in Colbridge's camp.

Colbridge's camp. Only yesterday and already it seemed a lifetime ago. She wondered how Ranald fared and wished he'd been taken, too, not left behind to deal with Colbridge's recovery when they discovered that she had disappeared with all the prisoners. He could be more comfortable here, as she was now, than he could living in a rough camp. And surely he could continue to assist her, or find employment among the many trades required to run a keep such as this; one where he could make a good life for himself.

Aileana luxuriated in the deep softness of the feather bed, so different from the pallet she was used to. Blankets and linen sheeting kept the autumn chill from her skin. Embers glowed in the banked-down fireplace, awaiting someone's attention to stir them to life. As she drowsed, she pictured the fire flaring up, and recalled the heat that had blazed last night in Toran's eyes as he touched her. He wanted her. That was plain, though he'd kept his caresses slow and gentle, his voice low and soft. She'd been nearly helpless against her own body's yearnings, and yet he had not taken advantage of her, had not tried to force her to do what they both wanted.

And she wanted him, though she should not. She had finally found her Voice and forced him to leave her alone, though the sudden absence of his touch had brought tears to her eyes. He possessed the will to defend against her talent, perhaps to overwhelm her, but he had submitted to her. This time. Would he do so again? Or would he become more and more immune to her will? As strongly as the attraction pulsed between them, she dared not enter into that contest. Her talent had kept her safe and untouched these two years. She could not risk being less than inviolable. Not for any man, no matter how attractive, powerful or wealthy.

Once taken, no longer untouched, but still

possessing her Talents, she would be vulnerable to the attentions of any man. That is what she risked with Toran. For when he tired of her, or when his clan forced him to marry someone suitable to be the wife of the laird, she would lose all of her protections—his, and the fiction that had carried her safe this far.

Irritated now, Aileana threw back the covers and quit the bed. Grabbing the poker, she stirred the embers of the fire and threw on some kindling to encourage a blaze to match her own frustration. A glorious day, comfort she had not known for years, if ever, and she could not let herself enjoy it for fretting over the laird and his intentions. It was not to be borne! She would protect herself as she always had, she vowed, and would not allow such thoughts to spoil the day.

As the fire started to come back to life, a soft knock sounded and the door to her chamber swung open. Elspie trundled in, green dress over one arm, and a tray of oat bread and cheese propped on the opposite hip.

Aileana caught a glimpse of a boy passing by the door as it swung closed, but her guard of the evening before was not visible.

"Ye'll be wanting to ready yerself," Elspie said as she put the tray on the small table so she could shake out the dress and hold it up for Aileana to don. "There's a bright mornin' without to be enjoyed, and Senga would be pleased to show ye the herb garden, now that ye'll take her place as healer."

The cloth sliding over Aileana's head muffled her voice, but she managed to squeak, "Take her place?" as the dress slipped onto her shoulders. "What do you mean, 'take her place'?" she demanded when she could see Elspie again.

"Aye," Elspie continued, waving Aileana to the chair and handing her the breakfast tray. "Old Senga is long past her prime. She's had no help these last two winters. The talk in the Hall is that ye're to become the clan's new healer."

"I'm not a prisoner, then?"

"Prisoner? What nonsense is that?" Elspie waved a hand to encompass the room and its comfortable furnishings. "Does this look like the dungeon, then, lass?"

"There was a guard on my door last night."

"Oh? No' a guard, I'm sure. 'Tis likely the laird wanted someone nearby if ye had need of aught during the night, since this keep is new to ye."

"How kind of him," Aileana replied drolly around a bite of bread. The frown Elspie gave her told Aileana the note of sarcasm in her voice had not been missed.

Aileana still had her doubts. Call it whatever Elspie wished, there had been a guard outside her room last night. But this morning, Elspie was her only company. Elspie didn't look much like a jailer. Aileana thought she could outrun the older woman with one leg broken, and without the use of her Voice. And what of Elspie's news? Aileana had only arrived last night. How could anyone know about her, much less be discussing her fate in the Great Hall? Anyway, she doubted that her future would be decided by common gossip. Talk in the hall was one thing, but... "What of your laird's wishes?"

"Ah. Ach, now, our Toran knows 'tis in the best interests of the clan, and himself, to keep Senga content."

"Why?"

"Would ye want the master of herb lore angry with ye?" Elspie asked with a smirk. "'Twould be impossible to eat or drink anythin', were it so."

Aileana picked up a piece of cheese, sniffed, and nibbled carefully on a corner, suddenly fervent in the hope that Senga was looking forward to having help. Elspie laughed.

"Dinna fash yerself, lass."

"That's easy for you to say," Aileana replied, then shrugged, put the whole piece in her mouth and chewed. "You aren't being put forward as her successor. What if she's not ready to be replaced?"

"Clan Lathan is an old clan, small now, but we've been here for many a year. The healer is well respected in the clan and always will be. Besides, Senga had an apprentice before, but a McDinnan lad caught the lass's eye and suddenly she left."

"And there's no one else to apprentice to the healer? No child?"

"There's none with the wit or the patience to take on the learnin' that Senga demands."

"So I arrive, ready-made a healer, is that it?"

"Aye, lass," Elspie smiled with satisfaction.

"What if my ways are not hers?" Aileana stood, setting aside the tray covered now only by crumbs, and began to pace, fearful again of this new situation she found herself in. What if Senga found her lacking in some way? And told Toran? What would she do then? She had no other training, no other skills, except as a healer.

So, that was why Toran had brought her to the Aerie. But if Senga did not accept her, what would

Toran do? Send her back to Colbridge's camp?

As Aileana paced, Elspie backed out of her way, toward the door, concern plain on her face. "What if I have no wish to remain in your Aerie?" Aileana continued, standing still as the thought occurred to her. "What then?"

"That ye'll have to discuss with the laird," Elspie answered, a frown knitting her eyebrows together. "It'll be up to him what's to be done wi' ye."

Aileana decided she did not want to know what Elspie meant by that. For now, as to whether Toran considered her prisoner or guest, it would seem this morning she was to be accorded the privileges of a guest, and the freedom of the keep, at least so far as the herb garden. But everyone would be looking at her, wherever she went. She needed to pull herself together and be dignified, or at least calm. She could not look flustered or fearful, no matter what happened today.

But to replace the clan's healer, when she'd just arrived yesterday? That remained to be seen.

****

Colbridge stalked through the remains of his camp, snarling at anyone who dared cross his path. Few tents remained standing. Most had already been packed for travel into the few wagons they had horses left to pull, as were supplies and stores. Those signs of progress did little to ease his frustration. His prize prisoner stolen, along with his Healer. In a camp of nearly two hundred armed men, it should not have been possible. And they hadn't just walked out on their own. But where had they gone? Farther north or west into the mountains?

The sentries on duty at the time had been whipped and now suffered the care of Ranald and the lesser healers. Hurts that Aliana could have righted quickly would linger, diminishing Colbridge's fighting force. But an example had to be made. The sentries had been careless of their duty. By God, he'd taught them to care. It was a lesson they'd not soon forget, and if they did, there would be plenty of scars on their backs to remind them.

His own hurts were mended, though the damnable weakness persisted. Curse the woman, stolen away just when he needed her. His slow recovery was delaying the advance.

He approached the area where the prisoners had been held, noting the leathers still tied round the trees, the only sign this area had once held men, men who now roamed free in the forest to rebuild a fighting force and attack his rear when he moved out. Many of the leathers showed teeth marks and ragged edges. They hadn't been cut; they'd been chewed apart. Fresh fury crested, and he cut the strips from the trees and tossed them into a pile. By God, he should use them to string those guards up. What were they doing while the prisoners gnawed through their bindings to gain their freedom? Whipping had been too good for them. Perhaps a more permanent example would have an even greater impact on their vigilance. The guard captain, for instance. Or the lot of them.

Then Colbridge spotted one of his men approaching with a prisoner whose hands were bound behind his back. Good. Let him try to get to those leathers and chew them off.

"This man has news you should hear," the guard told him and stepped back.

Colbridge, temper still frothing, snarled, "Well?

Speak up, man!"

"Aye, sir," the man started, then hesitated before continuing. "The other captives, they won't stay nearby. They'll likely follow the Lathan to the Aerie."

"What do you mean they'll follow the Lathan to the aerie? What aerie? And who is the Lathan?"

"The Lathan. Clan Lathan," the man answered, clearly confused. "The clan nearest to us. Their stronghold, the Aerie, isna close but it's less than a day's ride west—farther into the mountains."

"Why go there if it's so far?"

"The other clans are even farther away," the bound man replied. "The ones on foot will follow the men on horseback, though it may take them two more days."

"And when they arrive, will the Lathan receive them?"

"Oh, aye, certainly, since he likely ordered them freed."

"Ordered them freed? How could he do that when he didn't know they were captured?"

"What? How could he no' ken it? He sat right here among them. When his men came to retrieve him, he likely ordered the others freed to cover his own escape."

Fear widened the bound man's eyes when he saw Colbridge's fist clench.

Colbridge's rage threatened to choke him. "He was here?"

Clearly hesitant, the bound man continued. "Aye, tied up with the other prisoners. I saw him there when I they took me to the healers to bandage this cut on my arm. I wasna sure till I saw his torc."

"Torc? Torc! The man I took prisoner wore a torc.

He wasn't a MacAnalen laird?"

"Nay, no' one of ours. The MacAnalen wears no torc."

"He was the laird of the nearest fortress?"

"Oh, aye. The Aerie's a fine fortress. 'Tis set on a high tor. They say it has never been taken."

"Never been taken? What do you mean?"

"If they don't want ye in, ye don't get in. And they can last forever in there."

"Why are you telling me this?"

"Because when he escaped, he left me behind. The Lathan laird sat among us alone. He should have sent for his men to help us fight ye off, but instead he watched us get slaughtered, and walked away without me when it was all over."

Colbridge could barely credit what he heard. His fury raged as close to madness as it ever had. A strange laird had been in his hands. Now he was gone. Aileana with him. And instead of being able to turn south before winter moved in, he would have to get her from a castle reputed to be unassailable. They could be delayed here for weeks more—months, if they had to mount a siege. Colbridge shuddered.

"I had the Lathan here, and no one told me? You did not tell me!" Colbridge drew his sword. Both men facing him stepped back, but it was too late to run. In a flash Colbridge separated the prisoner's head from his shoulders.

His guard stepped back even farther, face white, hands out, not daring to run, but terrified to stand too close. "I did not know. Don't kill me, too."

It did him no good. Colbridge's wrath demanded blood and his sword flashed in the sun. Others who had started to carefully approach, not knowing what caused the commotion, stopped short, gaping at the sudden bloodshed. But they ran when he threw his head back and howled his fury to the sky.

Chapter Seven

Toran stood on the ramparts with Donal, watching as a small group of riders arrayed themselves at the edge of the glen below the Aerie, along the opposite trees. "They've found us, and quickly, too. Did they follow? Or did some poor MacAnalen captive point the way, I wonder?"

"It doesna matter," Donal retorted. "That lot are here, and they'll bring along the rest, soon enough."

"Their leader still lives or they wouldna come. So that's the answer to that. He willna give up."

"We saw nary a siege engine in that camp. They canna do much against us without at least one," Donal remarked thoughtfully and nodded toward the forest. "But there are plenty of trees to cut down. Given the time, they could build them, or use the logs as battering rams against our gates." He gestured toward the main gate into the Aerie and continued, "We'll need to post more archers there, but the approach up the ridge is easy enough to defend." He turned back toward the invaders' scouting party. "I dinna see many supply wagons in that camp, either. From the look of them, they've been on the march a long time."

"More than two years, according to the Healer," Toran answered, and wondered how the dark-haired lass had survived in the midst of the rough camp. She thought she'd been safe there. Toran wondered how long that would have remained true. "A long time to be away from hearth and home," he muttered, turning his back on the scene outside the Aerie to regard the activity in the bailey, below.

"If there's truth in what the MacAnalens told ye while ye enjoyed their company," Donal said with a smirk, and Toran groaned in exasperation. Donal would not let him forget that, ever. "Then," Donal continued, "most have no home to return to. If Colbridge didn't break their clans, the Sassenach already had in the fighting at the borders. They're mostly lost men, with none to look to except that toady bastard leading them around our countryside. And they've nowhere to go save squatting at our door." Toran nearly grinned at Donal's aggrieved tone.

"They'll leave soon enough."

"Aye, one way or the other," Donal growled.

With Colbridge's patrol in sight of the main approach to the Aerie, scouts that Toran had sent out would have to stay in the trees as long as possible and then make a fast break for the main gate, or take the longer, hidden way around the tor and the postern gate in the lower caverns. Toran allowed himself a moment of amusement, imagining the complaints as they climbed the many stairs and steep passageways up into the Aerie.

"We'll need to move some of the horses to the lower stable," he told Donal. "If Colbridge's archers get in range of the main gate, the postern will be our best way in and out."

"Aye. We'll move them after dark."

"I want three men to go back to Colbridge's camp tonight. Someone told Colbridge where we are. I suspect we missed freeing some unlucky MacAnalen or one was recaptured and tortured for that information. If our scouts find anyone else held in there, get them into the hills with their kin where they can be cared for."

"Aye. 'Twill be done."

"Quietly. We don't need any more Lathan captives in that camp."

"Aye, Lathan," Donal said with a straight face for once.

Toran's attention focused on the bailey as Aileana come out from the main hall, following Elspie. Her appearance stilled the activity in the yard. Toran sensed no animosity among his folk, merely curiosity, as people stopped what they were doing to watch her go by, offer a greeting or just nod and stare. It was more than the fact that she was a new face, a stranger among the clan. He'd seen plenty of visitors noted and ignored. Did her status as a healer fascinate them? Nay, this was different.

So, she gained noticed from all, but then, Toran mused, the Healer was hard to ignore. Even in this place and with these people who were strange to her and staring at her, she maintained an air of calm certainty that only added to her beauty. She acknowledged everyone she passed, but did not pause to return their greetings. Her thick, dark braid swung on her back as she crossed the bailey to the wall of Senga's herb garden and passed through the gate that Elspie opened. For a moment, the watchful stillness held, then the noise and movement resumed. Toran blew out the breath he had not realized he was holding.

"That's quite an effect she has on the folk," Donal muttered beside him. "As if she wears invisible armor, or royal raiment; all must regard her, but no one may approach."

"I think we have just seen why she remained safe and untouched in the invader's camp," Toran answered, as bemused as his companion.

****

"The wall's to keep the coneys out, or the long-eared pests would eat all that Senga grows, and there'd be naught for her stews and potions," Elspie prattled on as she opened the gate and gestured for Aileana to precede her. "Though why they hop their way into a busy keep like this is more than I ken. The main portion of grains and root vegetables and such we get from the fields in the glens, and from the villages hereabouts, o'course. We've a goodly store to carry through the winter in the cellars beneath the keep. But Senga likes her herbs, and this garden is a pleasant spot in the morning."

Indeed it was, Aileana thought as she noted with pleasure the neat beds of greens and herbs. If Senga tended this, she cared for more than greens and herbs; she had a bit of art in her as well. Aileana turned to take it all in, observing how the morning sun filled the generous space with light. Blooming vines climbed the rocky walls, some of the leaves turning russet or gold from the growing chill of the recent nights.

"It's lovely," Aileana said at last. "I can see why you like it so."

Elspie led her to a bench in the sun, and went through a doorway into what must be the kitchen, judging by the mouthwatering scents that wafted out of the door. The clatter of pots and pans rang over the sound of women's voices. Aileana couldn't make out what the women discussed, so she ignored the chatter and studied the layout of the garden. The rock walls were positioned to soak up the warmth of the low sunlight that illuminated them this time of year and extend the growing season. Savory herbs for the pot were kept separate from medicinal plants, which could be dangerous. Now that she'd had a chance to study the arrangement, she realized that flowers bordered the savory beds, while a low, thorny shrub bordered the medicinal beds, clearly signaling "keep away." Even the dullest kitchen lackey would be able to tell where to pick and what to avoid.

No such measures had been required in her mother's garden since only she and Aileana had harvested there. But in a large keep such as this, there might be several who helped in the kitchens, and children might enter to play or pick flowers. Aileana admired Senga's forethought.

Aileana had only a few minutes to herself to enjoy the sunshine and the scent of growing things before Elspie returned carrying a large basket and leading one of the tiniest women Aileana had ever seen.

"Good day, lady," the sprite greeted her, then dismissed Elspie with a regal nod and continued with barely a breath. "I'm Senga. I'm told ye ken something of healing and herb lore."

Elspie set the basket on the ground beside Senga, nodded to Aileana and left them alone.

Senga's eyes were a bright, sharp blue, set in a small face that was crowned by a wealth of white hair braided and wrapped around her head. Despite her tiny size, the spirit that shone from her eyes was formidable. Aileana had the sense that Senga weighed and measured her fully in one steely glance.

Aileana took a breath, then answered her. "Some, yes. Though I'm told your methods are different than mine."

"Aye?" The sharp blue gaze pinned her in place and the sense of being tested increased.

"What I know, I learned from my mother," Aileana spoke carefully, not sure what Senga was looking for and reluctant to be found lacking in some way. "But what you have here is more than she used, and more than I recognize. I would learn from you, if you're willing."

"Then ye'll be welcome to my garden when ye like," the old healer said with a nod that Aileana took for some sort of acceptance. "And I'll be pleased to show ye what's here whilst I pick some herbs for tonight's supper. There's nothing our wee laird likes better than my stew."

Aliana laughed at that. "Your wee laird?" she asked, incredulous that anyone, especially one as tiny as Senga, could describe the huge warrior as "wee."

"Aye, I've called him that since he was a bairn," Senga told her, then turned to a flower-bordered bed, knelt and began picking fresh herbs. "Toran's been hanging about my kitchen since he got old enough to crawl and clever enough to snatch a treat from my tables. A wee pest he was, but even as a bairn, he had a charm that no one could resist."

"I see that hasn't changed," Aileana answered, with only a little irony as the memory of her body's hunger for him suddenly swamped her.

It was Senga's turn to laugh. "Nay, lass, little has changed. He's laird now, and a good one. He's kept his charm. And he still visits my kitchen for a nibble whenever he pleases." Senga picked up the basket and gestured to Aileana. "Now walk with me."

"You're the cook and the healer?" Aileana asked.

"The healer, aye. My herbal is just beyond the kitchen, and I keep an eye on the cooking to ensure the health of the clan, but others do the work with the pots and pans."

Aileana could see why. She couldn't imagine someone of Senga's size lifting a pot full of stew. It would be nearly as big as she was.

Aileana listened with interest to Senga's tales of life in the Aerie and of its laird as they wandered the garden, filling the basket with herbs and greens. She impressed Aileana with her fierce loyalty to the man she'd known first in swaddling. Her tales of his childish antics did nothing to dilute her evident pride in the laird he'd become, but Aileana wondered how he'd won the hearts of his people.

Loyalty could be bought with rewards, or forced with fear, as she had seen Colbridge do countless times. Was it fair to judge Toran by the measures she'd learned from that tyrant? She'd had little experience with any other form of leadership save the coercion Colbridge used to keep his men under his control. Was a clan run like an army? Or more like the village she'd grown up in?

She'd noticed a sense of community among the few people of Clan Lathan whom she'd met that she missed when she allowed herself to think about the home she'd lost. She wasn't sure if it was real or a perception born of her own wishes. But it wouldn't exist if their laird mistreated them in any way.

"Does it not worry you, that the invaders could arrive soon?" she asked Senga as they finished the tour of the garden and stopped outside the door into the kitchen and the nearby herbal. The mood in the Aerie seemed calm and purposeful, despite the probability of a siege.

"Nay, lass. The Aerie's ne're been taken, no' by force, no' by siege."

"Never?" That might be so, Aileana thought, but it was about to change. Colbridge had defeated every force he'd met. The Aerie might take longer to subdue than a village, but Aileana knew he would persist until he prevailed—or died.

"Nay, lass, never," Senga responded with an undeniable air of certainty. "Ye're safe within its walls."

Aileana hoped that she was right.

A young woman with hair the color of acorns appeared in the doorway. "Senga," she said, her gaze moving from the tiny healer to Aileana and quickly back again. "Brea is asking for ye."

"She'll want what I've gathered," Senga answered then turned to Aileana. "This is Coira," she said, then turned back to the woman standing in the kitchen door. "And Coira, this is Aileana, a healer and guest of our laird."

Aileana nodded, but Coira kept her face still, her eyes watchful. Her clothes were too rich for her to be one of the kitchen staff, and Aileana wondered why she ran errands for the cook. Or was she just curious about the new guest in the Aerie?

"I'm pleased to meet you," Aileana finally said to break the silence as Senga frowned at the other woman.

Coira nodded. "I see Toran's eye for beauty did not desert him while he was gone from us."

"Coira!" Senga's tone brooked no argument, but the woman turned her back on them, went into the kitchen and out of sight.

"Who…" was all Aileana got out before Senga interrupted her.

"Pay her no mind," she advised. "She fancies herself the lady of the clan." She eyed Aileana and the corner of her mouth lifted just slightly. "She'll be disappointed in that ambition, I think."

Aileana frowned. What did Senga mean? Did Toran already have a woman, or did Coira merely hope to become his?

Senga returned to her kitchen, leaving Aileana sitting on a stone bench to enjoy the scents of the garden and absorb what she'd just learned. She was dimly aware of the voices outside its vine-covered walls, along with the clang of swords and the whoosh and thud of arrows finding their marks in the straw targets set up in the outer bailey. She could see men walking the ramparts on the outer wall, and realized that one of them was Toran. His well-muscled form was unmistakable, larger and more attractive to her eye than the other warriors nearby. She saw him turn from whatever had his attention outside the keep to speak to his companion, and his strong profile and the way his dark hair fell to his big shoulders captivated her. His gaze swept the interior of the bailey and paused on her for a moment before he continued his conversation with the man beside him. He'd noticed her, then looked away. He seemed focused on what his companion said to him, and his lack of regard for her made Aileana's heart drop into her belly. Had she been wrong about him, wrong about the attraction she felt growing between them?

Aileana sighed and settled herself more fully on the bench, listening to the sounds around her, inhaling the rich aroma of roasting meat and baking bread from the kitchen, feeling the warmth of the sun on her face. She forced herself to keep her gaze off of Toran, focusing instead on the soothing greens of the herbs and the bright colors of the flowers within the low garden walls. She listened to Senga's laughter and the answer of a deeper male voice from the kitchen. Someone must be begging a taste, Aileana thought with a sad smile.

****

"Damn, they've seen us."

Toran didn't bother to answer Jamie. He kicked his horse into motion and turned away from the trail that led up the tor to the main gate of the Aerie. It was pure bad luck to run into one of Colbridge's advance scouting parties so close to that path. Toran had been sending out scouts for days who had managed to avoid the invader's men Just his luck to meet up with them. Six in this patrol, mounted and well-armed, and they'd nearly run right into them. He and Jamie were too far from the gate to reach its safety and avoid a fight, or for help to reach them from the Aerie. They would have to lose the six in the forest.

After a moment, he realized his friend hadn't followed. Toran looked back just in time to see Jamie reach up to pull the baldric containing his longsword over his shoulder. As he did so, an arrow buried itself in the flesh under his arm, nearly knocking him off his horse. It happened so fast that Toran didn't have time to think. He spurred his mount back to his partner and grabbed his arm to reseat him. Then he took the reins that lay slack in Jamie's hand and, pulling the injured man's mount behind him, kicked his horse into a gallop. He had to trust Jamie to hang on any way he could despite the pain he must be in.

The movement seemed to jar his partner out of the shock of his injury enough to take back control of his horse. Jamie grabbed the reins one-handed and pulled them from Toran's grip, swearing continuously as they rode headlong through the forest.

"What are ye doin'?" he gasped. "The Aerie's back that way."

Toran didn't like the catch he heard in his friend's voice, but they didn't have a choice. As long as Jamie could ride, they would ride. He was still on his horse, so the injury might not be as bad as it looked. At least, not yet. But he doubted that Jamie would be able to fight. They had to run.

"We'll never make the gate before they catch us." Toran threw the comment over his shoulder as he ducked a low branch. "We've got to lose them in the woods."

They had found the main body of Colbridge's army and needed to get that information back to the clan, but they'd have to lose their pursuers to do it. With only a few horses left, the invaders' wagons were overloaded and most of the men were on foot. That meant they were a day away from reaching the glen below the Aerie's tor, maybe longer. But they were clearly coming.

Toran was determined that at least one of them make it inside the Aerie's walls with the news. But there were too many in the scouting party for them to be able to stand and fight, even if Jamie could swing a sword, which he couldn't manage in his condition. And Toran knew he couldn't take them all by himself.

"Head for the burn," Jamie called weakly. "Thick trees…they'll get separated. Maybe we'll lose a few…of them."

If he'd had time for it, Toran would have wept at the way Jamie sounded. His normally strong, deep voice crackled and he wheezed between words.

The pounding horses' hooves behind them rumbled like thunder in the stillness of the thick forest. Shouted oaths echoed among the trees, making their pursuers sound like a much larger group than they actually were and sending chills up Toran's spine. Despite being in unfamiliar territory and having to duck tree branches as they rode, at least a few of the pursuers were drawing closer.

Toran guided Jamie down a ravine that led to the burn and halted. Jamie pulled up beside him. The turnoff was well hidden behind a thick stand of trees. If they'd gotten through without breaking any branches, chances were good that their pursuers would miss it and keep going deeper into the forest. They waited, breathing hard but as silently as they could, until they heard the group of riders pass. Toran turned to Jamie with a grin that immediately fled his face when he saw his friend's condition. Blood soaked the side of Jamie's leathers, and his face had taken on an ashen cast that did not bode well at all. Swallowing, Toran pointed down to the burn.

"Can ye ride on?" he whispered.

"Aye," Jamie gasped through his labored

breathing.

There was no time to waste. Toran led them into the shallow burn and followed it around the base of the tor. Jamie slumped over his horse's neck, dripping blood onto his mount and into the water. Toran hoped that he could stay in the saddle long enough to reach the postern.

Toran had ordered the Aerie's scouts to avoid using the postern unless the situation was dire. Even by his rules, this qualified. So he kept them to the burn to hide Jamie's blood trail, only leaving it when they reached the approach near the cavern entrance. They went carefully—quietly and slowly. If any pursuers found them here, there would be no hope of getting inside the cavern. They could not betray its location. So they waited, and he listened and watched.

After an eternity during which Jamie's breathing became so shallow that he could no longer hear it, Toran moved them forward through the trees. He pulled up near the entrance and grabbed his friend's reins as his horse nearly kept going right past him. Jamie slumped in his seat, white and barely conscious. Toran had to get help, now. He dismounted and led the horses inside to the iron gate that barred their way. He quickly located the hidden key and used it, then relocked the gate behind them. The horses followed him quietly out of the passage and into the big cave.

The injured man kept trying to spur his horse into motion, clearly unaware of where he was.

"No, Jamie, 'tis all right. We're inside. Let's get ye down from there."

As soon as Toran touched him, Jamie collapsed into his arms. Toran lowered him carefully to the floor of the cavern, shaken by his friend's cold, pasty skin. Blood covered his clothes and dripped down his saddle. It had taken too long to get here. In protecting the postern, Toran feared that he was close to costing Jamie his life. He could not waste any more of Jamie's time.

"Old friend, I've got to leave ye for a few minutes and get Senga. Ye're safe here. Rest a moment, and I'll be right back with help."

When Jamie didn't respond, Toran gripped his uninjured shoulder briefly, then ran for the stairs.

Chapter Eight

Toran reached the top of the stairs out of breath and gasping, but still at a run. "Senga!" The kitchen hallway was empty. He kept yelling her name as he burst into her herbal. Also empty. Gasping and swearing, he ran for the Great Hall, still calling for the old healer.

As others took up the cry, Toran saw Senga's tiny form being hurried across the Hall toward him. Someone with legs longer than hers finally picked her up and carried her. The growing rumble of voices barely penetrated his fear and urgency. He pushed through the crowd gathering around him and saw Senga's lowered brow and firece stare as she assessed him. He knew blood soaked his clothing, but help was making its way toward him. That was all that mattered.

"Hurry! Jamie's wounded. Bad. Postern," he urged, and pushed the man carrying tiny Senga toward the hallway stairs. He turned to follow, but Donal stopped him with a hand on his shoulder.

"Are ye well?" Donal asked. The sharp scent of Jamie's blood on his clothes filled Toran's nose.

"Winded from the stairs," Toran answered shortly, grabbing Donal's arm and following Senga and the others who filed swiftly out of the Great Hall. "Jamie's blood. None of mine. Jamie's still below—too heavy to carry up." Toran's breathing was still ragged, but he knew Donal heard the worry in his tone.

Donal's frown turned fierce as they started side-by-side down the stairs through the caves. "How bad?"

"As bad as it gets."

It was far, too far, this climb down through the tor while Toran fretted. Once they arrived in the entry cavern, Toran pushed through the crowd that had gathered and encircled Jamie's pale, still form where he lay on the stone floor in a growing pool of his own blood. Blood soaked his clothes and a foamy trickle bubbled from his mouth. Toran's mouth went dry when he saw the arrow shaft protruding from where the shoulder cap met the mail shirt Jamie wore under his plaid.

Donal gasped and turned to Toran, grabbing his arm. "How did this happen?" he demanded.

Toran shook his head. "We were on the trail back to the main gate," he said in a low voice as they watched Senga examine Jamie. "A group of riders spotted us. Jamie was reaching for his sword—" Toran cursed softly for a moment, then continued. "He had the devil's own luck. There wasna a thing to do but run for it. We lost them in a thick patch of trees. Then we followed the burn to hide the blood trail in the water, and I got him back here as soon as I was sure we weren't followed."

Donal nodded, subdued by the grief and exhaustion on Toran's face. "Ye did the best ye could, lad," he said, then turned his attention back to Jamie. Senga knelt by the still form on the floor of the hall. Her face betrayed her sorrow as she looked up at Toran and shook her head. "He breathes yet, but not for long. There's naught I can do."

"Nay," Toran cried, dropping to his knees. "I shoulda got him back sooner."

"Nay, lad," Senga said. "It wouldna done any good. The wound's too deep. The arrow's in his lung and he's drownin' in what doesna bleed out."

Shock and anguish burned their way from Toran's belly to his throat. "Nay. No' Jamie." He gripped Jamie's shoulder and swore. There had to be something they could do to save him. Then Toran remembered the strange sensation in his bound wrists, and how Aileanna had healed the punctures in his arm on the ride to the Aerie. The Healer!

"Someone get the Healer," he ordered, his voice booming around the cavernous space and carrying up the stair. "Get Aileana. Quickly. Now!"

He heard several people start up the stairs at a run.

Donal, disbelief evident in his raised eyebrows, shouted, "Nay!"

The footsteps on the stairs faltered.

Toran looked up at him in disbelief. "Nay? Nay?" He clenched his fists at his side, glaring first at Donal, then at the faces gathered around them. "Will ye let Jamie die then?" he barked at Donal.

Donal had the grace to look abashed, but continued his objections. "Will ye have a stranger, new come from an enemy camp, have knowledge of the postern? That it exists? Where it is?" He pointed toward the wide fissure in the cave's wall where daylight reflected off of angled surfaces from outside. "Many more than this man will die if word of this gets back to the invader."

Toran looked down at his dying friend, and knew he had to take the risk. "That won't happen," he said in a calmer tone. "She's with us, and with us she stays.

She can save him. He is yer kin and friend, too."

Donal started to object again, and Toran surged to his feet, grief supplanted by fury. "I'm laird here. Do as I say! Someone bring the Healer, now! Run!"

In the same tone of command, but more softly, he knelt back by Jamie and said, "Stay with us, lad. Help is coming. Jamie, hear yer laird. Stay with us." He saw no reaction to his words, only the same shallow breathing, the same bubbling froth of blood at the corner of Jamie's mouth, so he kept repeating it over and over, "Stay with us…hear yer laird, Jamie, stay with us…stay with me."

****

Suddenly, a hand gripped his shoulder and pulled him aside. Furious again, he surged to his feet, only to find her, the Healer, sinking past him to kneel beside the injured man. Toran clenched his fists, but stepped back to give her room.

She did the same thing he'd seen her do to Brodric MacAnalen in the camp, moving her hands over Jamie's body, pausing to listen, then moving more. Toran watched, terrified yet fascinated, holding his breath. Finally she turned and looked up at him.

"You must pull the arrow from his side," she said, quietly. Toran hesitated, shocked that such rough treatment could do anything to improve Jamie's condition. But he knelt beside her and at her urging, put his hands on the wooden shaft. "Wait!" she commanded, still quiet, but urgent. "Do as I say if you want your friend to live. Move slowly; pull it straight and don't twist it unless I tell you to. Pull a bit, then wait for me to tell you to before you pull again. I will heal what I can, but if you pull the arrow too quickly, he'll finish bleeding to death before I can save him."

Toran was not sure he believed any of this was happening, but after a glance at Senga and seeing her remorse, he realized that there was no other option. Senga nodded at him. Her message shone clear on her damp face: do what the Healer instructed and have a chance of saving Jamie, or watch his childhood friend die before his eyes. "Aye," he finally managed to say. "Tell me when."

"Now," she commanded, after placing her hands on Jamie's chest.

Toran pulled, and the shaft slid a fraction, then caught. His own breath hissed between his teeth, but the Healer stayed silent. He dared a glance at her face and saw that her eyes were closed below a frown of focus.

"Pull again," she said. "Slowly."

Toran tugged the shaft out a little further, feeling the resistance of the arrowhead's points in Jamie's torn flesh. Thank the saints that man had passed out, for the pain would have been monstrous. Toran's teeth clenched on bile and his body shivered at the thought of bearing such agony.

"This time," the Healer said, her voice interrupting his thoughts, demanding his attention. She seemed weaker, somehow diminished. "This time, twist a bit upward. The arrowhead must slip past the rib or it will catch there and do more damage."

How did she know that? But Toran did as he was told and carefully, bit by bit, turned the shaft as she directed, then waited for her nod before pulling again.

"Stop!" she commanded and he froze, heart in his throat. He watched as her hands smoothed slowly over Jamie's chest, following the path the arrow had taken.

"The next tug will remove it from his body," she said, breathing heavily, almost panting now.

Toran risked a glance in her direction to see her pale and sweating and felt a shiver run up his back.

"There will be blood, but do not worry. It will stop."

He risked a glance at Senga, but she was focused on Aileana's hands, her gaze intense, as though she, too, had the Sight and it was boring into Jamie's body, overseeing the work being done by the woman at Toran's side. Aileana moved and he looked down to see her fingers curved onto Jamie's side on either side of the arrow's shaft. "Now."

Toran held his breath and pulled. The arrow came free, along with a gush of red that quickly coated the Healer's fingers before slowing to a stop after she reached into the wound. Toran watched, fascinated and terrified at the same time as her hands continued to move, covering the wound, slipping back along Jamie's chest, then down his belly and across to the other shoulder, coming to rest on his chest. Finally, she sat back, bowed her head, and stilled. Toran saw that a bit of color had come back to Jamie's skin—not much, but a bit. Aileana's breathing was still labored, her eyes closed. Her hands lay in her lap as if spent, bloodied, unmoving. Blood soaked the skirt of her dress where she had knelt by Jamie. Toran supposed his own clothes were soaked as well, but he cared not.

Then Aileana's head came up and her eyes opened. She looked first to Senga, as if she did not see the crowd encircling them, watching her magic. Senga met her gaze fully, and that seemed to give Aileana a bit of strength to replace what she'd lost healing Jamie. "He'll need your warming poultice for tonight," she said softly, and Senga nodded, seeming not to care that she was taking instruction from one who could have been her apprentice. "And water. When he wakes in a few hours, as much water and mead as he will take. He will sleep again, but each time he wakes, make him drink. He has lost much blood, much strength." She started to rise, but stopped and turned back to Senga. "Keep him warm. Blankets. Warm the mead."

"Aye." Senga nodded and put a hand gently on Jamie's chest. "Can we move him to his bed?"

"No, not yet. Cover him here. Bide with him…here. Perhaps tomorrow…"

Toran heard the catch in her voice as she paused between words, and realized that her own strength was flagging and about to fail her. "What do ye need, Healer?" he asked, putting a hand on her shoulder. He was shocked to find that she felt…cold.

She gave him a small, pale smile. "Food and drink. Then rest. I'll be able to tend him again tomorrow." Suddenly, she blanched and collapsed into Toran's arms.

"Senga!" he cried while pulling Aileana up against his chest. She was so still, so pale, so cold, as though she had taken her own life and gifted it to Jamie.

Senga left Jamie's side and reached out to Aileana, where she lay in Toran's arms.

"She breathes, though weakly. She's spent." At the panicked look in Toran's eyes, she continued, "Nay, no' like that. She'll no' die on ye. She's merely worn out, poor wee lass. This Healing she does, well, it's strange, and more than a mite hard on her. Take her to her bed, now, and keep her warm until she wakes. Then do as she said—food and drink, as much as she will take, and let her sleep again. Stay with her, Laird. I'll stay with Jamie."

Toran nodded, comforted by Senga's words. He stood, cradling Aileana to his chest, relieved to see hers rise and fall as she lay in his arms. When he looked up, the faces of his clan met him, surrounding the tableau that he, Jamie, Senga and Aileana made. Some looked relieved, and tears shone in many an eye, but there were also those, Donal included, who frowned at the woman in his arms, disapproval of Aileana's gifts clear on their faces. He heard someone hiss "witch" clearly in the silence, but couldn't identify the speaker. He saw Coira near the back of the crowd, glaring at Aileana. Such animosity gave him a chill, but he set that aside for later.

"Do you wish to challenge the wisdom of yer laird and yer healer, do so later," he growled at those gathered around him. "What's done is done. For now, let me by." The circle parted, and Senga nodded to him with a strange, wise look on her face. A small smile replaced it just as he turned to go. Toran noted that for later consideration, too, snugged Aileana closer to lend her the heat of his body, and mounted the stairs. Donal followed close on his heels all the way up into the keep, but said nothing. When they reached the door to Aileana's chamber, it was Donal who held it open for Toran to pass by with his burden.

"I'll send Elspie," he offered, then closed the door behind him. Toran laid Aileana on her bed, and heaped blankets and furs on top of her. Then he bent to stir the fire. Not knowing what else to do for her comfort, he found a rag and dampened it, then sat on the edge of the bed and began wiping the blood from her cold hands, stroking them much as he had when her hands had cramped on the ride to the Aerie.

There came a soft rap on the door, and Elspie pushed it open a crack and peeked in. "Is she well, Laird?" she asked quietly, entering the room at Toran's nod.

"Senga says so, though it's hard to credit, looking at her."

Elspie stepped to the other side of the bed and shook her head. "Who can see her, the way ye have her buried, Toran!" She started pulling covers off of Aileana. When Elspie got the pile reduced to her satisfaction, she stood back, hands on hips. "The idea is to keep her warm, my laird, not to cook her in her own juices."

Toran had nothing to say to that, but he didn't have to say anything as Elspie offered, "I heard how it went, below." She frowned as he tucked Aileana's hands under the blankets. "She saved Jamie, she did, and what thanks for it from the clan? A few fools who believe the tales of witches that travel with the smoke from the south, do they? Not foolhardy enough to challenge their laird, I'll wager."

"Not yet," Toran allowed. "What she can do seems unnatural, I'll admit. But I've only seen her use her Talent, she calls it, to help others. No one can gainsay that. Even Senga approved."

"Aye, she would. She's had the care of us since most were bairns. She'll knock some sense into those hotheads, if it's needed."

"I hope ye have the right of it, Elspie," Toran replied evenly, "so I don't have to." After Elspie left,

Toran said aloud what had been on his mind, the one thing that he could tell no one, the one thing that was tearing him in two. "The clan needs her. But I need her. And I don't know how I can have her, if she's to be our healer."

****

Aileana woke to find Toran dozing in a chair next to her bed. How long had she slept? A glance toward the window showed her weak afternoon sunlight. Ah, she hadn't quite slept the day away, then. Good. She could check on the man she'd saved from the arrow wound before nightfall. He was probably fine. Senga was a good healer and would tend him well, but it had been Aileana's observation that as the sun sank, so did the spirits of the injured, which sometimes led to a worsening of their condition.

Taking a deep breath, she began to make small movements. Fingers and toes first, then arms and legs, then a satisfying stretch. Other than ravenous hunger and thirst, she seemed no worse for the wear.

She turned on her side and regarded the man sitting vigil over her. He must be exhausted, she thought, to sleep on in broad daylight. The injured man must've been dear to him, indeed. Weren't warriors trained to rouse at the slightest movement or sound around them? But no, that could not be, else they'd never get a night's sleep. Though he'd certainly demonstrated how light a sleeper he was when he surprised her in her Healing tent that morning she'd thought to check on him.

There was no help for it. She needed to get up and take care of necessities. She lifted the covers aside and sat up. At her movement, Toran's eyelids popped open and he sat up, too, and reached for her.

"Aileana. How are ye? What do ye need?"

"I'm fine, Toran, truly. I just need a few minutes of privacy, and then something to eat and drink before I go check on my patient."

Toran stood to take her arm and help her gain her feet. "I'll send for something to be brought up."

Gently, she patted his chest and then stepped away from him. "Thank you. While you do that, I'll change and be ready when you come back."

"I'll send Elspie to ye."

"Nay, you needn't bother her. I'll be done in a moment."

Toran gave her a skeptical look, then nodded. "Verra well. I'll return in a few minutes. Be careful, lass. Ye may not have quite all yer wits about ye yet."

"My wits are just fine," she answered, fixing him with an insulted stare. "Now go, please."

Toran nodded and left her in peace. She quickly stripped off the bloodied gown and silently thanked Elspie for insisting that she needed more than one. The blood had soaked through to her undershift, and she removed that, too, then washed the sticky skin below it with the rag and warm, clean water someone had thoughtfully placed on the table next to the fire. After taking care of necessities, she pulled on clean clothes and inspected the bedding. Yes, it would have to be changed. Her patient's blood had stained the sheeting, but fortunately had not penetrated to the woolen blankets and furs above it. Sighing, she began stripping the bed just as Toran reentered with a tray, followed by Elspie carrying another.

"Aileana, what do ye think ye're doing?" Toran barked.

"Here now, lass," Elspie complained when she saw what had upset Toran. "That's no work for a lady. Come sit by the fire and eat while I take care of the bed."

Aileana gratefully ceased her efforts. The strength she'd gained from resting was deserting her quickly. She sat obediently under Toran's withering stare. He meant well. She took the tankard he handed her and drank deeply. Ah, cider. Wet and cool, it tasted wonderful. And the sweetness of it would revive her faster than almost anything else. She emptied the tray of food quickly, then drank down another tankard of cider. Toran leaned against the wall, looking like he would have preferred to hand-feed her if she'd allowed it, but there was no need. She knew her limits, and she'd been through this kind of recovery many times before, though never after healing someone so near death. The experience frightened her, but it also gave her even more confidence in her Talent, and in her ability to know just how far she could go and still protect herself.

Elspie finished changing the bedding as Aileana devoured the food and drink she'd brought. She bundled up the bloodied sheets and secured them against one hip with her elbow, then picked up the trays. "Shall I bring more?" she asked as she headed for the door. Toran straightened and went to open it for her.

"Nay, but thank you," Aileana replied. I'll be fine now."

"And I'll bring her down to supper later," Toran promised. "Have no fear, we'll see the Healer fully restored."

"That's good then," Elspie said as Toran closed the door behind her.

"Toran, I need to go see…the man I Healed."

"Jamie. His name is Jamie. My cousin and my oldest friend." He knelt by her chair and took her hands in his. "Lass, I dinna ken how to thank ye for saving his life. I thought he was lost to us."

"He'll be fine after he rests for a few days," she answered, squeezing his fingers before pulling her hands from his and gripping the arms of the chair. She did not deserve his thanks. "Toran, I need to apologize. It's my fault he was injured."

"What?"

"If not for me, Colbridge would not be here. He might have turned south after defeating the MacAnalens. Instead, he's set up camp across your glen, he's attacking your men and trying to break into your keep. All because he wants me back."

"Do ye truly believe that?"

"Aye, of course."

"What about the fact that I stayed a day longer with the MacAnalens than I should have and so was taken in the battle and then caused all of their prisoners to be set free? Do ye think that might have caused a bit of resentment among the invaders?"

"Perhaps. But…"

"But nothing, lass. Aye, he wants ye back. Ye explained why to me the first night ye were here. And ye have the right of that. 'Tis hardly fair, though, to put the blame for everything on yer slender shoulders when mine are broad enough to share the load. I brought ye home with me, after all." A droll grin lit his face, causing Aileana to snort, but then he continued more seriously. "But more than that, a warrior canna ignore the insult we gave him. He's here because of me, because of what I and my men did in his camp. And even if I had no' been there and had no' met ye and none o' the rest of it had happened, ye said yerself he's bent on conquering the Highland clans. He would have shown up here eventually, with or without ye. This way, the timing works in our favor, not Colbridge's. Winter is coming on. His force is small and shrinking by the day. 'Tis better to defeat him here and now when he's worn and at the end of a long march than to face him again in the spring with a larger army and all summer to harass us. My presence in the MacAnalen camp and yer presence in the Aerie only served to hasten the inevitable."

"Ye make a strong case, Laird Lathan." Aileana sighed as the weight left her shoulders.

"I'm right, and well ye ken it."

Aileana nodded thoughtfully. "Aye, you are. And thank you for that. The guilt was tearing me apart."

"Ye have nothing to feel guilty for, lass." He stood and held out his hand to her. "Now, if ye're ready, I'll take ye to Jamie."

Chapter Nine

Toran sat alone by the fire in the Great Hall, sipping wine and pondering the rumblings of discontent within the clan that had reached him. He had to find a way to deal with the situation in the Aerie before it grew into something much more threatening than disgruntled mutterings.

He had tapped into the expensive cask of French burgundy, one of the few benefits of the Auld Alliance with France against England. That treaty had led James IV and many Highland lairds to attempt to divert England from its war with France by attacking the border, which had led to their deaths at Flodden three years before. The dead included the old MacAnalen and Toran's father and older brother. Toran had never expected to become the Lathan. But now he was, and he had things he must deal with.

He took another sip and savored the taste, letting the wine roll around on his tongue before he swallowed it. So different from mead or ale or whisky. Like velvet in the mouth, warm and soft on the way down. It was proof that there were desirable things that came from outside of the Highlands. There were many, actually...spices, fabrics, books...and an unusual woman whose kisses tasted warm and soft like the wine but were so much more intoxicating. Which was why he sat here staring into the fire, soothing his troubled mind with a rare glass.

Some of his people feared Aileana was a witch. He kenned it. That was only fair, given what so many had seen down by the postern. And the tale grew as it spread, as tales often did. The way she saved Jamie's life would be as fearful to some as it was wonderful to others. But some even reviled her for the fact that Jamie still lived! Toran shook his head. How anyone could see anything but good in what Aileana had done that day was more than he could fathom.

He noticed movement out of the corner of his eye. Glancing away from the fire, he saw Aileana crossing toward the hallway to the kitchen and Senga's herbal. She was intent on her destination, looking neither right nor left. After spending one day resting and regaining her strength, and another alternating with Senga sitting vigil at Jamie's bedside, she seemed revived. A touch of color tinted her cheeks. Her movements had regained their former regal grace. Toran stood and started after her. The wine held not nearly the attraction that the woman did.

As he reached the entrance to the long hallway, Coira stepped out of the kitchen and challenged Aileana.

"What are ye doin' here?" she snarled. The memory of Coira's icy glare as Aileana swooned in his arms after healing Jamie flashed before his eyes. He'd been warned by several of the clan about Coira's ambitions, and about her arrogant treatment of the fosterlings and the serving folk. But it was that glare that had burned its way into his memory because she'd never shown him that expression until then. Toran feared that this chance meeting would develop into a confrontation that Aileana was not yet recovered enough to withstand.

But as he watched her square off with the other woman, he also knew she wouldna appreciate his interference, so he paused just out of sight beyond the entrance to the hallway and listened.

"Are we to accept yer witchery because ye healed Jamie?" Coira continued, with barely a breath. "Or did ye? Why has no one seen him since ye bespelled him?"

Aileana's reply was barely audible, her voice soft. She seemed unbothered by Coira's accusation. "You haven't seen Jamie because he took a fever and Senga has confined him to bed until it passes," she replied. "He'll be fine."

Toran peeked around the corner in time to see Aileana gesture down the hall toward the kitchen and Senga's herbal. "You can ask her yourself if you don't believe me. She's preparing some medicine for him." At Coira's snort, Aileana clenched her hand into a fist and brought it down to her side, but continued calmly, "I am what you see: a healer working with Senga. Nothing more. What do you think I'm doing?"

The volume of her voice had risen, so Toran ducked back out of sight.

"That remains to be seen, does it no'?" Coira's sarcastic reply sounded as if she was ready to spit into Aileana's face, or worse. Toran was tempted again to intervene, but just before he stepped into the hallway, he heard Aileana's even reply.

"It does, I suppose. Only time will prove my place here."

"Time is something ye'll no' have, no' if I have anything to say about it."

"Anything you have to say, you'd best take up with your laird."

"My laird, is he? I've seen yer gaze on Toran. And ye've managed to catch his eye, too, it seems. I won't have it. Stay away from him, if ye know what's good for ye. He's to be mine. He seems to have forgotten that of late, but mark my words, I'll soon remedy that."

"I prefer not to," Aileana replied evenly, much to Toran's amusement. The Healer had depths he had not suspected, and greater strength than he had imagined. "Now, if you'll excuse me," she continued, "I've work to do. Senga expects me."

There was a brief pause, then Toran heard Coira taunt, "Oh, 'Senga expects me,' indeed. Does she now? I won't excuse ye, except to see ye marched out the front gate and back to the invaders' camp where ye can starve with the rest of 'em."

The silence that followed Coira's last cutting remark worried Toran enough for him to step from his hiding place into the hallway. He half expected to see Aileana's tear-streaked face downcast from Coira's spite. But the sight that greeted him stopped him in his tracks. He caught a glimpse of Aileana disappearing into the herbal. Coira stood alone, her back to him, hands on hips, fairly vibrating with anger.

It seemed that Aileana had returned the favor Senga had described to him after Coira had rudely turned on her heel and left Aileana in the garden. Senga's tale wasn't the first hint he'd had of Coira's temper, but coming from Senga, he hadn't been able to doubt the source. And now this. Well and good. He'd seen her anger with his own eyes and heard her venomous words with his own ears. She could not deny it after this.

He crossed his arms in front of his chest, content to wait to be noticed, knowing that would unsettle her all the more. Nay, this shrew was not the face Coira showed to him; rather he got all of her sweetness and light, fawning over him, tempting him to her bed. But perhaps it was just as well that he saw this side of her now, before she got even more out of hand. He didn't like her threatening Aileana. He wouldn't accept it from anyone, certainly not from Coira.

At that moment, Coira turned and found him watching her. She paled, but tried a small smile and hesitantly stepped toward him nonetheless. He glowered at her, and his expression coupled with the fact that he had yet to speak, clearly worried her. Good.

"Toran? I didna hear ye come up behind me." She put a tentative hand on his wrist and brushed her fingers up and down. "Well met, then. Perhaps ye'll join me…"

"I heard ye." Toran's flat statement cut her off in mid-sentence. "Every bitter word." He removed his forearm from under her touch and held up his hand instead. "Have done, Coira," he said, so sharply and coldly that there could be no mistake about his intent. "I'll no' have ye treating my guest as ye just did. She doesna deserve yer ire. Nay, yer display of temper, and yer superstitious drivel, does ye no credit."

"Yer guest?" Oddly, Coira seemed to take heart from his anger as she rounded on him, hands on her hips, and Toran saw that her temper was once again about to get the best of her tongue. "Yer guest, ye call her? What does that make me, I wonder?" Suddenly, as if she finally took heed of the thunderous expression on his face, she modulated her tone, but her words were just as harsh. "Donal has warned ye that she will do us harm, healer or no'. Have ye lost all sense over her, then, Toran?"

"Nay, Coira, but it seems ye have."

"How so? Would ye set me aside for the witch? O'course, if ye'd rather have her skills in bed, then I suppose ye'll have her as whore instead."

"Remember yer place, lass." Toran kept a tight rein on his temper as his anguish over the very conundrum that Coira named rose to clog his throat. He narrowed his eyes and kept his gaze steely as one tear trickled down her face, then another. False tears, he had no doubt, as false as her heart.

"My place is at yer side, Toran. 'Tis why I was sent here. Or have ye forgotten the alliance others intend for us to make?"

"I havena forgotten," he finally spat, his words following one on the heels of another, allowing her no chance to interrupt, and no chance to mistake his meaning. "But ye seem to have forgotten that yer presence here was an enticement only—one that I've yet to agree to. We're done," he growled, "but make no mistake. It's no' because of Aileana. Yer behavior has been related to me." Her actions had burned away any hint of ardor he'd ever felt toward this woman, nor could he summon any compassion. He would not tolerate her lies. "It's because ye show a nasty streak to others that ye've kept from me while ye tried to seduce yer way into the laird's bed. Aye, I ken yer ambition to become the lady of the clan. It willna happen, Coira. 'Tis no matter whether I ever have the healer or no'. I'll no' have ye. Is that plain enough for ye?" Any alliance he'd contemplated with her distant clan was of little value if her duplicity reflected what he could also expect from them.

"Aye, Laird Lathan," Coira replied, her tone haughty despite her damp cheeks. "Ye've made yerself quite clear. Go to yer witchy whore, then."

Toran held onto his temper with both hands. He wanted nothing more at this moment than to draw his dirk and silence her malicious mouth forever. But he could not, would not, treat one of the clan in that way, even one merely fostered here. He was no Colbridge, to shed the blood of those who displeased him, no matter the provocation. Instead he made his next words a clear command. "Stay away from Aileana."

Finally seeming to come to her senses, Coira backed away as he spoke, then paused, poised to answer him.

He stopped her with a glare. "Say another word to her, or to anyone else about her," he warned, "and I'll ken it. Ye'll no' like the consequences, Coira, I can promise ye that." Toran clenched his fists by his sides, which should have been enough of a caution for her to make herself scarce.

But she ignored him, chin up, eyes flashing. "I only mean to warn ye, Toran," she said, her tone a contrite lie against the fury in her gaze. "She'll see ye dead or ruined, and someone else will be laird o' Clan Lathan."

"Are ye a witch now, to tell the future with such certainty?" he taunted, bemused by her lack of sense.

"We dinna tolerate her kind where I'm from." Was that fear he saw now, behind her anger?

More gently, he replied, "We do."

Coira didn't deign to answer, but brushed by him into the Great Hall. He watched as she mounted the stairs leading to her chambers, silently daring her to turn back or to speak her venom to anyone else. He was glad he had not allowed her tears to sway him; he knew they were as false as the rest of her. A breath escaped him. That was done, then.

Or was it? Coira had made friends among the clan, and her wiles were effective. His interest in her had proved that. She'd nearly snared him in her web. She'd soon have a new champion and be stirring up trouble for him, no doubt, and for Aileana. As much as he wanted to stay away from her, it would be best to keep an eye on Coira, at least until the siege was over and he could send her back to her home or marry her off into another clan—preferably one far, far away.

****

Aileana entered Senga's herbal with her head down and her ears still ringing with Coira's taunts. How was she supposed to deal with someone who treated her like that? With all she'd done for the clan, who was Coira to tell her she had no place here? Worse, she'd threatened Aileana with the one thing that Aileana feared most: labeling her Talent witchcraft and condemning her to banishment or death.

Aileana had forced herself to calmness while Coira railed at her, but that calm exterior was rapidly unraveling. She lifted a hand to see it shake, then clenched her fingers into a fist and dropped it to her side.

"Healer, whatever is the matter?" Senga asked her. "Ye're trembling."

The question startled Aileana. She turned toward Senga's voice to see the old healer standing at a low cabinet crushing green herbs between her hands. She'd been so wrapped up in her own misery that she had forgotten that Senga would be in the room, waiting for her. And the sympathy in her voice further unraveled Aileana's control. Had she heard what Coira said? Was calling Aileana "healer" Senga's way of reminding her of her value? A tear slipped onto her cheek and turned away from the older woman, too embarrassed to let her see it.

"'Tis naught but a bit of rudeness I must swallow," she answered.

"Why do ye think ye must allow anyone to be rude to ye?" Senga asked kindly, brushing bits of green leaves from her hands and turning to regard Aileana.

"Because I'm a stranger here. And I bring strange abilities that many do not trust."

"But in time, ye'll no' be a stranger, and all will learn to be glad of yer skills, dinna ye ken?"

"Not if some have their way."

"Pah," Senga hmmphed, waving away the idea. "Some will have far less say in the matter than they think." After a moment, she continued. "Dinna let the likes of Coira fash ye, lass. She's more jealous of the attention Toran has paid to ye than any fear she might have of yer talents."

So Senga had heard—at least some of it. "That may be so, but if she calls me 'witch' and spreads that libel then I may never have the chance to make a place for myself here."

"Lass, this is the Highlands. Most of us have a greater respect for the old ways here than yer folk do in the south." Senga gathered the pile of herbs she'd crushed in her apron and brought them to the table where Aileana stood. "Coira is fostered here, didna ye ken it? She comes from the isles to the south and west, where they be too cozy with the Sassenach for my taste." Senga worked as she talked, placing the herbs in a neat pile in front of her on the table, then dividing the pile into thirds. "And as for the Sassenach...nay, they were too long under Roman rule and have forgotten how to respect the auld ways. They give their priests too much influence over matters best left to those of us who ken the ways of the land, the healers, the seers. Wise women are respected here. Especially auld wise women," Senga said with a wink. "Yer only problem is that ye're no' ancient, like me."

At Aileana's sniff, she said, "And dinna worry about makin' a place for yerself here, lass. Ye've already done that."

"Maybe with you, but not with everyone else. Even Toran has avoided me lately, and he brought me here."

Senga regarded her for a moment, then moved to her store of dried herbs. "Give 'em time, lass. Give 'em time. And dinna worry about the wee laird. He's just been a bit busy of late, what with yer former companions due to arrive on our doorstep. And once Jamie is up and around and telling the tale of how close he came to the angels, and how ye saved him, trouble like Coira wants to bring willna have a chance. Now, speakin' o' the laddie, do ye want to help me make this potion for him?"

"Aye." Aileana summoned a small smile. "I'd like nothing better."

"Take these and put them over there, then," Senga said and held out several small pots.

Aileana moved to do her bidding.

Despite Senga's advanced age, she always seemed

to be in her garden planting, weeding, and picking, or in her herbal, drying, grinding, concocting—all the things that Aileana had helped her mother do many times. Senga's grip might be weakened by age and her eyesight dimmed, but neither was apparent to Aileana. She still measured and mixed with the skill of a much younger healer. Aileana had watched her with growing admiration the past few days after she'd recovered enough from healing Jamie to work with the older woman. They were starting to develop a companionable connection that Aileana found a surprising source of joy.

"How long have you been healer to this clan?" Aileana asked when the older woman finally stopped muttering to herself. She was adding a pinch of this and a bit of that to the pile of herbs she was assembling for the decoction that was just starting to simmer on the brazier, giving off a bitter scent. Aileana recognized bits of willow bark among the rest.

"Many years, lass," she answered, her bright gaze meeting Aileana's. "Since the laird's da became laird." Senga stilled for a moment and looked away. It seemed to Aileana that she looked inward to that day so long ago. "Bain, the auld laird, was a fine, muckle...big...man, much like his lad," she continued, finally. She pursed her lips before adding, "The day I became a healer was the day he became laird, and our fates were sealed." Senga's gaze returned to the present and met Aileana's. "But that's ancient history and of no interest to a young lass like yerself. Here, stir this while I add these last bits."

Aileana moved beside her to the small iron pot on the brazier, stirred, and watched the herbs she added swirl into simmering liquid. The steam rose with a scent both fresh and pungent at the same time. "Have a care, now," Senga cautioned. "Stir, and dinna let it boil. It must simmer for a few minutes, then be set aside to steep. Watch for the color to change from green to yellow, then take it off the fire."

Aileana nodded and kept her eyes on her task. She heard Senga moving about the room, muttering as she put away the jars and vials her dried herbs and potions were stored in.

When she finished ordering her workplace and perched on a stool next to her, Aileana knew the time had come to ask the question that she needed but also dreaded the answer to.

She stirred the pot whose contents had faded to a pale yellow, then set it off the brazier to steep. "What do you mean, 'your fates were sealed'? Why did you never marry, never have children of your own to follow your craft?"

"Ach, 'tis the root of the matter ye seek, then, aye?" Senga lifted her hands and spread her fingers out in front of her, then placed them, still splayed, on the tabletop. "So, it happens that long ago, I loved a young lad. But he loved another. So he married her." Senga tapped a finger distractedly. "They had a son, a fine, braw lad he would become. But his ma died giving birth to him. My lad grieved so for his lost lady that he ne'er looked to another, but devoted himself to his son and his clan. And I remained as I am."

"Oh, Senga, I'm so sorry," Aileana whispered. How could a lifetime go by with no relief from such sadness, and perhaps such stubbornness? A chill skittered along her bones that past heartbreak could still be affecting them today.

"He refused you?"

"Oh, aye, that he did." A small, sad smile played at the corner of her mouth, then disappeared as she remarked, "Loudly."

"Do you hate him, then, the son of your love and his lost lady?"

"Hate him? Nay, lass. I love him as if he were my own. He's a bit of my own laird, living still. Ah, there, I've said it, haven't I? Now ye ken it all. I protect him as I can, with the skills that I have."

"How long has Toran been laird?" The last of the tension in Aileana's chest loosened at the mention of his name.

"Since Flodden. His da and brother died there. He became laird—something he never wanted. But laird he is and a good one. Fair and far-seeing. Perhaps he has a touch of the Sight, himself. He's been forging alliances with the neighboring clans."

"That is why he was with the MacAnalens?"

"Aye, and a good thing, too, for he brought ye to us."

****

Toran was with the blacksmith early the next morning inspecting his repairs to shields and blades when word came that Angus MacAnalen was on the approach to the main gate, riding hard. "Let him in, quickly!" Toran ordered. "We'll continue this later, Parlan," he said, handing a heavy longsword back to the smith. "Keep at it; yer work is good, as always."

"Aye," the big man replied, and Toran took off at a run. He arrived just as Angus passed through the inner gate into the outer bailey.

"Lathan," he hailed Toran as several lads ran up to take his horse.

Toran stood with fists on hips as Angus approached. "What brings ye?" Toran asked. "Is there more trouble?"

"Aye," Angus answered. "And good news, as well." He dismounted and handed the reins to one of the lads who stood by. "Walk him to cool him down," he said with a nod to the groom.

"Let's go inside where ye can fill me in over a cup," Toran offered, and began moving toward the gate to the inner bailey. "The lads will see yer mount cared for."

"I must get back as quickly as I can," Angus said, pacing alongside Toran. "The MacAnalen's life depends on it."

"The MacAnalen? Ye found him alive?"

"Aye, more dead than alive, but still breathing. I'm here to ask a boon, Laird Lathan. My hope is that the Healer can save him."

Toran froze in his tracks. "She canna leave here."

"Without the Healer, he will die, and soon."

"There's naught yer healer can do for him?"

"He's tried everything he kens. That the laird still breathes speaks well of Craig's skill, but he lies in a deep sleep and we canna rouse him. After the tales we heard in the camp, I'm thinking her ways may be different enough to succeed where my healer has failed."

A chill swept over Toran and he resumed leading Angus into the keep. Events such as this—aid rendered or denied—could set the course of relations between clans for generations. This was more than a simple request to borrow a skilled member of Clan Lathan. It was an appeal from one chieftain to the laird of an ally. Denial of the appeal could mean war.

But to risk Aileana? How could he? And how could Angus ask that of him? She was safe behind the Aerie's walls. A journey to Augus's hideout meant avoiding enemy patrols, something a party large enough to protect her would have difficulty doing. If they kept the group small enough to avoid detection and luck turned against them, there would be little chance of keeping the Healer out of Colbridge's hands.

Inside the Great Hall, Toran signaled for ale as Angus settled onto a bench close by the fire.

"Ah, warmth!" he sighed. Toran took a seat across from him. They both took cups from the serving girl.

"Hungry?" Toran asked while she waited.

"A bite would not go amiss," Angus replied and Toran sent the girl for a tray.

"The MacAnalen's condition must be grim for you to risk running Colbridge's lines in broad daylight to get here," Toran said.

"Aye," he agreed. "I waited until their patrol was well gone before making a break for the gate. 'Tis unlikely I'll be able to do that twice. And we've seen patrols in the area near the caves. They may be looking for us or for deserters from their camp. We've spotted strangers heading south alone or in small groups, two or three at a time." He took a sip. "We've talked to a few then let them pass. They're eager to escape our winter weather, it seems. And traveling back the way they came is the only path they ken out of the mountains." He set the cup aside, leaned forward and continued. "Since our escape, Colbridge has few horses left. He uses those for his patrols. So the men desperate enough to escape do so on foot. If they make it out of the mountains, they might survive."

"There are many ways to get lost in these mountains. Most willna make it."

"We've followed a few of them for a couple o' days to see them well on their way. They're worn, but they're tough, and they havena turned back. That's the good news. Colbridge is losing men every day that the siege continues. The deserters say that rations are short in that camp and Colbridge's temper is worse by the hour. But the men he has left are ranging close to our hideout. As it is, we havena dared a fire. Smoke would be seen during the day and the glow at night. We're living on bannocks and bring the horses into the cave at night for warmth."

"Are the women and weans with ye?"

"Nay, I sent them on to Iain MacIntosh right away. That was a fight, let me tell ye," Angus said with a quick but mirthless chuckle. "Some o' the lasses were eager to pick up a sword. But they went for the good of the bairns. And to carry news of the invaders to Iain."

"Aye, that was well done."

"I had little choice. We couldna risk them."

"What about sending the MacAnalen to him?"

Angus took a pensive sip. "Iain is too far away. The MacAnalen wouldna survive the trip."

"Perhaps there's another answer," Toran hedged. "Ye ken the risk to all of us if Aileana were to fall into Colbridge's hands again."

Angus could only nod. "I ken what I'm asking. But ye ken what it means to my clan, do ye no'?"

"Aye, Angus. I'm afraid I do."

"How goes it here?" Angus changed the subject as the tray of food arrived. "Ah, hot stew and real bread! I canna tell ye how tired I am of oat cakes." He put a thick slab of cheese on a piece of bread and eagerly bit in. A bite of the meaty stew followed immediately.

"Well enough," Toran said while Angus groaned his appreciation. "If ye think it safe, start moving yer men here at night. We'll make room for the lot of ye."

"It'll have to be done a few at a time," Angus agreed when he finished chewing. "Unless ye're ready to end the siege and attack the camp?"

"Nay. With the cold coming on, and what ye said about deserters, the longer we wait, the fewer men he has to fight with and the better for us."

"Verra well. Brodric will come with a few of my men first. Ye ken him, and he can identify any MacAnalen ye havena' already met. We wouldna want any of Colbridge's men to sneak in among 'em."

"That'll do. In the meantime, ye can rest in comfort and enjoy another hot meal. I've been sending patrols out at odd hours. One will go out tonight."

"So ye'll send the Healer back with me?"

Toran shook his head, making the decision that he had no doubt he'd come to regret. "Nay." At Angus's stricken look, he continued quickly, "I willna send her, but I will take her. I'll come, along with enough of my men to keep her safe. But we must wait until dark."

"Aye." Relief was evident in the sudden drop of Angus's shoulders. "There's no way we'll get out past the invaders in daylight now that they've seen me arrive." Angus took another bite and chewed thoughtfully for a few minutes. Toran left him in peace. Whatever he had left to say, he'd say soon enough.

"Now that I mention Brodric, well, he told me a bit of a strange tale after we got free."

Toran kept his face impassive, remembering Brodric's performance of his feigned illness that drew Aileana among the prisoners and allowed Toran to steal her from the camp. But he suspected that he knew what Angus was about to say.

Hearing no comment, Angus continued, "He told me that after the Healer did, well, whatever it was that she did to him, he felt better than he has in months. And he's no' been plagued by the pain in his hip that has been with him since a fall from his horse early this summer."

"Indeed."

"Indeed, that tale is what convinced me to come." Angus lifted his gaze from the food in front of him to Toran's. "If the tales are true, if she is a witch, then surely she can help."

"A witch? Or a healer, a wise woman, or a seer?" Toran prompted.

"So it seems. Whatever she is, she's the only hope the MacAnalen has." Angus went back to eating, and appeared content to drop the subject, warning given.

Toran wondered what Angus would think if he'd seen how Aileana healed Jamie three days past. He could scarce credit the memory, even though he'd watched with growing horror as Jamie's blood coated his hands. Senga's despair at her own impotence had been terrible to see. He kenned what damage an arrow lodged in muscle would do. Besides the torn flesh, bleeding to death was a real possibility. Jamie's wound had been much worse, and yet he still lived.

But for Senga's confidence in Aileana's abilities,

Jamie would be gone from them. Donal might have succeeded in arguing against bringing Aileana down to provide her aid. Toran had been too stunned by Donal's defection to be terrified of her, or of what she was doing, until it had all been over. And then, he'd been terrified for her when he saw the toll the healing had taken on her, the price she'd paid to save Jamie's life. It was something he'd never forget, holding her nearly lifeless body in his arms, and looking up to see the faces of his clan. If not for Senga's evident concern for her, what might have happened?

He pulled his wandering thoughts back to the present. Angus was still focused on the food in front of him and didn't seem to have noticed Toran's distraction.

"How did ye find the MacAnalen?"

"We searched for our missing, and we found some of them, none hurt as badly as the laird, thanks be to God." Angus's frown deepened. "Colbridge's men have dumped the bodies of our dead in a crevasse, but we havena been able to get close enough to identify them. He keeps a patrol nearby, knowing we'll try to go there. We know who we're missing, o'course, but no' until we've seen their bodies will we count them dead." Angus heaved a deep sigh. "'Twas ill done, that day. Our men dead, our village burned. We've no homes to return to, once this Colbridge is gone."

"Ye'll rebuild. We'll help ye," Toran promised, not liking the set of Angus's shoulders.

"Aye, then, let that day come soon," Angus said, straightening, a small grin playing around the corners of his mouth. "Or we'll guest with ye 'til spring comes again."

Chapter Ten

Toran faced Donal on the practice ground, breathing heavily and leaning on his sword. As laird, Toran knew he had to set the example, so he sparred with Donal or anyone else, as often as he could, just as he took his share of watches on the ramparts.

He signaled for a cup of cold, clear water, and drank it down in a gulp as soon as it was handed to him. Sweat sheened his body and ran down his chest and back despite the chill in the air. But Donal eyed him and he knew if he didn't pick up his sword in the next few seconds, Donal would, putting Toran immediately on the defensive. So with a deep breath, he hefted his longsword and with no other warning, began their third mock battle of the day.

It was the best way Toran knew to pass the hours until dark, when they would leave for Angus's cave.

The siege had been underway for nearly a week, and autumn was suddenly well advanced. Toran agreed with Angus that the colder weather signalled Colbridge wouldn't be able to maintain the siege much longer. Morning mists now turned to heavy frost that coated the glens with diamonds that melted away in the weak sunlight—beautiful, but portending the deadly cold and snow to come.

Colbridge's remaining men had continued trying the walls without success, but their failures made no difference within the Aerie. Donal was a strict arms master who never relaxed his guard. Shouts and clangs, the familiar din of fighting, had echoed around the outer bailey all day. There might be a hostile force camped at their feet, but training never ceased.

"That's water that coulda been poured on the invaders," Donal remarked, his parry countering Toran's thrust precisely, with no wasted motion. Though odd for a man of few words, Donal often used taunts or conversation to try to distract his opponent, and to force his students to learn to deal with the distractions that occur in battle before they had to face them with their lives at stake. Two could play that game.

"'Tis a good thing we have an endless supply." Toran swung his blade, watched Donal twist out of the way.

Donal grinned and picked up the pace. "Aye. Boiling water works as well as boiling oil or pitch to keep them off our walls."

"And Senga says it's easier to treat our men for scalds than for the burns they get from hot tar or pitch. That damn stuff sticks," Toran continued, turning to parry another thrust just before it connected with his shoulder. Thick practice padding protected them, and Donal was as skilled an instructor as he was a fighter, but Toran had no wish to suffer bruises at his hands, either.

Donal used the momentum of his twist to step sideways and around Toran's back.

"Plunging a hand into a bucket of cold water has saved many a lad from deeper burns," Toran added, his breath coming faster as he met Donal's challenge.

Donal, damn him, seemed unaffected by the pace he set

Donal jumped out of the path of Toran's sword and pulled his dirk. The claymore was long and heavy enough to be challenging to wield two-handed, but to fight one-handed with it took considerably more strength and skill. Donal now faced him with sword and dirk. Toran heaved a sigh and pulled his dirk from its sheath, too.

"One less jeopardy we face," he continued, as if the level of difficulty had not just doubled, or trebled. From the corner of his eye, he saw several people stop to watch as he and Donal sparred. He feinted with the sword and stepped in to threaten with the dirk. Donal saw him coming and danced out of the way.

"Thanks to our walls, none here face jeopardy. Save ye." Donal grinned as the flat of his claymore thwacked Toran soundly across the back.

Damn! That was his weakness, Toran berated himself, and probably how he'd been ambushed during the battle in MacAnalen territory. He dropped his weapons and raised his hands, palm forward, his heart pounding. "Have done," he said, conceding the match.

"Well fought, Laird," Donal said, sheathing his dirk and dropping the point of his claymore into the dirt. He took Toran's arm in an iron grip and chided, "Except for that last."

Toran shook his head. "One day that ploy will fail."

"Not soon enough," Donal answered, suddenly grim, "or I wager ye wouldna lain in the Healer's tent, laddie."

"Aye," Toran admitted, picked up his weapons, and then slung an arm over Donal's shoulder, walking with him toward the great hall and tankards of mead to slake the thirst they'd both worked up. "But it turned out for the best. The Healer is with us now."

"Is she, lad? Despite her helpful ideas, do we truly know where her loyalties lie?"

Toran dropped his arm from Donal's shoulder and faced him. "Aye. Ye saw what she did for Jamie. What she's done for others since then. Would ye turn aside from her when she saved his life and helped many more?"

Donal shook his head, his expression turning stubborn. "Lad, she's got ye bewitched and besotted, it seems. Aye, what she did for Jamie was fair miraculous, but there's the problem. What else can she do? What dinna we ken?" Donal gripped his arm, urging him into the Great Hall. "I'm not the only one of yer clan who has concerns, lad. What she did lies in the realm of fables, no' healing as we ken it. Ye canna dismiss this. I see the way ye watch the lass. No good can come of it."

"It already has, Donal."

"Perhaps. And perhaps it would be best to leave her with Angus."

"Nay. I'll no' do that. She belongs with us."

"I hope ye're right lad, I do."

****

Dinner in the Great Hall was never a grand affair. The clan's laird preferred to keep a more casual, comfortable home than had his father, the old laird, who sat at the high table and ran the servants ragged. Even with guests in attendance, Toran maintained the informality of the Hall. It was the way he preferred it to be, and after all, what was the point of being laird if he could not live the way he wished in his own home.

Tonight, Angus joined him at an early dinner. It would be their last chance for a full, hot meal for the next few days. Toran took his obligation seriously to treat Angus to what comforts he could offer before they ventured out into the cold night to rejoin his clansmen and carry out the plans he and Toran had made. He and Angus sat at table, Toran at the head and Angus at his left, cups of wine in hand.

Though it had become Aileana's habit to take her evening meal with Senga, or in her chambers, Toran requested that she attend tonight after her preparations for the trip were finished. He was quite interested to see what Angus made of the Healer in her new setting.

"I have to say, I've never seen the like before," Angus told him as they waited for her. "Many clans hereabouts have healers, wise women, and seers among them, but none that I know of have the skill this healer is said to possess."

"Nor I."

"'Tis a rare thing, it seems. Is it better known in the Lowlands? In the camp, it seemed strange that Colbridge's men respected her wish to remain untouched. Was that due to Colbridge's orders? Or because they already knew about healers like her?"

"Why would healers from the south have special talents that we havena seen here, and why would they have to remain untouched?" Toran wondered aloud. "How do new ones get born if that's the case?"

"It defies logic, it does," Angus replied. "Perhaps that was only her way to protect herself."

Aileana entered the Hall then. Toran stood, and after a surprised moment of delay, the rest of the men in

153

the Hall did, too. Aileana stopped, dismay on her face at the sudden display in her honor, and then started forward again as Toran held out his hand to her.

"Laird Lathan," she said quietly as she touched her fingers to his palm. That contact shot a frisson of want through Toran. She had never before offered her touch without being involved in healing an injury. Was she becoming comfortable enough with him to forget her safeguards?

"Healer Aileana," he replied, matching her formality for the moment. "I believe ye met Angus MacAnalen while he guested with Colbridge in the camp? Nay?" Toran hid the sense of loss that nearly overwhelmed him when Aileana retrieved her fingers from his. Angus offered his hand across the table, but Aileana merely nodded.

Angus inclined his head and smiled warmly at her, accepting her slight with good grace.

"Healer," Angus said, "we did not meet. But ye took care of some of my clansmen. And soon, ye may save our laird. For all of that, I am in yer debt."

"You owe me nothing, sir," Aileana responded primly. "I simply did what I was called to do."

"Aileana, please join us," Toran invited, and pulled out the chair to his right, keeping the table between her and Angus.

She sat quickly, clearly uncomfortable, but doing her best to be polite.

"Supper is on the way," he told her. "Would ye like some wine while we wait?"

"I don't know," she replied with a small frown. "I don't believe I've ever tasted any."

Toran noted Angus's raised eyebrows, but chose

not to explain Aileana's simple background. "Indeed," he said. He poured her a cup and placed it before her.

Aileana picked it up and sniffed the dark red liquid. "How can something smell warm?" She looked at Toran, but he simply smiled at her and nodded.

"Taste it. It's good."

Aileana took a sip, then raised her eyebrows in surprise. "It's very good," she said after she swallowed.

Angus chuckled, but Toran laughed outright. "Aye, that it is."

When the food arrived, Toran was pleased to see Angus dig in with a will, and even more pleased that Aileana nearly matched him, bite for bite, between sips of wine.

"Healer," Angus began after a glance at Toran, who nodded permission, "how do ye like living in the Aerie?"

"It's very different," she replied after a moment's thought. "Different from anything I've ever known."

"What do ye mean?"

"Look around you, Angus. It's a grand fortress. I come from a village, and spent the last two years with a traveling army. I've never lived anywhere like this."

Toran was amused to see her run her finger around the rim of her wine cup as she spoke.

"Would ye like some more, Aileana?"

"Yes, please."

Toran poured just as Senga walked into the Great Hall and beckoned to him.

"If ye'll excuse me," he said to Aileana and Angus as he rose, "Senga wants me for something. I'll be back shortly."

Toran met the old healer halfway across the hall.

"Is there something amiss?"

"Come with me, Laird. There's something ye should see before ye leave."

With no further explanation, she turned and led him from the Hall. He glanced around as they exited and saw Angus and Aileana deep in conversation across the table. He was tempted to turn back to see what subject had them both so engaged, but one did not ignore a summons from the clan's healer. So he followed her up the stairs toward the solar. There, in the hallway, Toran nearly shouted with joy at the sight that greeted him. Jamie walked toward them and smiled, bringing a healthy pink to his cheeks.

"Jamie, ye're on yer feet!"

"Ye have a wonderful grasp of the obvious, Lathan. And glad I am to be up and about, especially after coming so close to singing with the angels.

"They wouldna have ye, ye fool. Ye canna sing a note." Toran clasped his old friend in a careful embrace. He remembered just in time not to pound him on the back. He wasn't sure Jamie would appreciate that particular display of affection yet. "Ye're the best thing I've seen for days."

"He has recovered very well," Senga announced. "I willna say he's ready to resume his duties to the clan, but some time spent walking about the keep and a few good meals should see him completely restored."

"That's great news," Toran responded with genuine feeling. "Thank ye for yer care of my old friend." Toran slung an arm over Jamie's shoulders as his friend stood between him and Senga looking sheepish. "He wouldha' been a real loss to the clan."

"Now, Toran," Jamie interjected.

"And if ye tell anyone else I said it, I'll deny it."

"Then it will be our secret," Senga said with an uncharacteristic wink that surprised a laugh from Jamie.

Toran didn't realize how much he'd missed the sound of his old friend's laughter until he heard it now. It nearly brought tears to his eyes. To cover the emotion, he spoke. "So, Jamie, Senga, dinner awaits in the Hall. Will ye come?"

"Go along with ye, lads," she told them. "I've work yet to do."

"Thank ye, Senga," Jamie said, solemnly before Toran turned him toward the stairs.

"Don't thank me, laddie. Thank Aileana. She saved yer life when I couldna."

"Did she, now? Then I will do that," Jamie answered by way of a leave taking.

Toran went first down the stairs, knowing that Jamie would not hesitate to grasp his shoulder should he falter or stumble on the treads. He was surprised to see Aileana still deep in conversation with Angus. They both looked so serious. What could they be discussing with such intensity?

As he and Jamie entered the Hall, cheers and shouts of greeting rang out. Jamie was forced to acknowledge every person as they made their way to the table where Aileana and Angus now watched their progress. Angus looked puzzled over the uproar, which didn't surprise Toran since he hadn't been told about Jamie's injury and miraculous recovery. Aileana looked around her. Her face was impassive…no, he glimpsed a hint of a smile playing at the corners of her mouth. Was she pleased to see Jamie up and about? Or pleased to see the reaction to his return to health, one that did not include labeling her a witch?

Finally, he and Jamie reached Aileana.

"Jamie, ye may not remember Aileana, but she saved yer life when ye were as close to dead as I've ever seen a man who's standing now on his own two feet, and tended ye with Senga through yer fever."

"Aye," Jamie responded, suddenly solemn as he sketched a bow to the Healer. "I ken the lady. I've said my thanks before, but the more I hear the tale, the more I ken that no thanks will ever be enough to balance what ye did for me. And the toll it took on ye."

"'Twas only what I'm meant to do," Aileana replied softly. Her gaze met Jamie's briefly, then dropped to the floor. "I took no lasting harm."

Aileana's simple words brought a flood of memories back to Toran and a frown to his face. She'd looked to be near death herself before she'd finished with Jamie. She'd nearly scared the life from Toran that day.

At Angus's raised eyebrow, Toran quickly shook his head. He'd tell him later…if they got the chance. Toran could see Kyle heading toward them. The time had come for the night's patrol to go.

"Laird, I've come to collect ye. If ye're ready?"

Angus nodded and glanced around the group, catching first Jamie's, then Toran's, and lastly Aileana's gaze with a nod and murmured thanks for hospitality and for the risks they were about to undertake on his clan's behalf. Again, he held a hand out to Aileana. This time, she briefly touched her fingers to his palm. Was it the wine? Toran wondered if Angus felt the same thing when they touched that he did and a spurt of jealousy shot through him at the thought.

"I'll just be a minute," Aileana told Toran. "I need my cloak and supplies."

Toran nodded and watched her as she hurried to the stairs.

"Walk out with me, Toran, if ye would," Angus said as he turned to follow Kyle. Jamie was pulled away by some of the men.

"That seemed to be quite a conversation with the Healer," Toran said as soon as he and Angus moved out of earshot of anyone in the Hall.

"And one ye'll wish to hear about. What's the saying? Latin, I think? In vino veritas. In wine there is truth. Yer healer put away three cups fairly quickly. And despite the meal, the wine loosened her tongue."

"Indeed? What did she have to say that took wine to get past her lips?"

"I asked her about her life before Colbridge took her from her village. I don't think she meant to say it, but she mentioned that her mother worked as the village healer until her death…long after she'd married and had a child. When I pressed, she said that her mother's methods were like hers."

"She told me she must remain untouched to retain her Talent."

"Then she did it to protect herself. She's probably told that tale so often in the time she's been with that army that she nearly believes it herself."

"I can understand her lying to Colbridge and to the men in that camp. But she lied to me."

"Give her a chance, Toran. Now that the wine has let the secret slip to me, perhaps it'll be easier for her to tell ye, too."

"Aye, perhaps." Angus's news rocked him. If Aileana had finally told the truth, then she was no different than any other woman, despite her Talent.

Kyle handed the reins to Angus's large, dark horse to him.

"Ye've got blankets and sacks of food," Toran told him. "Not so much as to slow ye down, but enough to last a few days."

"Thanks for that," Angus responded as he swung into the saddle.

A stable boy led Banner, similarly laden, up to Toran. As he mounted, Jamie approached with Aileana. He leaned down to pull her up to sit in front of him.

"Have a care, Toran," Jamie told him as he stowed Aileana's pack behind Banner's saddle. "Colbridge may not have many horses left, but he uses them well. Remember how his patrol came upon us suddenly. Dinna let them do the same to ye this night."

"We'll be careful."

"Look for Brodric tomorrow night, late," Angus added.

"There'll be extra men on the gate," Jamie promised. "We'll be glad to have him and the rest of yer men, when ye can get them here."

"If Aileana needs more time with the MacAnalen, we'll send word with Brodric," Toran promised.

With that, Kyle led them through the open gates and out into the night. Toran wrapped an arm securely around the woman in front of him, but despair weighed on him, growing heavier the more he thought about Angus's revelation. Aileana had lied to him. She should have known she had no need to. He'd promised to keep her safe, to give her a home. Hadn't she understood him? What had he done to make her feel threatened enough to perpetuate a lie like that? A lie that had laid waste to his hopes for her and one that had kept him sleepless and anxious since he'd brought her home. Aroused. Frustrated. Irritated.

Then something else bothered him. The memory floated just out of reach, but he finally retrieved it. She'd told him days ago that she was the daughter and granddaughter of Healers. He'd been too distracted to realize what that might mean.

He'd been torn between his duty and his heart's desire. And for what? It had all been so unnecessary. He'd been prepared to sacrifice his need for Aileana for the good of the clan. For the laird, the clan came before everything else. It always would.

As they rode silently down the trail from the Aerie, he took a deep breath, then turned his face to the sky. Stars glinted overhead. His breath formed a dense fog as it left him. But the cold was nothing compared to the icy dread lodged deep within him. The only way to get the truth was to risk getting an answer he did not want. He must confront her. If she held to this lie, he would know that she did not want him. He would know that she was capable of other lies. And if she was capable of other lies, what else might she conceal? Was Donal right to suspect her? Did she have Talents she had yet to display? Could she do things that were dangerous to the people of the clan? How could he know for sure?

****

Aileana leaned against Toran and thought about the last time they had ridden like this, his arm wrapped securely under her breasts, holding her firmly against his broad chest. Perhaps it was the wine she'd drunk with dinner, but despite the risk they were taking in leaving the Aerie, she rested comfortably in Toran's arms.

But her mind was troubled. She'd told Angus something she should have told no one. Because of the wine? Where had her caution fled while her mouth ran amok? He'd asked about her home and once she started talking, she had not been able to stop. Not even before telling her deepest secret. It was if everything she'd kept locked inside her for the past two years had boiled over and spilled out. And worse, if he related their conversation to Toran, then she was lost.

Of course he'd told Toran. Or he would. Unless she could ask it as a boon for saving his laird?

They were surrounded by Toran's men. Kyle led the way with Angus at his side just ahead of them, communicating with the riders behind him when necessary with hand gestures and nods. Everyone was silent. Even the horses seemed to know not to make any noise. The night sky was moonless and no darker than it had been when viewed from within the Aerie, but it seemed blacker, muffled and still. The stars still glinted above, but their light seemed not to reach the ground.

Aileana held her breath as they made their way silently and uneventfully off the tor and into the forest.

Rather than relaxing as they gained the thicker trees, the men seemed to become even more watchful and alert. Aileana sensed Toran's tension through the hardness of his muscles at her back. She thought to turn and ask him what was wrong, but realized quickly that she dared not speak. And with that thought, any comfort she'd enjoyed in his arms disappeared. She also put her worries aside. They had more immediate problems.

Any sound she might make, for any reason, would not be welcome. She fervently hoped that no one got the urge to sneeze. They had waited for dark to make this trip because it was safer. But safer clearly did not mean safe. Despite their precautions, Toran and his men expected trouble and were on the alert for it. She wondered at the relationship between the Lathans and the MacAnalens that they were willing to risk so many lives, including hers, on the hope that she could save the MacAnalen laird.

Aileana jumped as an owl hooted above them, but managed to hold back the startled squeak that almost escaped her lips. The hand that Toran had wrapped around her ribs stroked up and down as he quickly tried to soothe her. She exhaled and nodded, not daring to speak. Toran hugged her a bit more tightly to him, then relaxed his grip. Her forbearance was noted and appreciated, it seemed. They rode on.

No more startled owls alerted to their presence, much to Aileana's relief. Under the trees, the night was even blacker than she'd thought it was as they left the Aerie. How Toran's men thought to see any adversary they might have to fight was beyond her comprehension. They now rode in a line, led by Angus, who knew where they were headed. She could barely make out the dark rump of Kyle's horse just in front of Banner's nose. Then she saw Kyle's pale hand flash upward, fingers spread, then close into a fist. The message was clear. Halt. Toran had pulled on Banner's reins almost before Aileana noticed Kyle's signal, and had let go of her to signal to the rider behind them. Now they stood still, waited and listened. Aileana tensed as Banner shifted under them. Toran reached forward and patted him on the neck, stilling him, then placed his hand at her waist, ready to grab her and go, or signal again, whichever was needed. The silence stretched on. Aileana strained to hear any sound, but detected nothing. What were they waiting for?

Suddenly she heard what Angus must have: horses, several, moving across their path well ahead of them. A shiver ran up her spine. She held her breath, waiting to see if they would be discovered, fearing the battle that would result if they were. All it would take was one nicker, one whinny, from one of their mounts, and they would be discovered. But clearly, the Lathan horses were better trained than that. The patrol passed well ahead and off to their right. They waited long minutes more in tense stillness, giving the patrol time to get out of earshot, before Aileana saw Kyle's hand come up and slash forward. Toran repeated the signal for the rider behind him, then replaced his arm around Aileana's waist as Kyle's mount moved silently forward, tail swishing. Banner dropped his head and stepped forward without Toran's urging.

They continued on in the same careful silence for what seemed to Aileana like hours more, but it was still full dark when the incline they'd been climbing under the cover of trees opened out to reveal a rocky hillside and the mouths of several caves, visible only as an impenetrable deeper black in the pale glow of starlight.

Two soft hoots, not unlike those of the owl that had started Aileana earlier, sounded, announcing their presence. Toran urged Banner forward to stand beside Angus's mount. Angus was on the ground already and walking forward to meet the man who had emerged from the mouth of the largest cave. Toran handed Aileana down to Kyle, who was suddenly there to steady her, then dismounted and went to join Angus and the other MacAnalen at the mouth of the cave. Kyle stayed by Aileana after she pulled her supplies from Banner's pack, but took her arm at Toran's signal. After some low voiced conversation with the two MacAnalens, Toran waved, and Kyle escorted her forward to meet them.

"Aileana, yer help is urgently needed," Toran told her in a low whisper. "This is Angus's cousin, Craig. He'll take ye to the laird now. I'll be along in a few minutes. If ye need anything, tell Craig, and he'll see that ye get it."

After hours of silence, Aileana could only nod. Craig turned and moved away. Aileana quickly followed. She feared losing sight of him in the deeper blackness of the cave.

Fortunately, they didn't go far. A man lay swaddled in plaids just at the edge of the starlight. As if there was any doubt that this was the laird she'd been brought to save, Craig pointed. Aileana dropped to her knees beside the unconscious man and gently laid her hands on the wool covering his chest, then swept them upward onto his throat, face, and head. With a gasp, she pulled them away. Chills coursed through her. He was quiet, empty, but still breathing. This was even worse than the blankness that she'd feared upon seeing Toran's head wound for the first time. The body living, the mind completely gone. Sighing, she sat back on her heels and looked up to see Craig still hovering over her.

"Where did you find him?" she whispered, hoping to disguise the dismay that swamped her.

"At the edge of the loch below the village, Healer."

"In the cold water?"

"Aye, mostly. At first we thought him drowned, but he still breathed, though barely, and with his battle wounds, well, 'twas little surprise that he refused to awaken."

"Who is your healer?" Aileana asked, dreading the coming confrontation.

"I am," Craig answered, and Aileana nodded. He'd done his best, saving the body in all the ways he knew how, but there had been no saving the mind. She supposed that the MacAnalen, wounded by one of Colbridge's men, had managed to get away from the battle and gotten as far as the loch before he collapsed. He probably was nearly drowned by the time they found him.

Aileana lifted the blankets from the MacAnalen's still form. Just to be sure, she told herself, forcing her hands to his chest and using her Talent the best she knew how, despite the aversion she felt to the emptiness within this body. If she could not save him, she could not barter for Angus's silence.

Oh, how close this poor man had been to the final escape from his enemies, only to be pulled back by the care and concern of his clan. She repeated her earlier touch, running her hands over his head and neck, listening for any hint of self within. There was nothing. His body lived, for a while yet, but his spirit had departed. He was gone. And she was lost.

Aileana bowed her head and recalled the blessing for sending the dead on their way that her mother had taught her so many years before. "Go swift on angels' wings," she whispered. "God grant you grace."

Then she lifted her hands and stood, turning to face the MacAnalen healer. "His body will live a few days yet," she told him, "but his spirit has already gone. You did the best anyone could do for him, but the loch..."

"Nay!" Craig's exclamation startled her into backing away from him. "They said ye could save him," he continued in a softer, pleading tone.

"No one could," she replied, saddened by the man's distress. "He had already gone when your men found him."

Aileana felt Toran arrive at her back. Craig's protest must have alerted him. She glanced around and shook her head. Angus, on Toran's heels, gasped.

"Dead?" The anguish in his voice grated on her conscience.

"Nearly so," she told them. "Your healer did all that was possible, but your laird was too far gone. There's nothing left for me to"—Aileana's voice broke on the admission—"there's nothing I can do. I'm sorry."

Toran put an arm around her shoulders and pulled her close. "Ye tried, lass. That's all anyone could ask."

"Nay," Craig snarled. "She did naught but place her hands on him and declare him too near dead to save. Where are her potions? There must be something..."

"Aileana?" The hope in Angus's voice nearly broke her heart. At least it was hope and not censure. Though that might soon follow.

She looked Angus in the eye. "Angus, I'm truly sorry. His body will carry on for a few hours yet, but his mind, his spirit is gone. I can sense nothing of him left within."

"How do ye...what if ye tried again?"

"I will if that is what you wish, certainly. But the answer will be the same. In a day, two at the most, you will bury your laird."

"Witch!" The accusation echoed within the cave's dark walls. Aileana whirled around, not sure who had spat out the word like an oath.

"Nay." Toran swore as he, too, looked for the accuser. "Angus, ye ken the truth. Aileana risked herself to come here. She does not deserve such just because she canna do what ye wished."

"Aye," Angus replied, looking around at the members of his clan who had awakened and come to see what was happening near their laird. "We owe our thanks to the Lathan and his Healer for coming to our aid. I'll hear no more like that from any man here."

Silence greeted Angus's demand for a long moment, then a man stepped forward. "What right do ye have to order us?" he complained and Aileana recognized the voice that had named her witch. "Yer brother still breathes, still lives. Ye are no' laird yet."

"Ye have the right of it, Colin," Angus acknowledged. "But the clan has followed my lead since the battle. And while ye may no', several of the others ken full well what the Healer has done for us."

"Aye," Brodric said, stepping forward into the starlight to stand by Angus, his expression completely serious for a change. "The Healer is no' a matter that concerns ye, Colin. And as for Angus's leadership, I'll warn ye no' to challenge that. The lairdship will be decided by the full clan at the proper time. Ye'll no' debate it now over the laird's still-warm body. I'll no' have it."

"Angus," Toran said, and Aileana hoped that by

breaking into the rising tension, Toran could distract and diffuse the MacAnalens' upset. His commanding presence, at the very least, would force them to be still and listen, and to remember that they had strangers in their midst.

"We've no wish to intrude on MacAnalen clan concerns at a time such as this. But it's too late to make the trip back to the Aerie in safety. I ask guest-right for the day. We'll take as many of yer men as ye wish to send with us after dark tonight."

"Of course," Angus said. "Ye havena need to ask. Ye bring us food and blankets as well as hope in yer offer of shelter and in the person of the Healer." He smiled sadly at Aileana. "Have yer men make camp and get some rest. We'll table this discussion until a more appropriate time and place. In the meantime, Craig will keep watch over the MacAnalen."

"I'd like to join him, if I may," Aileana offered.

Angus cut a glance in Craig's direction.

"It is customary for a healer to attend," Craig replied evenly.

"The rest of ye, return to yer pallets and get some sleep. We've new supplies and will have a decent meal to break our fast when the sun rises."

Aileana risked a glance at Colin, but he seemed to be bowing to Angus's leadership now that his objections had been heard, or now that it was clear that his clan supported Angus—and Aileana. He sketched a shallow bow to Angus and turned away. Aileana breathed a sigh of relief, and was not surprised to hear Angus do the same.

Chapter Eleven

In the cold light of day, Toran could see just how foolhardy their trip here had been. These mountains were riddled with caves where men could hide. They were on Penwyms hill above the old MacAnalen village, which was where he kenned they'd be bound before he ever agreed to this trip. It was the very place he'd suggested to Angus as they made their escape from the invaders' camp. But they were a long way from the Aerie and help, should the need arise.

Toran understood why Angus had not moved his men closer to the Aerie. They had yet to bury their dead, for one, and if any of the clan still lived, the only chance of finding them meant that they must remain nearby for as long as possible. But time was running out, both for any survivors still unaccounted for, and for the clan's ability to remain hidden from Colbridge's patrols. The fewer men who remained here, the better their chances of staying hidden from their enemies while they searched for their missing kin.

The clan was up and about, moving quietly in the chill morning air. Several of the men were packing their meager belongings for the return trip to the Aerie. Those who were staying were intent on their chores keeping the camp clean and hidden, while others were out hunting or gathering firewood. In Angus's absence, someone had come up with the idea to dig a pit in the floor of a nearby cave and place a small fire there. It was completely hidden from view and hot enough to produce almost no smoke at all. And if it was detected, at least there, it would not lead anyone directly to the survivors. Fresh meat combined with the provisions the Lathans provided meant the first hot food these men had eaten in weeks. There was no question that morale had improved overnight, despite the grim news about their laird.

Aileana had stayed with the MacAnalen and their healer until dawn, when Angus relieved her from her vigil. She'd slept for a few hours on the pallet Toran had laid out for her, then joined him in a light meal from their travel provisions. She didn't have much to say; rather, she watched the entrance to the cave where Angus sat with his brother.

Now that she faced him, he was reminded of what Angus had told him as they left the Aerie. Anger forgotten in the perils of their journey and the events after they'd arrived resurfaced as Toran recalled that she had chosen Angus to share her truths with instead of him.

Sitting and waiting grated on Toran's nerves. The death watch was only part of it. Waiting for the sun to set and the prospect of the harrowing return to the Aerie was only part of it. Waiting for Aileana to confide in him—aye, that was the worst.

Why had she trusted Angus over him? Had the wine truly loosened her tongue so much that hadn't realized what she was saying? Or had she sensed in Angus's calm demeanor someone with whom she could lay aside her burdens?

What must he do to prove himself to her? Surely

she could no longer fear him, if she ever did. He'd cared for her, fought off challenges from his own people for her. He'd shown her in all the ways he could think of that she belonged with him. He wanted her, fiercely. And she wanted him, too. Of that he was certain, despite her reticence.

Must they forever test each other, never quite sure, instead of sharing the passion that was between them and allowing it to grow?

For the moment, he had only one way to measure her. If she could only trust him enough to share with him the secret that she had shared with Angus, then he could believe she might be willing to accept his love and his clan.

Their sparse meal eaten, she played with her empty cup, twisting it first this way, then that, with nimble fingers. She glanced at him, then away again at the cave where Angus was dimly visible. Then back at him. She sighed.

"I suppose Angus told you about our conversation."

Aileana's simple statement broke the lengthy silence and caused Toran's heart to swell in his chest. Here it was, then. The truth he needed to hear from her.

"Aye." He barely got the word out past the catch in his throat.

"Are you angry with me?"

Toran found that he had it within him to forgive her for all his sleepless nights and bad tempers.

"For protecting yerself? Nay. That would be foolish."

She kept her eyes downcast. "For lying to you."

"I canna say that I approve of that. But why carry

on with the lie even in the Aerie? Even with me?"

Aileana looked at him then, and folded her hands around the cup in her lap. He saw that her cheeks were stained with red. She quickly dropped her gaze before she answered him. "I did not know how I would be received. Whether the same precaution would be necessary...as it was in the camp. I feared you would treat me as a captive is treated."

Toran managed to swallow the anger that scalded from his chest to his throat and put all the sincerity he could muster into his reply. She thought him no better than a barbarian to claim her as a prize of war? Use her? Over her objections? Gods. "But I didna. I would never force a woman. Ye ken that now, do ye no'?"

"Do I? You've touched me, kissed me, even when I told you it was not allowed."

Toran frowned. He couldna deny it. He had. But he had also fought his urges and resisted the temptation to do more, much more. "Can ye blame me for wantin' ye, Aileana? I do, more than ye ken. But I didna harm ye, did I? I willna."

"You'll leave me be?"

"For now, aye. But no' forever, Aileana. We mean something to each other. Ye feel it as I do." He reached out to touch her, but drew his hand back, forcing himself not to betray his frustration by balling it into a fist. She wanted him to leave her be. He had to give her time, no matter the pain this restraint caused him, and right now, it was causing him plenty. He was nearly bursting from wanting her, and the anticipation of holding her lush body in his arms, her rear snuggled against him for the long hours of the ride back tonight was near to killing him.

She didn't answer him for the space of several heartbeats. Toran held his breath, never taking his gaze from her as she struggled with her answer. The camp around them seemed to disappear. There was no one near. Only her.

"What are you saying?" she finally asked and Toran found he could breathe again. She did not deny the connection between them. "That we're attracted to each other? Aye, I suppose we are. But I'll not be your mistress, no matter what we might feel for each other."

"I ken that, lass. I do," he said, relief making his voice gruff. "When ye're ready. Only then."

"When I'm ready for what?"

Toran gritted his teeth. It seemed that Aileana was deliberately avoiding understanding him. But she was talking to him. That gave him hope. He could not risk scaring her into closing away from him again. He meant to have her, to bind her to him and to his clan forever, but if that meant waiting, biding his time while he drew her out and let her adjust to the idea, he would find the strength to do it.

Somehow.

But, no. He had to prove to her that he was serious about a future with her. "To become my wife and the lady of my clan."

"What?"

Toran glanced quickly around, but no one else seemed to have heard her startled exclamation.

"There will be time, lass. All ye need. And when ye find that ye are ready, we will marry."

"Marry?"

What did she think they were discussing? Damn, she was gripping that cup so tightly, her fingers were turning white. He'd only meant to reassure her that he would no' dally with her and cast her aside. At least she was no longer looking toward Angus. Her attention was solely where Toran wanted it: on him.

"Or we can handfast if ye wish to take more time to be sure of...of me."

"Isn't that the same?"

"Nay. We simply promise to marry in the future and if we don't...well, it will be merely a betrothal. But if ye decide ye do no' wish to wait for the priest and the kirk, then 'tis a simple matter to make the betrothal into a marriage."

"Oh?"

Heat climbed up Toran's neck into his face. Ballocks! This was not going the way he'd intended at all. Not that he'd intended to have this conversation here, now, under these circumstances. She deserved more. To be cosseted, wooed, until she could admit she cared for him, too. Not this too frank, too abrupt discussion. It was not the way to win a lady. But she'd asked and he had to answer.

"If ye let me love ye, lass, then 'twill be done. For the rest of our lives. 'Tis up to ye."

Aileana looked away. The rosy flush in her cheeks contrasted with the bloodless pallor in her hands where she still gripped the cup. Then a shy smile lifted the corners of her mouth. But it was her eyes that captivated him as she captured his gaze with her own. They shone. Whether the glimmer of tears meant sadness or of joy, he wasna sure, but the depth of her emotion—that she couldna hide.

"Aye," was all she said, but it was enough. Aye, she felt this bond between them. And it would not be denied. She would choose the time and the place. He was not heartless. He could understand that after years as a captive, it she needed to control her own destiny, especially when taking a step as permanent as the one he proposed. He would woo her for as long as she wished, if that was what it took to convince her to become his. But first, he had to get her home safely.

****

Night had fallen an hour ago. The Lathan men were ready to ride, the MacAnalens sharing mounts. They could go faster that way than with men on foot accompanying them, but the burden on their mounts was much greater, which slowed them. And if they were discovered and had to fight, it could prove disastrous. Having the MacAnalens with them also meant that they must risk the approach to the main gate, rather than having the postern as a backup if they were pursued. But they had little choice in the matter. Toran had promised Angus safe haven for his clansmen. And, he reminded himself, he'd promised Aileana to return her home safely. But he would not divulge the Aerie's most precious defensive secret to another clan. He could not let his eagerness for her distract him from the real dangers they would face on the return trip.

Toran walked among the mounted men one last time, checking for anything loose that might rattle or clink and betray their presence to an enemy patrol. His men were well-trained; he'd give Donal credit for that. There was nothing to find. Their mounts were more restless than usual carrying the double load, but they'd distributed the weight of two riders among the strongest horses, and once they were underway, the horses would settle down. In truth, Toran should ride with the heaviest MacAnalen since Banner was the biggest and strongest of the Lathan mounts. But he refused to relinquish Aileana to any one else. If they were attacked, he could best defend her and he would not share the risk for her life or freedom with any of the other men, even Kyle. She meant too much to him.

Aileana was already seated atop Banner, looking concerned, but calm. Toran swung up behind her and settled her against him, reveling in the warm roundness of her body nestled between his thighs. "Are ye ready, lass?"

"Aye."

"Good. I'll have ye home before false dawn."

Toran turned to Angus, who stood at Banner's withers. "Keep ye safe, Angus, and send more men as ye can spare them."

"I'll do that," Angus replied evenly. "We'll meet again in a few days, Laird Lathan." He faced Aileana. "Keep ye safe, lass," he said solemnly, "and take the gratitude of the MacAnalens with ye as ye go."

"Angus, I'm sorry." Tears tinged her voice.

"Dinna say it, lass. Ye did what ye could. Now we must wait."

"Aye," Toran replied for her and nodded to Kyle, who led off, followed by Toran and the rest of the riders.

The first few hours passed uneventfully. They proceeded as they had on the trip out, silently, in single file, communicating by hand signals. Aileana even dozed in his arms. They stopped more often than on the outward journey because of the horses carrying two riders. They also shifted riders to further rest the animals carrying the greatest burden. Over Aileana's energetically pantomimed objections, he stayed with her as she moved well away from the others to take care of her personal needs. She had sense, and there was no doubt by her silence that she knew how dangerous any conversation would be, even when she clearly wished to forbid him to accompany her on such a private mission.

Hours later, Toran was beginning to think that they might reach the main gate without incident. True, the closer they got the the Aerie, the closer they got to Colbridge's camp and the chances of meeting one of his patrols went up. But this late in the deep, dark hours of the night, Toran hoped that most of Colbridge's men would be abed, not ahorse and looking for trouble.

Aileana stirred in his arms, awake and, he suspected, trying to ease numbness in her hips and seat from the long ride. He gave her a gentle squeeze to let her know all was well. Unused to long hours in the saddle, she must be uncomfortable. But Kyle would soon call another halt to rest the horses. She would not have long to wait to get down from her high perch on Banner and walk off some of the stiffness she must be feeling.

And speaking of stiffness, all the stirring about that Aileana was doing against his thighs was giving Toran's body ideas of its own. Apparently, Aileana was aware of the hardening fullness at her back, for she suddenly sat up straighter and grabbed his thigh.

Then Toran heard what had alerted her and gave the signal to halt. Horses, moving in their direction. The trees muffled the sound and made it hard to distinguish exactly where the riders were, but the hoofbeats were getting louder.

Aileana tensed in front of him. Toran waited, listening, praying that this patrol would pass them by as the last one had, not run right into them. It took only a moment to ken that they were going to be close, too close. Kyle turned his mount around as Toran signaled the riders behind him to turn back they way they'd come. If they moved quietly and fast enough, they might still avoid a fight.

Then one of the horses stumbled over something in the dark and neighed its distress. No one spoke, no one swore, but the damage was done. The hoofbeats, nearer now, veered directly toward them.

"Form up!" Toran ordered and the MacAnalens dismounted to allow the Lathans to fight unencumbered. Weapons clattered against tack. Toran considered putting Aileana down among the armed MacAnalens, but could not do it. He had no choice. If he set her down, she could be trampled, or lost, or worse, picked up by one of the patrol and carried off into the night, back to Colbridge's camp. Nay, better she stay with him. They would win or die together. She was his to protect, and so he would.

"Stay on Banner," he told her tersely. "Ye'll be safer with him than on the ground. Stay low so I can swing a blade above ye."

"Aye," she answered tightly, and he kenned she must be terrified at the prospect of going into battle.

"Dinna fash, lass," he told her, though he knew she would, and truth be told, he was worried enough for both of them. "If something happens to me, Banner will take ye home."

The first rider blundered into the middle of their line and was quickly dispatched before he knew what happened. Two of his companions were cannier, pulling up and engaging the end of the line where there were fewer defenders to harry them. Toran parried the blow aimed at his head and beheaded the attacker for his temerity, then whirled Banner around to parry another blow.

A sword cut barely missed Aileana. She shrieked and ducked lower on Banner's neck. Toran's heart leapt to his throat at her cry. He was more terrified than he'd ever been during battle. Normally coldly calm until the fight ended, he was keenly aware of the woman clinging to Banner's mane between his knees, distracting him. He saw Robbie gut the next attacker headed his way, and gave him a quick salute with his bloody blade.

In another moment, it was over. He heard Kyle call "Report," and let go a breath when he heard all of his men reply. Only then did he lift Aileana up from her crouch over Banner's neck and back into his arms. The warm wetness along her side coated his fingers.

"Lass, are ye hurt?" he cried, nearly panicked at the thought of her suffering a mortal wound here in this dark forest. Who would care for her?

"I'm all right," she choked out between terrified sobs. Toran, frantically patted her down and finding no wound, realized the blood was not hers, but her attacker's.

They would have to finish the ride home with the smell of blood on her dress. It would not bother the unflappable Banner, but it bothered Toran more than he was willing to admit. They'd had a close call. And they weren't home yet.

Toran breathed a sigh of relief until he heard

hoofbeats racing away from them through the trees. A lone rider, escaping the fray? They could not allow a report of this confrontation to get back to Colbridge. If that rider had heard Aileana's shriek and knew a woman rode with them, Colbridge would search, hoping to find Aileana, and would be after them before they could reach safety. And when he realized the Lathans were not locked up inside the Aerie, but able to roam the countryside at will, he'd redouble his attacks on their walls. Instead of just lay siege, he'd search for ways other than the main gates in and out of the fortress. Time marched against Colbridge. The longer he maintained the siege, the worse off he was. The last thing Toran wanted to do was give him an alternative, not yet.

"Kyle, Robbie, after him!" Toran ordered, swinging Banner around, fighting the urge to pursue the quarry. "Everyone else, pick up yer riders. Let's move!"

Toran pulled Aileana tighter against him. He snapped the reins and Banner took off. One by one, he heard the rest of his men fall into line behind him. Stealth was no longer a concern. They were close enough to the Aerie that speed would have to win the day. They rode. They encountered no more of Colbridge's patrols. Instead, as they started up the trail to the Aerie's gates, Kyle and Robbie joined up with them.

Then the outer gate stood before them, and Toran shouted for the night watch to let them in. Just as they swung open, he heard horses pounding up behind them. It was too dark still to see, but it had to be another patrol. If Toran didn't get his group inside the outer gate quickly, they'd be caught between the gates, or risk allowing the battle to spill into the outer bailey.

"Ride!" he shouted. He had to get Aileana safe inside the gates before he could return to the fight.

Inside the bailey, he handed Aileana down to one of the stableboys. He spotted Donal up on the rampart with the watch standers, making sure they were ready to mount a defense, inside or outside the walls. Toran raised a hand in salute, then turned Banner and raced back to defend the gates.

The last of his group approached the gate, but a group of six riders was coming on fast. Toran pulled his claymore and rode them down, swinging with deadly precision. Kyle joined him on one side, Robbie on the other and they beat the patrol back down the trail away from the gate before the Aerie's archers could take aim. By the time the survivors turned tail and ran for the glen, only two of them remained alive to report to their leader that the gates of the Aerie had opened.

Kyle and Robbie took off in pursuit, but Toran called them back. "Let them go," he growled. "They won't tell Colbridge anything he doesna already ken. There's no way he didna hear this."

Kyle started to protest, but Toran shook his head, disgusted with the turn of events. "Get inside. We need to plan how to get the rest of Angus's men in without getting them all killed."

****

Hours later, after a bath and some sleep, Aileana felt recovered from the terrifying return to the Aerie. She walked along the rampart, nodding to the men standing watch there and paying close attention to those she and Senga had treated in days past. Most of their injuries had been minor and Aileana's healing touch had speeded them back to their duty sooner than it would have been possible without her. But were they returning to the walls too quickly? She trusted her talent and Senga's judgement, but that did not stop her from harboring concerns about her patients.

Senga claimed that her old bones were no longer suited to climbing the stairs to the ramparts, and it gave a clearer picture of the men's fitness to see them at their posts rather than lounging in the great hall or fidgeting in the herbal. So she passed the rampart walking duty to Aileana.

The more tasks Senga gave Aileana, the more a sense of belonging grew within her, so she welcomed anything that Senga saw fit to turn over to her. She hoped that as word of her healing spread, and as more people in the clan experienced it, her talent would no longer be feared, and she would be accepted.

She paused out of the wind, next to the entry to an enclosed staircase and peered over the wall between two merlons onto Colbridge's camp, where she could see figures move along the edge of the trees, in and out of the patchwork of tents, and from campfire to campfire. The small army already had the look of long habitation. Tents showed travel wear, dirt, and stains. Whenever they weren't trying to breach the Aerie's walls, men lounged wearily around cooking fires or could be heard moving about deeper within the forest.

Most were too far away to identify, but a few stood out. Colbridge, with two other men, paced behind a fire, well lit by its brightness as if to say, *Here I am, and there's nothing you can do about it.* Aileana had seen his aggressiveness demonstrated too many times to mistake the scene he set. No doubt their foray last night had provoked this display.

Another man approached the group. Ranald! Aileana smiled in recognition, but her smile turned sad at the thought of how he must be faring in the camp. She heard the faint cadence of voices in the distance, but by no means could she overhear what Ranald and Colbridge discussed, though she supposed their conversation might have something to do with her. Or with Toran. Thinking of him made Aileana smile again as she pictured his broad shoulders; his strong, yet gentle hands; the sheer masculine beauty of his face. Warmth spread through her, and she imagined she heard his voice amid the others that echoed around the keep. Nay, she did hear him.

"I canna explain how she does it," Toran was saying, sounding irritated, and Aileana realized his words were carrying up the stairs in the tower she huddled against. "But Senga accepts her, and explain or not, we need her. She is training her up in her potions and herbs. What she can't heal that way, she can heal her…special…way."

Toran had talked to Senga about her? Why? Yesterday at Angus's camp, he seemed to accept her answers, even though his expression had been fierce. What had gone wrong now?

"Aye. But she lied to ye and even if she has now told ye the truth, it concerns me." Aileana recognized Donal gruff voice and understood the frustration in Toran's. Donal didn't trust her, and made no secret of it. Why had he told Donal about their conversation?

"It concerned me, too," she heard Toran reply, and her heart sank as Toran acknowledged Donal's suspicions. "But we've seen no sign of her doin' anything unseemly save lying to protect herself."

Donal's voice was louder when he replied, "At least ye've seen that there are limits to her power. She canna raise the dead. But I still say it doesna mean she's safe to have within our walls, no matter what Senga told ye."

She realized the two were ascending the stairs. She quickly moved away from the tower, into the wind. With her back to them as they exited the tower, they would not know she'd overheard.

She clutched her shawl tighter around her and leaned over the wall to better see outside. A large hand gripped her shoulder and pulled her roughly aside, behind a merlon.

"Aileana! Stay back! Colbridge's men can see ye here," Toran growled. "A lucky shot by their archers, a following wind, and well—" He paused and gripped both her shoulders more gently, entreaty and...was it fear for her on his face? "Be careful, lass."

"Aye," Donal added, doing exactly what Aileana had done moments before, peering out at Colbridge's camp. Then he swore. "That son of a cattle thief! Toran, take a look at this."

Toran released his hold on Aileana, reluctantly, it seemed. Without his touch, the wind blew colder and she was bereft of support. She gathered her shawl again and joined the men.

"Damn, what's he doing?" Toran muttered.

Donal cut a frown in her direction, but Toran kept his eye on the approaching riders.

"It's taken him long enough to decide on a parley," Toran muttered, "if that's what this is."

Aileana peered carefully over the wall. Colbridge led two other riders at an easy canter across the glen. Finally the riders stopped just out of range of the Aerie's archers. Colbridge kicked his mount a pace forward.

"Laird Lathan!" he called out. Aileana ducked down, out of sight from the glen, afraid to be seen by that man.

"Aye," Toran replied, mildly. "Have ye come to surrender?"

"Surrender?" Aileana could not mistake the fury in Colbridge's voice. Toran's taunt had hit home. "Never. I'm here to accept your surrender. And to retrieve something of mine that you took. I want it back—undamaged." Almost she stood to peek out at her former captor, but common sense held her back, since she was the only thing within the walls of the Aerie that had once "belonged" to Colbridge.

"Something of yers?" Toran's voice held nothing but innocent bemusement. "I can't imagine what that might be. Since…guesting…with ye," Toran continued, more forcefully, "I've received nothing from yer camp save insults and feeble attempts to scale my walls."

"You can't sit behind those walls forever," Colbridge challenged angrily. "You'll come out, and when you do, it'll be on my terms. Send Aileana out, and I'll spare your lives."

Aileana blanched. He was after her. Of course he was. "No," she whispered. "I won't go back." But she could not imagine Toran giving her back to Colbridge. She stared up at Toran, looking for reassurance. Surely he wouldn't.

"Aileana is spoils of war," Donal spoke up, his

voice pitched to carry into the glen. Then he leaned over the wall, and smirked. "She is our property now. To do with as we wish. Later, we may toss her back to ye. But for now, we'll keep her."

"Harm her at your peril," Colbridge shouted.

"Why is she so valuable to ye?" Toran finally asked after a glare at Donal meant to silence him.

"That's my business and none of yours. But if you or any of your men violate her, then she will be useless to me and to you."

"Surely ye can't mean to ransom her? Or marry her off for an alliance? That's no' yer way, is it?" Toran said, deliberately misunderstanding Colbridge's concern.

"My way is to offer you one chance to save the lives of your clan. Open your gates. Send out the Healer and surrender, or die."

"Nay, I dinna think we'll be taking ye up on yer offer. But perhaps I'll consider a ransom. If ye want her back, pack up yer camp and return to where ye came from. Dinna trouble us again, and I'll see her returned to ye."

Aileana could not contain her gasp of dismay, but Toran either did not hear her, or chose to ignore the reaction of his "property." She stared up and him in shock, waiting for some signal, some sign, for him to step aside and quietly tell her it wasn't true. Could he truly be bargaining with Colbridge to send her back? Hadn't he spoken of a special bond between them? Of handfasting together?

He continued to favor Colbridge with the mildest of regard and ignored her completely. She would not let him see her cry. She would not! All his words had been lies. She'd been right, and Senga was wrong. She was nothing to Toran but curiosity and a challenge. She turned and ran for the stairs, intent on getting as far away from her "master" as she could within the walls of the Aerie. He didn't trust her. He'd told Colbridge as much. He knew the truth about her Talent; that she would not lose it with her maidenhead. And before he sent her back, he'd do the one thing that Colbridge believed would ruin her forever.

A laird could do whatever he wished with female property. There was nothing she could do to protect herself now.

Chapter Twelve

Toran heard Aileana's gasp when Donal called her their property. He became painfully aware of her distress when she ran from them, and deeply regretted that she'd been hurt by the taunt, but he could not leave a confrontation with Colbridge. It was bad enough that Donal had spoken up and interrupted the conversation between his laird and the invader, much worse that his words had wounded Aileana. But it would be worse still for the laird to appear weak before their besieger by leaving the confrontation in the hands of one of his underlings to go after her.

He censured Donal with a hard look and received one in return that was equal parts anger and embarrassment. Aye, Donal kenned just how he'd overstepped. Toran gestured him away and turned back to Colbridge.

Thankfully, after they traded only a few more threats and insults, Colbridge abruptly jerked his mount around and rode back to his camp. Toran quit the rampart on the run, determined to find Aileana and clear up the misunderstanding. Damn it, she'd just begun to trust him!

He found her in the empty hallway outside her chamber, crying, as she tried to open the door. Thank God, it was stuck. If she'd locked herself inside, she might never come out after what she'd just heard.

"Aileana, wait," he called after her. She glanced around and redoubled her efforts to force the door open. Her flushed, tear-streaked face nearly broke his heart. "Aileana, I was goading Colbridge. Ye're no' a prisoner. Ye ken that."

She paused, then apparently gave up on opening the door and ran to the far side of a large table set against the wall, as if she needed protection from him and that barrier could keep her safe, which finished breaking his heart in two.

"Not a prisoner? Then let me leave. Not in a year and a day. Now."

Toran's breath caught in his throat at her appeal. He began to move around the table to her.

"Don't," she commanded, putting her hands up to ward him off. "You lied to me. I'm no guest here, nor do I belong here. I'm as much a prisoner as I was in Colbridge's camp, allowed the freedom of the keep only because I can do something you need. You care nothing for me. I heard you say it."

Toran stood still, assessing. Her back pressed against the wall, tears streamed down her face, but then she leaned forward and splayed her hands on the tabletop, challenging him. He admired her spirit, even as he damned himself for hurting her.

"No, Aileana. I didn't lie to ye. I lied to Colbridge. Ye're no' a prisoner. Never that."

Her hesitation heartened him even as her words betrayed her fear. "I don't believe you."

He fought to keep his voice calm and quiet as he continued. "I willna negotiate with Colbridge over ye. I willna give ye back to him."

"Perhaps not, but you'll still hold me against my

will."

"Where would ye go, lass?"

"'Tis none of your concern."

Toran sighed, reaching for something, anything, to tell her that would convince her. The only thing he could think of was a promise he did not want to make, but it was all he had.

"When this is over"—he paused, grimaced at what he was about to offer to regain her trust, and continued—"when he is gone, if it is what ye truly want, ye may leave."

At his words, she straightened, still poised to flee, but listening to him.

"But that is not what I want," he continued. "I want ye to stay in the Aerie, make yer home here, with us."

"As your healer," she stated, flatly, not moving.

"Aye, of course." Toran said, but before he could go on, she interrupted.

"Why is that any different than the life I had with Colbridge's army? I had a purpose there, too. But I've spent the last two years learning that having a purpose is not the same as belonging."

Aileana fisted her hands on her hips, and marched around the corner of the table, coming to stand toe-to-toe with Toran. "He's a tyrant. What makes you any different than him? Because you have the Aerie? I'm told he has a keep in the south. Because you inherited a clan? He has one, too—misfits and lost men, all, but he's made them his. Why do you think you're so different?"

"Because," Toran finally interrupted her tirade, angered at being compared to her former captor, "because ye ken I'm no' like him. Yer anger is speaking for ye. Ye dinna really mean that."

"Don't tell me what I mean or don't mean."

Toran sighed. "Have ye no' seen enough by now to ken the kind of man I am? Have ye no' seen better from me than that?"

"I don't know what to believe."

"Then believe this." He touched a finger to her damp cheek, and felt the warmth spread between them, melting his ire. "I dinna take what doesna belong to me, lass. If ye dinna belong to me, if ye truly do no' wish to stay with me, then I'll let ye go when it's safe to do so. But ye feel how I want ye. And ye want me, the same. I feel it, too. We have something together, ye and I. I dinna claim to understand it, but 'tis there."

She pulled back from his touch, stared up at him as if he'd lost his mind, but didn't step away. Emboldened, he stroked the side of her face, wiped a tear stain softly with his thumb. "Ye feel it, too. I can see it on yer face, and feel it in the way yer heart beats faster when we touch."

She continued to stare at him, a deer frozen in the hunter's sights, ready to bolt.

"I am sorry," Toran whispered against her hair. "I've ne'er wanted ye to run from me, to make ye cry over something I've said or done."

"It wasn't just you who said those awful things," she said, softening a bit, he hoped. "It was Donal, too. But you didn't deny them."

"Ye ken why I couldna, no' then. But ye understand how I feel about ye."

She tensed under his hand, then exhaled slowly and he watched her shoulders drop slightly as her fear and anger turned to something else. Ever more gently, he captured her breath with his own, caressed her lips with his, slowly. She stood still as Toran continued to drop light kisses over her face, tasting the salt of her tears. He wanted to soothe her, but he also wanted her passion. As he continued to coax her, Toran's need rose within him like the tide. He took her in his arms, held her. She hesitated, as if stunned, then wrapped her arms around his neck and clung to him.

"Oh, Toran. What are we to do?"

He answered her between kisses. "What we want…what we need…what we must."

He lifted her, crossed to her chamber and freed one hand to turn the latch, then kicked the door open. When Aileana did not protest as he carried her inside, he closed and locked the door behind them. Setting her on her feet, he stroked her back, lost in the way she fit against him, her head tucked onto his shoulder, breasts to his chest, hips to his hardness. As if she belonged there. As if she had been made just for him.

He kissed her again, pulled her up on her toes and nibbled her earlobe, her throat. He slid his hands along her sides, caressing her, then he set her away from him. He smiled as she watched him, her uncertainty reflected in her wide eyes as he untied the shawl she still wore. "I willna hurt ye, Aileana," he promised. "I willna make ye cry, no' again, never again. But I willna let ye leave me. Ye are mine."

Her chin lifted, and he feared he'd said the wrong thing, but she reached for his face, and pulled him down to kiss her again. "Aileana," he murmured, moving his mouth over hers, tasting her. She responded with her lips, and her pulse beat faster under his fingers as he slipped his hands down along her throat to untie the bodice of her dress.

****

Aileana burned. The moment Toran touched her, she was lost. His remorse doused the flames of her anger, and his kisses ignited needs she had never known to be within her. Fire ran under his fingertips and trailed across her skin. Yet her core was molten liquid, seeping down her belly to scald her thighs with heat and longing, leaving behind a void that must be filled. She barely knew what was happening between them. She could only feel. Toran's hands, Toran's breath, his hot, demanding mouth, his steely muscles moving under satiny skin as he caressed her, coaxed her, enticed her. Won her.

Her hands moved over him almost without her direction, unlacing his shirt, unpinning the plaid from his shoulder and pulling it down to his waist. Those were all things she had done as he lay unconscious on her surgery table, movements she knew and did not have to think about. She ran her fingertips across his chest, and it was broader and stronger and more heated than she had ever imagined in her deepest longings. His breath hitched as she slid her palm down to his waist. His belt fell next, and the plaid slipped to the floor. She slid her hands up under his shirt, memorizing each ripple of muscle along his tight belly, the silky slip of his chest hair between her fingers, and the tiny knots of his nipples. Toran's groans.

At any other time, his voice captivated her with its deep resonance. But his wordless sounds of passion were intoxicating. They stole her breath, stopped her heart, and drove her mad with longing. That she could bring a man of such strength, wisdom, and goodness to moaning out his need for her gave her a sense of power beyond anything she'd ever known before. He was hers, and she was his. Nothing had ever felt more right to her, more real.

Toran released her to step out of his boots. His gaze pinned her as he reached for her. She could only stare at the man her hands now knew, broad and strong, and hungry for her touch. So she reached out to him and he breathed her name.

His eyes were dark and fierce as he pulled her hands away. He bent to unlace her clothes, finally pulling the layers from her as quickly as he could.

Cool air caressed her skin, and Toran's gaze roamed freely over her body, a license no man had been allowed 'til now. Suddenly shy, she thought to cover herself just as he lifted her effortlessly and laid her gently on her bed.

Even when his touch left her skin, Aileana was aware of him. She knew she would be able to find him on the darkest night in the deepest forest. But when they did touch, her heart beat with his, and his hot blood seemed to course through her veins. His hunger for her was a living thing. She missed that knowing as he leaned over her from where he stood by the bed, so she reached for him.

"Are ye certain, lass?" Toran asked, his voice deep, his brogue thick with his need. "As much as I want this, I willna, if ye dinna want it, too. It's too important."

Was she certain? How could he doubt it? She'd never wanted like this, never needed, not like this.

"What have ye done to me?" she asked, her voice a soft reply to his harsh demand. Some called her a witch, but this man had bewitched her in truth. She answered for him, before he could speak. "You've made me need you more than I need breath. Aye, I'm sure, Toran...Laird Lathan..."

"Laird Lathan, is it?" Toran asked, and his quick grin betrayed his relief at her answer as he knelt over her, straddling her slim thighs with his strong ones. He pulled his shirt over his head, revealing his need to her.

The time for shyness had passed. "Aye, laird. If you'll have me," she replied, reflecting his grin for one brief second before he bent down to her.

"Oh, I'll have ye," Toran promised, leaning in to kiss her throat, her breasts, her belly. "As long and as often as ye like." His kisses moved lower, while his hands stroked her hips, her thighs, her breasts, anywhere in his long reach. Aileana reveled in the strange yet wonderful sensations running through her from all the places that Toran touched. In answer, she raked her fingers through his long dark hair, stroked his shoulders and upper back, reaching for him, desperate to touch him, too.

She tensed as his fingers caressed her molten center and tested the barrier of her innocence that he found there.

"Ah, lass," he murmured, "we'll take this slow."

His mouth followed his fingers. Embarrassed, Aileana tried to pull him back up, but he would not be deterred. She gasped at the dizzying spiral of sensation his touch produced as he kissed her thighs then traced upward with his tongue. The clenching need in her core turned sharp, almost painful. Sliding his hands under her hips, he lifted and opened her completely to his teasing mouth. "So sweet, ye are," he whispered, his hot breath adding to the delicate torture. "Like honey."

With each stroke of Toran's tongue, Aileana surrendered to the sensations he produced in her. Her body tensed, arcing up, twisting, while in her core, a wanting the likes of which she'd only heard about from love-sick village girls wove a tighter and tighter spiral. Behind her closed eyes, she saw streaks of light, much like the ones she'd once seen in the dark of a late summer's predawn sky. She felt herself spinning ever upward to meet those falling stars.

What was this rapture? Her heart beat furiously, but her breath caught with each groan Toran gifted to her. How could something as simple as his touch, the heat of his mouth, the sound of his voice drive her to madness?

Finally, when she could no longer sense the earth beneath her and Toran's touch became more than she could bear, she exploded across her starry sky.

When she could breathe again, she opened her eyes to Toran's satisfied smile. His hands rested on her thighs, his fingers warm where they played on her skin. He stroked up her belly to her breasts, paused to kiss each tightly puckered tip, then moved up to drop gentle kisses on her mouth. He wrapped her legs around his waist, then covered her, taking his weight on his arms. His hardness rested where his tongue had worked such magic. "There's more?" she asked softly against his mouth, though she knew full well what was to come.

"Aye, lass, much more. There may be a wee pain at first, but that will be gone in a moment, and then ye'll feel pleasure again."

"Aye," she answered, uncertain despite her healers' knowledge. Knowing and doing were two very different things. Then his shaft breached her entrance, filling her, stretching her, intruding little by little as her body accepted his invasion. He was silky, then hot, then unrelenting as her moisture flowed over him and he suddenly thrust into her.

A quick, sharp stinging shocked tears from her eyes. But Toran's soothing murmurs and gentle kisses helped her forget it. He filled her completely and she gripped him tightly as she fought to relax, to breathe, to allow herself to know this man in a way she'd known no other. She'd wanted him since she first saw him, and he'd wanted her, too. Oh, how he wanted her. The evidence burned deep within her body. After a few deep breaths, she managed a nod, then took his face in her hands. His look of surprise amused her. She gave him a small smile as she stroked his cheek and ran her fingertips over his lips, then tangled her fingers in his hair and pulled his mouth down to hers. Slowly, gently, he began stroking in and out, letting her become accustomed to his size and pace. The fire rekindled deep in her middle as his passion rose, and hers climbed along with his. His heart pounded in time with the powerful rythym of his loins. His need for her burned in his kiss, and she gave herself over to him completely.

He was struggling to be gentle with her, but Aileana soon decided that was a battle he was about to lose. Full of a sense of power like nothing she'd ever known before, she arced up to meet his thrusts, demanding more. He groaned her name into her mouth as he tensed. Suddenly he began kissing her wildly, devouring her breath as if he had no other. His fingers gripped her shoulders, then his hands slid under her head and lifted her mouth closer to his as he rocked their bodies in his ardent rhythm. She slid her hands down his broad back to grip his buttocks where they clenched and relaxed with each stroke, pulling his hardness deeper into her core. She wanted him, all of him. As her nails bit into his flesh, his climax took him, and he pushed even deeper, crying out her name as he leapt over the edge. The power of his release shocked her into another of her own, and they soared, breathing one breath, hearts beating as one, together.

****

Aileana awoke with the dawn the next morning. For a moment, she didn't know where she was and expected to open her eyes to the interior of her sleeping tent. But the softness of the bed beneath her and the warmth of the deep covers quickly brought her back to the present. Toran...her eyes flew open and she looked over her shoulder. No, not just the warmth of deep covers, but the warmth of a very large man sprawled at her back.

Toran! He wasn't supposed to be here. Senga would box his ears, if she could reach them. Or perhaps not. Aileana smiled. She had slept soundly the night through, and had not even been aware that Toran had remained in her bed. Surely Senga could not complain about the comfort his presence gave her.

She yawned and stretched, then turned to curl against Toran's massive chest, resting her head on his shoulder. She draped her arm across his belly, intending to let sleep take her again, but found that she could not resist exploring the warmth of his skin under her palm. Her fingers trailed upward, sliding into the silky hair on his chest. When they brushed across his nipple, she found a tiny, hard bud. Under it, the beat of his heart, at first slow and lazy, begin to increase in pace. He was awake.

"What will Senga say when she finds out where you spent the night?" Aileana asked softly, still brushing her fingers across Toran's chest.

"Perhaps she'll no' discover it," came the lazy rumble beneath her ear. "If we do no' tell her, who will?"

"Elspie has a habit of coming in without more than a quick knock on the door," Aileana warned him.

"Ach, Elspie will never tell on me."

Aileana propped her head up on one hand and continued to trace lazy spirals on Toran's chest with the other while she eyed him. His eyes were still closed, but his smirk was almost more than she could bear and she grinned back at him even though she knew he wouldn't see her.

"Elspie tells on everybody. She's the worst gossip in the Aerie."

"So, then," Toran said, opening his eyes as he grasped her wandering hand and urged it lower, "what if we give her something more interesting to talk about?"

As her hand skimmed over his belly to his hip, Aileana discovered that Toran was naked. "Do you always sleep this way?" she asked as he released her hand and lifted his to stroke the side of her face and neck.

"At home, aye. Away from the Aerie, the ground's too cold and hard to sleep like this."

"I do have some familiarity with sleeping on the ground. This bed is much better."

"Ah, so ye approve of the bed, do ye? What of the man ye find within in?"

"I approve of him, as well."

"In bed or without?"

"I suppose I must approve both, because I'd rather not do without."

"Lass!" Toran's laugh was loud and Aileana took her hand from his hip and put it over his mouth.

"Ssshhh! Someone will hear you!" He lifted her hand away and kissed her fingertips, her palm, and her wrist.

"Let them. We lack the ceremony, but are we no' married, Aileana? Since the moment I claimed ye?"

That gave her pause. "Is that what ye meant, back there in Angus's camp? Are we married?"

"Aye, we are. Ye told me that ye loved me, and that this is where ye wished to be. I told ye that I wished for ye to remain here with me. I offered a betrothal, if ye'll recall, when ye were ready. But I neglected to tell ye the most important thing before our passions overtook us yesterday. I love ye, too, Aileana. I never want to lose ye again. I want ye beside me, always."

The look on Aileana's face was a joy to behold.

"Then I suppose we are, my laird. Married. A ceremony would be nice, but the churching can wait."

"We'll do what ye wish, lass." Toran's satisfied smile teased her. "But for now, do ye ken where I'd like yer hand to be fasted at this moment?"

"I believe I do," Aileana answered with a wicked grin and began to trail her fingers down his throat.

"Farther than that, lass."

Aileana moved her fingers onto his chest and filled them with the soft, dark hair she found there. Then she tugged.

"Ach, lass, no' there, and no' like that." Toran leaned over and kissed her on the mouth, then whispered against her ear, "Lower."

Aileana trailed her fingertips down his belly, following the line of hair that led even lower. She circled the indentation she found midway, and scratched lightly at the skin below it. Toran groaned.

"Ye're getting nearer," he moaned as his thumb trailed over her mouth.

Finally her questing fingers found the hard heat of his shaft. "Hmmm," she murmured as she gripped him.

With an oath, he collapsed back onto the pillows.

"Have I found it then, this place you'd like my hand to be fasted?"

"Lass, ye ken ye have. Come, let me love ye. 'Tis what we both want. What we both need. God, I thought I'd lost ye when ye ran from me."

Aileana smiled and leaned down to Toran's lips. She stopped just shy of touching his mouth. "I do love you, Toran. And I'm sorry I ran from you. I should have known you didn't mean those things you said."

"Ach, lass," he murmured just before his mouth took hers. He lifted her onto his body, trapping her hand between them. She shifted her grip on him and heard him groan in response. His groans deepened every time she shifted her hand around him, stroking and feeling him grow even larger in her grip.

"Ye're driving me mad, woman," he declared and Aileana reveled in the power of it. Then he sat up, lifting her with him so that she let go of his manhood. He moved her legs to each side, so that she knelt on the bed over him.

Suddenly shy as he gazed at her, she crossed her

arms over her breasts. Gently, he uncrossed them and placed her hands on his shoulders. Then he slid his hands down her sides as he bent to suckle at her nipples. Fierce fire ran from them straight to that place between her thighs, and liquid heat bathed it just as his fingers strayed between her legs to touch her...there. Aileana thought the pleasure could not get more intense, but it did as he stroked and explored every fold, then inserted one finger, then two, then three. Aileana arched in ecstacy as Toran's fingers filled her and his thumb circled over her bright nub. Finally, the sizzle of sensation became too much and she came apart in his hands. He held her until the trembling abated, then lowered her hips until she was poised over his rock-hard shaft.

"Gently, Aileana. Slowly and gently. Let yerself take me into yer body. It will be as before, but ye'll control the pace. The depth. The pleasure."

There was that need again. The emptiness that cried out for Toran to fill it. She smiled as he nudged at her entrance and reveled in the sensation of his slick heat filling her as she settled onto him. A shiver ran through her as she tightened around him and sank a little lower, taking more of him in. She let her head fall back as he groaned, reveling in the throb of his pulse in her body. Only he could make her feel this ecstasy. With small movements, she slid lower onto him until she'd taken all of him inside her. "Oh, Toran, this is wonderful." She sighed.

"And about to get better," he answered as he placed his hands on her hips and began to lift and lower her. She quickly caught the rythym and began to rock up and down on his length, nearly rising off him, then plunging down to take him to the hilt. As his groans filled her ears, Aileana felt her own pleasure spiraling out of control.

"Now, Toran," she breathed as she felt herself slipping over the edge into a bright maelstrom. "Now!"

His moan of ecstacy and the furious heat of his seed erupting into her core were his only answers.

Chapter Thirteen

Toran and Aileana were wrapped in each other's arms when the knock at the door came that Ailena had told Toran to expect. Elspie's voice preceded her as the door swung open. "Lass, do no' let our wee laird upset ye. Surely he didn't mean what he said yesterday...oh!"

Aileana had ducked under the covers, only her eyes and the top of her head peeking out, at the first knock. Toran, on the other hand, sat up, and was content to let the covers drape across his midsection.

"Good morning, Elspie," he said, smoothly, as Aileana blushed.

"Laird! I dinna expect to find ye here..." Elspie trailed off, glancing from her laird to what she could see of Aileana and back again. "Well..."

"We are well, indeed. Please send up some breakfast," Toran replied, nonplussed. "I believe we'll be here a while longer."

A sly grin split Elspie's face and the skin around her eyes crinkled. "Aye, Laird. I'll bring it myself."

"Good. Oh, and Elspie," Toran continued as she turned to leave, "make sure ye knock and then hear me tell ye to enter before ye open the door from now on."

Aileana couldn't help the gasp that escaped her at that pronouncement. Elspie blushed furiously and nodded, then left with haste.

"Now, where were we?" Toran asked, pulling

Aileana into his arms.

"We were discussing what to do now that our secret is out and the tale is likely being told from one end of the keep to the other," Aileana answered him archly. "I warned ye about Elspie."

"What better messenger, then…"

"Save you?"

Toran had the grace to look discomfited. "Aye, ye have the right of it, as usual. I suppose we should dress and go make the news known before Elspie gets word to everyone in the clan."

"Oh, I think we're minutes too late for that, already."

"Then let's have a handfasting ceremony today."

"Today? But…"

"Aye. We agreed to it at Angus's hideout, and now that we've bedded, we are married. And 'twould be more fitting for the laird to announce his marriage as soon after the event as possible. Rumors fly quickly. But would ye no' like a ceremony?"

"Not a large one, please, Toran."

"A small one then. Or we can wait for the priest and the kirk. I care not. I want ye by me forever. Starting today."

Toran smiled at the glint of tears in Aileana's eyes. "Oh, aye, Toran. Forever. Starting today."

Toran's heart was so full, it swelled to fill his chest. He could not believe how happy those six words had made him. She accepted him wanted him, and she wanted the ceremony to mark the occasion. "Who would ye like to bind us together, do ye think?"

Aileana appeared to give that a moment's thought. "Who better than Jamie?"

"Aye, he would enjoy that."

"I think he would. And while ye're about it, bring Senga, too. And Elspie would never forgive us if she missed this. She'll so enjoy telling everyone about it."

"I'll send Elspie to help ye dress while I gather the others."

"I love you, Toran."

"And I love ye, Aileana."

****

Aileana sat before the fire, brushing out her hair after her bath. Elspie had gone to fetch a "special" dress for the handfasting. Ailieana wasn't sure what significance a dress might have, especially since she had expressed a preference to wear her green kirtle. But Elspie had insisted, and Senga, the traitor, had sided with Elspie. Aileana supposed she could look it over and then politely decline to wear it if it were too awful. But she knew Elspie would have none of it and she'd wind up wearing whatever Elspie brought.

Senga, too, had left to fetch some special oil that she guaranteed would drive a man wild. Not that Toran needed any help in that department. Nor did Aileana, when she was in his arms. But a laird took a wife only rarely, and they were doing this with little notice, simply and with no fanfare. Let them have their fun.

Toran agreed to hold the ceremony in the privacy of his chambers. That was the way she wanted it: just between the two of them and their chosen witnesses. No one in the clan was more closely connected to both of them than Jamie; as Toran's closest friend and the man whose life Aileana had saved, he would do the honors.

But whenever a priest could get to the Aerie in the spring, Toran had promised her that they would hold another wedding the entire clan could attend in the small kirk outside the keep. Toran was quite certain that the invaders would be gone from their glen long before then. Aileana hoped he would be proven correct. And that Ranald would find a means to slip away and join her here before that happened.

Aileana regretted that her brother could not be here to see this.

Simple Aileana, healer's apprentice, becoming the lady of a Highland clan. True, a small one, and one under siege. But she hoped he would be happy for her, both in her chosen husband and in the new life that lay before her.

Toran offered her what she'd longed for: a home, a family, stability, perhaps even respect, if not for her Talent, then for her position as lady.

That was a bonus she'd never expected to reap. Or a burden. Time would tell. In the meantime, this fretting was getting her nowhere and Elspie would be back in a moment. Aileana stood and stretched. She went to the window and peered out, much as she had on her first night in this chamber. Wispy clouds scattered across an azure sky and a breeze stirred the limbs of the trees. It was a beautiful day. A beautiful day to marry a handsome laird.

Elspie opened the door and came in carrying a large box. Senga, right on her heels, closed the door behind her and set a vial on the table by the bed while Elspie opened the box. Aileana watched with some amusement their well-orchestrated movements. They were going to see their laird married, and it was up to them to make sure the bride appeared before him as beautifully as a bride should.

Then a flash of green within the box caught Aileana's attention as Elspie peeled away layers of paper that had been wrapped around the dress to preserve it. Forest-green satin filled the box. Gently, Elspie pulled the dress free and shook it out, then held it up for Aileana's inspection. Aileana's breath caught in her throat and she reached out to touch the fabric, relishing the silky slip of it along her fingertips. Toran would not be able to resist this.

"It's beautiful. Who did it belong to?"

"Toran's mother. Though I dinna believe he's ever seen it. Ye have her size, as I recall it. So we'll try this on ye. It should fit."

And it did fit, like it had been made for her. As Elspie did up the buttons, Senga watched with a teary smile.

"So beautiful ye are, lass. Our wee laird willna be able to resist ye."

"He hasna afore," Elspie quipped, "so why should he start now?"

Aileana blushed and the other women laughed.

"Sit, lass, and let me fix yer hair," Elspie ordered and produced several ivory combs set with small green gems from her pocket. It took only moments before Aileana's auburn tresses were swept up and held in place, grass-green crystals glittering brightly on the ivory combs. Elspie left a few tendrils framing her face and gracing the nape of her neck.

"There ye are, lass, a vision if I ever saw one."

Senga nodded. "I feel as if I'm to watch my own daughter marry. My heart's all a-flutter in my chest." She patted her thin bosom for effect.

Aileana went to her and hugged her close, then

turned and did the same to the startled Elspie. "Thank you both. You were right. This is a special occasion and it needs a special dress. I'm grateful for your care."

"Lass, we're grateful that ye're taking on our wee laird. He's been mad for ye since the day he brought ye home. We hope ye'll be happy together for the rest o' yer lives."

Jamie chose that moment to knock on the door, open it and peer in. "Are ye ready, Healer?"

"Aye, Jamie, we are," Elspie answered for her. "And a good thing that the bride was dressed, too, before ye came barging in here."

"My apologies, ladies. But the groom is getting impatient, and ye ken what that means."

"Aye," Senga snorted. "Grumping and growling and if he has to wait too long, cursing and swearing."

"We're still at the grumping stage," Jamie reported with a smile as the women filed out the door past him, "but moving quickly on to growling."

Aileana paused at his side and placed a hand on his face. Jamie jerked back from her touch. "None o' that now, lassie. Ye need yer strength to deal with the laird today."

"I simply meant to thank you," Aileana lied gently. "For seeing to us. I could think of none better than you."

"Thank ye, lass. Or should I say, Lady?"

"In a few minutes, perhaps."

Jamie grinned. "Let's get on with it, then. Yer laird awaits."

As she entered Toran's suite, Aileana drew a startled breath at the same moment he did, and likely for the same reason. He looked magnificent, and she knew from Elspie and Senga that the fancy dress suited her. Toran wore resplendent full ceremonial dress as if born to it. The Lathan tartan and a gold pin topped a fine shirt with a frothy laced jabot. The torc he rarely wore at home rested against his neck, the gemstones gracing its ends catching the light. Black leather boots shined to a mirror surface covered his feet and lower legs. He had pulled his midnight hair back with a ribbon into a queue. Aileana thought he had never looked so deliciously handsome.

And from the way he stared at her, his thoughts were trending in the same direction. Like he was the starving cat and she the cream. He looked so imposing that by rights, she should be terrified of him. But this was Toran, the man who loved her, who wanted to keep her by him forever—and a day. She gathered her courage, lifted her chin and approached him. He held out his hand to her.

"My God, lass, ye're a vision."

"You're in no danger of scaring the children either, milord."

Toran chucked and pulled her close for a kiss.

"Ach, none o' that," Jamie said, his voice cutting between them like a board blocking her way. "No' until after the ceremony."

Aileana turned to regard him with a smile and a raised eyebrow. His laird may have been grumping and growling, but Jamie clearly had no fear of him.

"Let's get on with it, then," Toran commanded, and settled Aileana by his side. Elspie and Senga took up their positions on either side of Jamie.

"Ye will first sign the Clan Lathan's Book of Protocol to record this event."

"Not a Bible?" Aileana asked.

"There is one," Toran told her, "and ye'll sign that when the priest marries us in the kirk. The clan's Book of Protocol is how we'll record today."

When they'd affixed their signatures in the heavy volume of bound vellum, Jamie cleared his throat and began.

"I have here the dress tartan of Clan Lathan," Jamie said for Aileana's benefit and picked up a slender length of woolen cloth whose colors were brighter and more distinct that the tartan plaid Toran had worn in the MacAnalen camp, but matched what he wore today. "Laird, yer hand if ye please."

Toran extended his right hand and Jamie tied a length of the tartan around his wrist. For a moment, Aileana was reminded of the damage he'd done there trying to escape leather bindings, but she blinked the vision away. This was not the same thing at all. This binding, he welcomed.

"Repeat after me," Jamie instructed, his attention fully on his laird. "I, Toran Lathan MacLathan…"

"I, Toran Lathan MacLathan…"

"…take ye, Aileana Shaw…to be my lawful wife…under the laws of the Kirk and the King…and to ye I pledge my life, my troth, and my honor."

Tears welled in her eyes as Toran repeated the vow to her. She wasn't sure she'd be capable of speech when her turn came.

Then it was her turn. "Give me yer right hand," Jamie commanded, and then wrapped the tartan fabric around her trembling wrist. "Repeat after me. I, Aileana Shaw…take ye, Toran Lathan MacLathan…to be my lawful husband…under the laws of the Kirk and the

King...and to ye I pledge my life, my troth, and my honor."

Somehow, Aileana got the words out. She could not help but be mesmerized by Toran's eyes as she spoke them. His gaze bored into her. He inhaled her every word, every breath, as though he was trying to absorb it all and remember this moment for the rest of his life. She had no doubt that she would never forget the look on his face as Jamie wrapped the end of the cloth three times around their wrists, binding them together.

"I pronounce ye married, laird and lady. No' 'til death will ye part. And now, Toran," he added with a wink, "ye may kiss the bride."

Toran wasted no time in pulling Aileana into his one-armed embrace, their bound hands clasped between them. His kiss was the sweetest Aileana had tasted of the many he'd given her. Tender, hopeful, joyful. She kissed him back, giving him with her lips and tears the full measure of her happiness.

After a moment, Jamie cleared his throat and both Elspie and Senga began to clap, then rushed forward to hug them both, spilling tears and laughter over them like a benediction. Jamie stood to one side, looking like a small boy not invited to the party, so Aileana pulled her free arm from around her husband and welcomed Jamie into the assembled embrace.

Toran's patience lasted longer than Aileana anticipated. Finally, he stepped back and the group broke apart.

"Thank ye, old friend," he said, offering Jamie his free hand. "And thank ye both, Healer Senga and Elspie. Now if ye all would be so kind, my wife and I would like some time together."

Elspie blushed, but Senga nodded sagely. Jamie grinned when Aileana forced Toran to raise their bound hands up for all to regard. "The first thing we have to do is to unwind all of this."

****

"Laird Lathan!"

Toran glanced up from brushing out a knot in Banner's mane. The stable boys didn't yet have the strength yet to groom his stallion as Banner liked it, though they did the best they could.

After the handfasting ceremony had been completed, and after another very pleasant interlude with his new bride, Toran had reluctantly departed Aileana's bed for the second time that day, reminded of Senga's advice to let the poor lass rest when Aileana fell asleep in his arms. Rather than being spent after their lovemaking, Toran felt energized, restless, so he'd obeyed Senga's advice and left to allow Aileana to get some much needed sleep.

He'd gone to alert Cook to concoct a celebration feast for that evening, and had been amused to find out that Cook knew, thanks to Elspie. Preparations were already underway. Then he wandered the keep, greeting his clan members and confirming the news.

Still restless, he had brought Banner out of his stall into the outer bailey so they could both enjoy the remaining sunshine while Toran worked. He finished brushing the knot loose as Donal strode toward him. No doubt about it, the day was about to become a good deal less pleasant.

But, of course, word of his and Aileana's handfasting must have finally reached Donal, who had been out hunting fresh game with several of the men since before dawn. Elspie efficiently spread her gossip, indeed. And the look on Donal's face was as thunderous as any Toran had ever seen.

"And how are ye this fine day?" Toran asked before Donal could speak, hoping to forestall the outburst that his expression foretold.

"What is this news I hear?" Donal demanded, ignoring Toran's question.

"What news is that?" Toran replied mildly, determined not to rise to Donal's bait.

"Ye ken what news, Toran. How could ye do it? Her, of all women?"

"Have a care, old friend." Toran clamped down on his sudden spike of temper, but there was only so much he would allow, even from Donal.

"I do care, Lathan, and well ye ken it. It's because I care that I question yer sense now. We've talked often enough, and ye know my objections as well as the concerns of many in the clan. So I'll ask again, how could ye, Toran?"

Donal's voice had gotten louder as he spoke, and Toran noticed several people passing had slowed, or even stopped to eavesdrop, so he kept his tone even and his voice low. "Aye, we've talked, Donal, but it's been clear all along that ye dinna listen. Everything she's done has been for the good of the people of this clan. Ye lack any basis for objecting to her presence here as a healer, or as my wife."

"How can ye say that?" Donal made an effort to lower his voice. Toran could see that it cost him. "Her magic is basis enough for me, and for many others."

Banner chose that moment to shift restlessly. Toran

doubted the argument affected the great warhorse. More likely, he was reminding Toran that he enjoyed Toran's hand at his grooming. Aye, Toran did, too. He found it soothing to brush down the big horse and see to him. Banner's needs were much simpler and easier to deal with than any other of Toran's charges. Such as Donal.

"The subject is closed, Donal. Let's take Banner back to the stable and go inspect the guard."

"And leave yer new bride for so long?"

A gasp from one of the onlookers distracted Toran into glancing toward them. Coira stood at the edge of the small group, eyes wide and mouth agape. Toran bit back an oath. So she had not yet heard the news. And she was exactly what he did not need to deal with at this moment. But she surprised him by staying back, her eyes narrowed, and continued listening intently as Donal challenged his laird.

Damn it all to hell, as determined as he was not to let Donal's anger get out of hand, Donal seemed just as determined to push him past all control of his own. Toran's tone, when he spoke again, was curt. "My new bride kens well my responsibilities to the clan, which I have never abandoned. And that as lady, she'll also have responsibilities that go beyond her skills as a healer. She is prepared to take them up."

"I'll just bet she is." Coira's voice echoed angrily around the bailey. "She's gone from worse than nothing to lady of the clan in his bed. I wonder if that was entirely the laird's idea, or if she's bewitched him into it."

"Coira!" Both he and Donal shouted at the same time. "Don't interfere," Donal continued at the same moment that Toran barked, "Silence!"

216

Coira's bravado fled at the combined attack and she blanched, then hurried away, to the snickers of several of the other onlookers. But Toran noted a few assessing glances following her retreat. Surely no one took her nonsense seriously?

"I am not bewitched," Toran said, keeping his tone level and his voice low. "I am a happily married man. Aileana is not a witch. She's a healer with an unusual talent, which has proven valuable to the Clan. We love each other. She is my bride. Be happy for me, Donal, can't ye?"

"Nay, Toran, I canna. I'm...sorry. I care too much for ye and for this clan to lower my guard. I'll have my eye on her, since ye canna do it, and I'll be watching for any hint of trouble."

"And ye'll come to me if ye see any...trouble," Toran said, deliberately using Donal's term. Toran didn't like the way Donal hesitated, but to be fair, Donal probably believed he'd done that already. Toran had to drive the message home. He would not tolerate any threats to Aileana, no matter how well intended. "Donal, ye'll take no action without the laird's permission, nor will ye allow anyone else to do so," he commanded, finally raising his voice slightly. "I will not be disobeyed in this." He left the consequences to Donal's imagination. Toran would kill anyone who harmed Aileana, and Donal kenned it well.

"Aye, Laird Lathan," Donal finally answered. "I'll come to ye first."

"Good. And send Coira back to her clan before first light—with an escort and enough supplies for the journey and the weather. She's worn out her welcome. But let it never be said that Clan Lathan failed to safeguard one of its own, be they fostered, guested or newly married into the clan."

"I hear ye, Lathan."

"Then get to it."

Banner chose that moment to toss his head and whinny for attention. Toran had delayed his grooming too long, it seemed, for Banner's patience. Toran patted his mount's nose in relief as Donal moved to obey and the onlookers went on their way. He agreed with Banner. Better to be doing something useful than standing around here arguing.

Chapter Fourteen

Colbridge had been cursing since the confrontation in the glen yesterday afternoon. His demands had been met by taunts flung down from the Aerie's high walls, and his temper, judging by the fierce expression on his face as he stared into the fire, was still something to fear. He'd barely paused in his ranting to sleep during the night and had kept the entire camp on edge, waiting to see what he was going to do next. Now a full day had passed and the sun sank lower toward evening. He had to be planning something, not just nursing his anger at the insults traded with the Lathan laird.

Ranald stood by, quietly. Sudden moves, he judged, could be fatal. That Colbridge's fury still burned hot after the shouted confrontation with the Lathan laird that had been barely audible from Colbridge's lines told Ranald that Aileana would not be returning. Not soon, not easily.

"He dares to mock me," Ranald heard Colbridge mutter under his breath. He turned from the fire to his two lieutenants who stood stiffly by, awaiting orders. "Never again! I'm bloody tired of this siege. I'll tear down his walls, stone by bloody stone, before winter arrives, and kill them all, including that witch. If he hasn't ruined her already, she won't live to help them or anyone else."

Ranald's breath froze in his throat. Kill Aileana?

"No!"

In the sudden silence, he realized with sick certainty that he'd spoken his objection aloud. Colbridge turned slowly to face him, placing his hand on his sword hilt.

"What did you say?" he demanded, advancing around the fire to where Ranald stood, unarmed, expecting death at any moment.

Damned fool! Think! Ranald bowed his head, attempting to appear as non-threatening as possible. "Sir, I spoke in error."

Colbridge pulled his sword. "Damned right you did. Give me one good reason why I shouldn't run you through where you stand?"

Ranald grimaced at the thought, but called upon his years of training as a warrior, desperately searching for an idea, an explanation. "I can get her out," he said, calmly, hoping to buy some time to think and to bring Colbridge's ire down a notch or two. "I have a plan."

"You have a plan, do you? For getting the Healer out of that…" He used the swordpoint to gesture at the steep tor, and the Aerie atop it.

Ranald couldn't take his eyes off the swing of the blade as Colbridge brought it back around and leveled it at his chest. "Why don't you tell me about this plan, then, cripple? What can you do, limping, that my army cannot?"

Ranald sucked in a breath, pulling his chest back a fraction away from the sharp tip. "Send me in," he said, quickly, but quietly, trying by his own stillness to calm Colbridge down. "An envoy, with an offer to end the siege. An offer to ally with them," he said, jerking back as Colbridge's frown deepened, and the sword point lifted from his chest to his neck.

"Ally? Have you lost your reason?"

"Just a ruse…" Ranald continued quickly, all too aware of the cold steel at his throat. "Just a ruse. They won't harm a cripple. Won't think I can do anything but carry a message. But Aileana will see me. I'll convince her to come out with me. Get her out, back here, where she can help you as she has these past two years."

That was the last thing Ranald wanted to do to Aileana. As much as he missed her, he would let Colbridge cut his throat before he would condemn her to life under Colbridge's rule. She was well rid of this camp and this mad man who had led them here. But he had to convince Colbridge that he meant every word.

Ranald could see Colbridge thinking, and breathed a sigh of relief when the sword left his throat. Then suddenly, it was back, just under his chin.

"Just a ruse, eh? A ruse to escape me and find what you think is safety with that Highland mob, isn't that what you intend?"

Colbridge teased and taunted before he killed, Ranald knew, and he watched the point of the sword slipping from side to side, just under his chin, with dread. Colbridge's jibe was too close to what had been in the back of his mind…escape from here, with Aileana.

"Nay, never. I'm the only one who can return her to you. The only one she will trust."

Abruptly, Colbridge resheathed his blade, and stepped in closer to Ranald, hissing right into his face. "She trusts you? You must be special to her, then. Lovers, perhaps?"

Ranald felt the confrontation sliding out of control,

and gulped. "No, no, nothing like that."

"I think you were. You want her back. And I think the Healer will come back to save you." Colbridge turned to two of his men. "Strip his shirt off him and tie him up between those two trees, where he can be seen by any who look this way from up there." He gestured toward the Aerie.

Ranald had no choice but to submit or Colbridge would kill him where he stood. He remained stoic while his arms were tied above his head. Then, disbelieving, he watched Colbridge pull his dirk and brandish it in front of his face.

"Now...I think we need more incentive for the Healer—a job she knows how to do. She must be compelled to save you."

Ranald shook his head, and despite the autumn chill, sweat broke out on his face and body. But he dared not speak. Colbridge was in a mean temper, and it would only be worse if he enraged him further.

"She must see blood," Colbridge continued, circling him, fondling the knife. He stopped in front of Ranald. "At first, perhaps only a little," he continued, and sliced Ranald's face beside his ear.

A warm, wet rivulet ran down his neck. He felt no pain, not yet, but he knew that was coming. Colbridge had the scent of his blood now, the sight of it, and he would want more. Ranald kept his eyes on the high tor and willed himself to silence, as Colbridge sliced his arm, his chest. But his eyes clenched shut and a scream nearly escaped his lips when Colbridge plunged the knife into the thigh of his good leg.

****

Replete from her wedding dinner, Aileana heard

the first sweet notes under the rumble of voices in the Great Hall. She looked quickly toward the sound. How wonderful! Music! She had not heard music in two years. One of the women had begun plucking a small harp, and gradually, the voices died down as more people stopped to listen. The tune started out softly, but soon picked up its pace and became a lively air. A few people began dancing, and as quickly as that, tables were pushed out of the way to make more floor space and others joined in. Aileana smiled at the cheerful scene they set. When the harpist was done, she set the instrument aside. As the appreciative calls and whistles subsided, one of the men began to sing, and others joined in. In moments, other instruments appeared and added to the happy din, spurring anyone not singing to take to the dance floor.

"Do ye like music?" Toran asked, leaning close to her ear.

"Aye, very much." Aileana smiled at her husband, feeling relaxed and content for the first time in a very long time. "I haven't heard any in years. I didn't know until the harpist started playing that I've missed it very much."

"Then we'll have it more often," Toran told her and sat back, smiling at her. "Do ye sing?"

"Me? Oh, no. Not at all. But I like to listen."

Toran nodded and Aileana turned her attention back to the people in the hall. Everyone was either singing along, or smiling as they listened to the chorus of voices.

Suddenly a commotion in the back of the room where most of the clan's children sat caught Aileana's attention. A sharp cry broke the singers' harmony, then

a high-pitched scream that silenced them in mid-word.
What was happening? She stood to better see what had
caused the disturbance. Toran rose to his feet by her
side.

"Ach, nay!" Toran exclaimed as she caught sight of
Coira, holding a young girl in front of her and a knife at
the girl's throat. "What's this?" Toran barked. "Coira,
put the dirk down and let the lass go."

Shocked silence filled the hall. The dancers quickly
cleared out of the space between Coira and Toran.

"Nay, Toran. No' until yer witch comes to me.
We've unfinished business, we do."

Aileana started to move but Toran grabbed her
hand, keeping her next to him. "Nay, lass," he hissed, "I
dinna ken what's she's about, but I dinna want ye
anywhere near her."

"She'll kill the girl."

"No' if I can help it," Toran vowed and turned
back to Coira. The other children had backed away
from her, but some of the men were starting to edge
closer. If Toran distracted her, that might give them a
chance to stop her without harming the lass under her
knife.

"What business is that?" Toran replied then to
Coira, raising his voice.

"She kens it. She stole ye from me. Bewitched ye
away from yer chosen mate, and yer duty to yer clan to
ally with mine. Now ye plan to send me away, and my
time is short. No one else here has had the wit to do it,
so it falls to me to rid the clan of the witch."

Toran stiffened beside Aileana. In contrast, her
knees weakened with Coira's words and she grasped
Toran's arm to steady herself. Had it come to this? A

witch hunt here in the midst of the Great Hall? On this day, of all days? But no, Senga had said Coira was more jealous of her than fearful of any witch, and angry that she had not been chosen lady. So what was Coira up to?

"Yer problem is with me, then, not the child," Aileana said, speaking up for the first time. Toran squeezed her arm with one big hand, but she ignored him. "Let her go."

"No' until ye come to me," Coira answered, tossing her head back. "Here. I'll no' risk marching into the midst of this lot." She glanced around at the nearby adults and everyone froze, but Coira seemed not to notice that some had already moved closer to her. "I'll deal with ye here."

"Aileana, nay," Toran commanded in a low voice, but she pulled her arm free and turned to face him.

"A child of the clan needs aid that only I can give," she told him softly but firmly. "Let me be. I can handle her."

"Nay, ye canna. She's no' in her right mind."

"It doesn't matter, Toran. I will do it." To do so might mean exposing her most threatening secret to the entire clan, but with a child at risk, she had no choice. If Aileana could not talk Coira into releasing the girl, she'd have to use her Voice to subdue her. She knew doing so would merely confirm in Donal's eyes that she was wildly dangerous, but if Coira would not listen to reason, there might be no other way. Aileana would cope with the consequences when the child was safe.

"I'm coming with ye," Toran said as she stepped away from the table and began to walk toward Coira. Aileana ignored him, focusing instead on holding her head high, and locking her gaze with Coira's. She couldn't do anything until she was close enough to touch the madwoman, and she feared Coira would slash the girl's throat in her fury before she could get that close. Toran's presence was like a solid wall at her back, ensuring that she could face an attack head on without fear of being flanked by anyone who sympathized with Coira.

"So this is what it takes to get ye to come to me, Toran," Coira snarled as she watched him follow Aileana. "Ye canna tell me yerself that ye banish me, but send yer minions to do it for ye. Did ye hope never to see me again, Lathan? Now that ye wed yer witch? I doubt ye expected to see me again, now did ye?"

Toran didn't answer. Aileana felt another presence arrive at her back and glanced aside. Donal! Shoulder to shoulder with his laird? Or ready to support Coira? It didn't matter. This was her fight. "Stay back," she told them, risking a quick glance at Toran. "Don't interfere."

They dropped back two paces, but they neither stopped, nor gave her more room than that.

She stopped a pair of paces away from the lass Coira held in front of herself like a shield. The child's eyes were wide with fear and tears streaked her ruddy face. So far, the blade at her throat had not broken the skin—a small miracle given the hatred on Coira's face as she stared at Aileana. "I am here, Coira. Let the child go."

"Come closer."

Aileana took a step forward. She could almost feel Toran's fists clench behind her. But he made no move to stop her.

"Closer," Coira demanded.

Aileana complied, her gaze never leaving the other woman's face. "I'm here as you demanded," she said calmly. "You promised to let her go. You can do so now."

With a cry that was more of a wail than an expression of outrage, Coira shoved the girl aside and swung the knife at Aileana. Aileana reached out just as Coira swung the blade, wincing as it plunged into her shoulder below the collarbone. Shocked by the sudden attack, she still managed to touch Coira's face, but it was too late to try to use her Voice. She heard the gasp that echoed around the hall. Everything seemed frozen. No one moved. Coira, still holding the hilt, sneered at her in satisfaction.

Then, almost dreamlike, Aileana saw Donal stepped around one side of her, Toran the other. Their dirks flashed in the middle, Toran's held at Coira's throat, Donal's buried to the hilt in her chest. Coira widened her eyes in surprise and she let go of the knife she'd plunged into Aileana. She took one step back, gaze still locked with Aileana's, before she crumpled to the floor.

Toran sheathed his dirk as he spun then grabbed Aileana by both arms. "Sit, lass," he commanded as someone shoved a bench their way.

Aileana had come out of her shocked daze when Toran touched her. She felt for the extent of her injury, and sighed in relief when she found the damage confined to the muscle and breast tissue above it. "Toran, help me," she said, relieved that her voice sounded stronger than she felt. "I need to help Coira, but you have to pull her blade out of me first."

"Nay, lass, wait for Senga."

"Nay. There's no time. Do it now, Toran. Don't make me do it myself."

Senga hurried up at that moment, took one look at the bloody tableau and sniffed. "We're well rid of that one."

"Nay, Senga," Aileana told her. "She's hurt, and needs my help. Tell your laird to remove Coira's blade from my shoulder. Then you can aid me."

Senga looked skeptical, but nodded. "Do as she says, Laird."

He started to protest, but both women gave him such determined looks that he had no choice but to comply. He gripped the hilt reluctantly and slowly, careful not to twist or shift the blade in any way, and pulled it free. Aileana fought to keep her expression bland, despite the pain that swamped her. She had a job to do. "Put pressure on my wound. This will only take a moment."

Senga pressed a clean cloth to the blood welling from the top of Aileana's breast and winced as Aileana paled against the pain. "Hurry, lass."

"Aye," Aileana gasped. But in a moment it was done. The wound was not healed, but the bleeding stopped, and she could do what she must before she finished with it. Senga insisted on tying another clean cloth over the still-gaping cut before she allowed Aileana to drop to her knees beside her wounded attacker. "Toran," Aileana commanded as soon as her head stopped spinning from kneeling over Coira, "this is just like the arrow in Jamie. Pull this blade slowly. I'll work as ye go. Don't stop, but go slow."

Toran knelt beside her and did as she bade him,

thankfully for once without any argument. Coira was badly hurt, but Aileana knew that this wound was nothing compared to the pain in her heart that had driven Coira to take such desperate action. Aileana had sensed it when she touched her face. Yes, Coira feared her. But most of what Aileana had sensed was a deep, abiding sense of loss, an aching emptiness that had stolen the rest of her breath after Coira's blade pierced her. Coira couldn't understand why Toran had refused her. His was the latest of many rejections in her life. Her clan had sent her far away. Aileana could not begin to guess what had happened to her there to drive her this far from home.

Aileana worked quickly, knowing her strength would be severely limited by the wound Coira had inflicted on her. Donal's blade had bitten deep in his bid to protect his laird's bride. Coira's lung was filling with blood. As Toran pulled the blade from Coira's body, Aileana worked quickly to stop the bleeding and mend the torn tissue Donal's dirk had left behind. Finally satisfied that she had done all she could, she did not allow Coira to awaken, but lay a healing sleep on her.

"Senga, keep someone with her. She'll sleep into tomorrow. But if she has any trouble breathing, come get me right away."

"Nay, lass, ye need to rest."

"I will. But Coira needs our care. She was sore troubled before she did this terrible thing. But now I think she'll awaken very sorry for her actions. We must guard her well, so that she has a chance to make a better life for herself."

"It will be done, lass. Dinna fash."

Aileana smiled at Senga, then at Toran, then at Donal. "Thank you, Donal, for protecting me. I know you believe I'm a threat but…"

"Nay, lass," Donal said, interrupting her. "After the grace I've just seen ye display, to risk yerself to save a child, and then to save the life of yer attacker and forgive her actions, well, Toran has been right all along. There's a good heart in ye, lass, and I'm glad to have ye in the clan."

"Thank you, Donal."

"And now, if ye'll help Senga get Coira settled and post a guard," Toran interjected, "I'll get Aileana to bed so that she can rest and recover."

"Wait," Aileana said, as Toran bent to pick her up. "Where's the lass Coira held hostage?"

"Here," a woman's voice answered. Aileana looked around to see the child, tears dried, sitting on her mother's lap. The mother looked more upset than the girl. Aileana took a step toward them and smiled when Toran took her arm to assist her to them. She knelt in front of the child and touched her cheek. "Are you well, lass?"

"Mommy says so," the little girl replied shyly.

"Ye sacrificed yerself to save my daughter," the woman said, fresh tears springing to her eyes. "That madwoman could have killed her."

"But she did not. She bore many burdens that wounded her, but I think she'll be better now. And as for you, little one"—Aileana turned her attention back and brushed her fingers across the girl's forehead. It would take so little of her talent to make the child forget…she reached gently and told her, using the Voice in a whisper that not even her mother would detect—*"It was just a bad dream. But your mother is here and all is well."*

A shy smile lit the girl's face and Aileana dropped her hand to her side. Toran helped her stand. "She'll sleep and remember this only as a dream," Aileana told her mother. "She'll be herself in the morning."

"Thank ye, Healer...Lady," the woman choked out before turning to hide her tears in her daughter's curly hair.

"Let's go," Toran said.

Aileana nodded. "I'm ready."

Toran scooped her up. As they started toward the stairs, someone started clapping. First it was one, then several, then it became a thunderous din that echoed around the Great Hall. Toran stopped at the top of the stairs and turned to look down on the people of his clan. "Ye've seen the worth of yer new lady. Let this be the last of the slander and of the violence."

Aileana blushed as the clapping began anew, punctuated by shouts and cheers. She could see Donal at the back of the room, overseeing Coira's removal from the hall with Senga. Before he left, he turned and caught her eye. A rare smile lit his face and Aileana smiled back. All was well. Then she winced at the twinge in her chest as Toran turned her away from the noise and into the hallway leading to his chambers. So, not quite all. She still had some work to do.

****

Toran watched Aileana settle in front of the fire. She seemed disinclined to talk, and he wasn't sure he was even capable of speech. Not yet. Not until his belly stopped trying to climb out of his throat. Gods! Coira had nearly killed her. A few inches lower and the blade would have pierced Aileana's heart. Bad enough the damage she had done, to mar Aileana's beautiful breast, to weaken her shoulder, hell, to cause her even the slightest pain at all. Toran couldn't think of a penalty severe enough to punish Coira for what she had done and nearly done.

The anguish of it was eating him alive. It was all he could do to stand quietly and let Aileana's attention be absorbed by the fire in the hearth and what healing she could do for herself while she waited for Elspie to bring the sustenance she needed.

"Laird?" Elspie voice roused him from his fretting. She stood at the door, tray in hand, hesitant for the first time in his memory to enter Aileana's chamber. Perhaps she sensed her laird's mood.

"'Tis all right, Elspie," he told her, his tone more gruff than he'd intended. "Come in. Aileana needs what ye bring."

Aileana lifted her head from her study of the flames in the fireplace. "I'm sorry. I've ruined the dress." Then she turned her gaze back to the fire.

The sound of her voice started Toran. She hadn't spoken since he'd brought her to her chamber.

Elspie put the tray on the table beside her and took Aileana's chin in her hand, studying her eyes. "Nay, lass. Moina will simply redesign the neckline," she told her. "Anyway, better the dress than ye." She put the tankard of sweet cider into Aileana's good hand. "Now, drink this down, and eat what I brought ye. Then ye can sleep."

Aileana obeyed Elspie without a word. Toran shifted where he stood, arms crossed, glowering at his bride. He'd never seen her so unresponsive after healing, even after she exhausted herself dealing with Jamie's wounds. But he'd never seen her attacked and injured, either. Perhaps she never had been, and despite her special Talent, or perhaps because of it, it was more of a shock to her than to others who had been through the same kind of thing.

Damn, he had not intended to spend the evening with her this way after celebrating their handfasting with the clan. Nay, he'd had a joyous, aye, even vigorous celebration in mind. Now that would wait until Aileana had time to fully recover. In the meantime, he'd deal with Coira.

He'd once thought to find a place for Coira in the clan, though not as lady, and cement an alliance with her people. That could not happen now, especially not after Toran meted out a punishment that fit her crime. At the very least, he must banish her as soon as she was well enough to travel. But her attack on the Lathan lady merited repercussions that could have their clans feuding for generations, exactly what Toran had wanted to prevent.

"Laird," Elspie's voice penetrated his thoughts yet again. "She's ready for bed, but she'll need our help."

"Nay," Aileana said. "I can manage."

"Elspie will help ye," Toran commanded, his tone making it clear that he would brook no nonsense. "As will I. Come, lass." He went to her and helped her stand while Elspie set the now empty tray aside. Gently, Toran started peeling her blood-soaked clothing from her while Elspie wrung a cloth out in hot water and began to dab at the wound.

"Ach, 'tis already nearly healed," she exclaimed. "Ye think I'd be accustomed to this by now, but 'tis still a fair miracle what ye do, lass."

Aileana gave her a tired smile.

Toran picked up her nightrail and as soon as Elspie finished cleaning the skin around the newly healed wound, lifted Aileana's arms and helped her into it. Then he scooped her up and deposited her gently on the bed. Elspie fussed with the covers, layering them to her satisfaction.

"Warm enough, lass?" Toran asked.

"Aye." He could barely hear Aileana's response, and her eyes were already closed.

"Do ye want me to stay with her, Toran?"

"Nay, Elspie. I thank ye for yer care, but I'll stay with her. I'll send for ye if I'm needed elsewhere."

"I'll warn Donal to leave ye be," Elspie said with a smile, picked up the empty tray and left the room, closing the door softly behind her.

Aileana was already deep into what she called her healing sleep. Toran wasn't sure how it differed from normal sleep, but he took solace that she'd consumed the food and drink that Elspie had brought her well enough. Toran took the seat she'd vacated by the hearth and stared into the flames. Now he would wait and sit vigil over his wife.

His wife.

How could he have let her put herself in danger like that? He was her husband. It was his job to protect her. But no, his stubborn, determined wife was all too capable of taking on challenges that would daunt a lesser woman—or man. She'd gone straight to Coira, sure that she could convince Coira to let the lass go. He'd nearly lost his dinner when Coira's blade had pierced her. He hadn't been affected like that in battle since he was a beardless youth. But the attack had not been aimed at him. He knew how to handle that. No, it had been aimed with deadly intent at Aileana, and he thought his heart would break from the shock of it. If not for his and Donal's quick action, Coira might have had time to strike again, and again, until even a talent like Aileana's would not have saved her.

It had been all he could do to hold his dirk at Coira's throat and not slice her open from ear to ear. No, Donal had come closer to finishing her off. But Aileana would not allow her attacker to die. She had more heart than sense, this one. So she thought that Coira would be somehow reformed by her healing? Toran didn't think so.

It was interesting that after all they had seen her do in her time in the Aerie, it was this simple thing—forgiving her attacker and saving her life—that had transformed Donal's opinion of her. It wasn't that he'd been determined to doubt and distrust her. He'd just needed to see her good heart for himself. Jamie's healing had been too sudden and too new. And Donal had not gone with them to try to save the MacAnalen. He hadn't seen the grief and remorse that failure had cost her.

What she had done for Coira spoke volumes about the kind of person she was, and had been enough to convince even an unrepentant skeptic like Donal. But gaining Donal's support was not worth this. Toran had never felt so helpless in his life. He vowed that he would never allow her to put herself in jeopardy for another person again.

Chapter Fifteen

When Aileana joined Toran on the rampart, it was still early morning when the sun hung just below the edge of the earth, and everything took on an eerie radiance, lit by reflections of the first trace of daylight. Aileana imagined that if she were ever to walk underwater, it would look and feel just like this. Despite its glow, the air was completely still, cold, heavy, and thick, pressing down on all it touched. Nothing moved. High, thin clouds streaked like claw marks across the deep blue of the sky.

Toran stared out at something in the glen. Donal stood stiffly by Toran, frowning toward Aileana but refusing to meet her gaze.

Toran had left her bed, reluctantly, upon hearing Donal shouting for him. Not very long after that, she'd been surprised when Elspie arrived at her door with food and drink to help her dress. She said the laird asked that she join him on the ramparts and had sent Kyle, who waited for her in the hall, to escort her. Aileana wondered at that, too. She knew the way to the ramparts.

For once, Elspie had made no comment. Aileana fretted over that. Elspie's silence was unnerving.

Kyle, who usually offered a friendly greeting or had a story to tell to amuse her, also made no comment. He hastened her straight to his laird at such a pace that she'd been forced to focus on keeping her feet under her, looking neither right nor left as they hurried along.

Toran's posture was guarded. He, too, refused to meet her eyes, and Aileana had no idea what would make him so closed off and...grave. When he finally opened his mouth to speak, he closed it again and motioned Kyle and Donal away without saying a word.

"Toran, what's wrong?" Aileana asked, worried by his strange behavior.

"There's something I must show ye," he finally said, but pulled her back when she turned to peer over the wall to see what had drawn his attention. "Not yet. First ye must tell me something."

"What, Toran? Tell me what's wrong. Is it Coira? Please tell me she hasn't been hung from the ramparts, has she?"

Toran grimaced and looked away from her, out over the bailey, where members of his clan went about their chores, a few of his warriors practicing their skills with swords and arrows. Aileana followed his gaze, seeing nothing unusual.

"This man ye call yer assistant..."

"Ranald. Yes? What does he have to do with Coi..."

Toran interrupted her. "Is he close to ye?"

"I've told you about Ranald," she reminded him. Nerves loosened her tongue, and all this grim solemnity made her uncomfortable. "He was wounded. His leg healed badly. He could no longer fight, but he had some skill tending battlefield wounds, so he became my assistant."

"I ken all that. Answer my question, Aileana. Is he close to ye?"

"Toran, what has happened?" His face, in profile, brooked no nonsense, and Aileana suddenly chilled, though no breath of wind stirred.

Toran looked at her then, and she scowled up at him. "Have you seen Ranald? Do the MacAnalens have him?" That would be good news; away from Colbridge, he could make a new home with them or join her in the Aerie.

Toran shook his head and sighed. He seemed to come to some difficult decision, and pulled her closer to the crenellation.

"It's no' good news, Aileana. I'm sorry to do this to ye, but I must make ye look. Is that Ranald?"

Aileana looked out over the glen into Colbridge's camp, and reeled as her blood sank to her toes. "Oh, no," she whispered against her fists quickly pressed to her lips. "Oh, no."

Toran gently shook her arm, and she blindly turned in his direction.

"So it is, then," Toran sighed. "I was afraid of that. He looked like the man I'd seen with ye in the camp." He pulled her behind the merlon and away from the horrible sight of Ranald, lit by firelight, hanging by his arms, blood running from his body in several places, head slumped onto his naked chest.

"'Tis Colbridge's doing," he continued. "Ye can be sure of that. He's trying to draw ye out, using the one person that he thinks ye care about."

"He's dead, isn't he?" Aileana managed to choke out through her tears.

"No, I dinna think so," Toran answered her. "He's no use to Colbridge dead. I think he believes Ranald was dear to ye...perhaps even a lover, and that ye will be compelled to go back to heal him, to save him. Colbridge canna get to us inside these walls, so he's trying to draw us out."

Memories flared bright and suddenly painful in Aileana's heart at Toran's use of the word lover, something they had so recently become. Husband. Wife. "You would let me go? You would help me save Ranald?"

Toran's expression grew even grimmer and he shook his head. "Nay."

"But, Toran, he'll die, horribly. Colbridge won't stop torturing him until he's dead."

"I can't help that, Aileana. As much as I might wish to for yer sake and his, I canna help Ranald, not by sending ye back into Colbridge's clutches. Ye're mine now. I won't risk ye."

"But he's…"

Suddenly a shout echoed up from the glen. "Laird Lathan!"

Toran pulled Aileana further behind the merlon, then peered out.

"Colbridge, the cocky bastard, alone, in the glen," he said, as Donal ran up to stand with him. "He must have seen us up here."

"Out of range?" Donal asked.

"What do ye think?" Toran's reply was terse. "Get the archers ready, in case he comes closer." Donal nodded and moved away to do his laird's bidding.

"Laird Lathan," the call came again. "I've something you should see. You and the Healer you stole from me."

Toran moved into sight and called back, "What do ye want, Colbridge?"

"Get the Healer," the reply came. "This is for her enjoyment, as well."

Aileana watched Toran's hands close into fists out of sight of the man below in the glen, then he turned and gestured her over. "Ye must be brave, lass," he said quietly.

Aileana slowly moved to stand next to Toran and lifted her chin. Her instincts were screaming at her to stay hidden from Colbridge, but she had no choice if she hoped to save Ranald.

"Aileana, so good of you to join us," Colbridge sneered, then gestured behind him. "You're late to the festivities, and I fear Ranald has already enjoyed himself too much."

Tears started afresh in Aileana's eyes as she once again beheld Ranald's slumped and bloody form.

"What do you want?" Aileana called out, silently cursing the tremor in her voice as much as she cursed the monster on the glen below her. "Why have you hurt him?"

"Why, you, my dear," Colbridge answered, as if nothing in the world was amiss. "I want you. Come back. Your lover needs you. He's eager for your touch."

"Cut him down!" Toran shouted at her side.

"No, I don't think so," Colbridge replied, reasonably. Then his voice turned hard. "In fact, I think I'll leave him right where he is, so the Healer can watch as I carve him up. I've already ruined his good leg. He'll never walk again. Not that he'll need to, by the time I finish with him. Unless you come back, Aileana. I'll let you save him. Or stay where you are, and watch him die. Slowly. In agony. And then it will be your turn, when I break down your walls. Everyone with you will die. You, will, too. As slowly as your lover." Colbridge laughed. "We'll see if you can Heal yourself."

Aileana gasped at the brutality Colbridge promised, and Toran reached over to take her cold hand in his strong one.

"She's no' coming out," Toran growled. "No' now, no' ever. Kill that man if ye must, but do it quickly. He's not yer enemy, Colbridge. I am."

"No," Colbridge refused, smiling. "I'm not finished with him yet. It's up to you, Aileana, how long he suffers. Whether he dies strung up like a pig to slaughter. It's your choice, Healer. Save him, or die like he does."

With that, Colbridge whipped his mount around and rode back to his camp. As he approached Ranald, he pulled his dirk. Toran pulled Aliana's face against his shoulder but he could not prevent her from seeing Ranald's body arc against his bonds in agony as Colbridge slashed his torso from shoulder to ribs.

****

Aileana opened the door to her chamber, her refuge, where she'd retreated after seeing Colbridge's horrible display, in answer to the soft knock that awakened her from her exhausted, grief-stricken doze. Toran looked down at her, observing, measuring, in that quiet way he had. The connection between them was strong, but she didn't need it. His grave countenance told her without words that the scene with Colbridge still weighed on his mind. She stepped back and waved him in, resigned to the coming confrontation.

"Whatever you have to say to me, come in and say it. You don't need to stand out in the hall."

"I have questions," he began, closing the door behind him and following her as she walked toward the hearth. "And I need honest answers. No' lies."

Shocked, Aileana spun to face him.

He gripped her shoulders and pulled her face up to his. His features were twisted with anguish and realized that he thought she had betrayed him somehow with Ranald...or soon would.

"Toran, put me down." When he didn't release her, but continued to hold her, his eyes searching hers for answers, she kicked him. "Put me down. Please! You're hurting me."

Toran released her as if she had suddenly become as hot as the flames in the hearth. He continued to stare at her, saying nothing, as he stepped back and crossed his arms over his massive chest. Aileana wanted to put her hands on those arms, to pull them around her so that she could sink into his warmth and strength. She felt safe when Toran held her, but she knew that he would not hold her now...and might never do so again. Ranald's torture was more than she could ignore. As soon as she could, she'd leave the Aerie and go to him. And somehow, Toran knew that.

"What do you want to know?" Aileana asked, wondering again if she would have any answers that would satisfy him.

"Why are ye here? And what is Ranald, to ye, really?"

Aileana sucked in a breath, fighting the urge to pound her fists on Toran's chest. "Why am I here? How can you ask that? You know why I'm here. You brought me."

"Did I? Or did ye somehow bewitch me into

wanting ye, into bringing ye? While ye Healed my head, did ye plant yer wishes there, too? Ye were conveniently at hand at just the right moment...or had ye planned that, also? To get inside the Aerie, learn what ye could, then report back to Colbridge? Only when I didn't release ye right away, Colbridge tortured a man ye care about, so ye'd remember yer duty and bring yer information back out. He has no interest in Ranald, other than using him to compel ye. He wants to know what ye know about the Aerie, and if ye fall into his hands, ye'll be forced to tell him everything. The moment he gets the chance, his men will be inside our gates to finish what their siege could not."

"No," Aileana said, and repeated it over and over as Toran raged. "No, that's not it; that cannot be."

"No, Aileana? Are ye so certain?"

"You must be wrong. Colbridge would never hurt me. He's trying to get me back..."

"Unless he thought ye could be used against him, against his men, to keep another army at fighting strength. He has to have realized by now that ye can be a danger to him."

That stopped her cold. "Oh, no." She turned away from him, unable to look at him and think at the same time. And she needed to think.

Toran came up behind her and turned her to face him. "Ye saw what he's done to Ranald. There is no way ye would be safe again in his camp. I will not allow ye to go. I canna."

Aileana stared, stricken with fear at this new world she found herself in. Nothing had been the way she thought. She'd been a fool, all that time. She thought herself at least safe there, guarded by her Talent and Colbridge's need for it. But that had never been true, not when he threatened her now. And Ranald, if he survived what Colbridge was doing to him, he would never forgive her for the agony he had suffered because of her. He was the last of her kin. If Toran's anguish meant he was turning against her, too, she really would have nothing, and no one.

The only thing she had left was her Voice—a talent that Donal would greatly fear if he knew of it. It would only take a touch, and the right suggestions.

She could go to Ranald and heal him. She could walk out though the postern, or she could have Toran escort her out the front gate, and forget he'd done it. She could control Colbridge with a touch and a word, something she'd never dared before because there'd been no threat from him to cause her to try it.

But could she really do this? Toran would never trust her again. She did not want to leave him. She wanted him. For God's sake, she'd married him, and she wanted the home with his clan in the Aerie that she had begun to love. She had fallen in love with him, deeply in love, even before she had given herself to him. Her breath caught. Oh no, had she come to this knowledge just in time to lose him?

No, it wasn't her fault that Toran had grabbed her and stolen her away, but she was glad that he had. Nor was it her fault that Colbridge was a brute bent on destroying everything and everyone that he encountered, but she could do something for Ranald. She bowed her head as tears sheened her eyes. She had no choice.

Toran reached for her then and folded her in his arms. "I promised not to make ye cry, and in my fear for ye, look what I've done."

"But I..." Aileana murmured against his chest. She had to tell him. Before she left. Before she disappeared from his life, possibly forever, if Colbridge caught her.

"Hush, it doesna matter," Toran said, soothing her.

"But, Toran, it does. Ranald is my half-brother. I don't want to leave you. I love you. But I have to save him," Aileana said, looking up into his deep blue eyes.

As he leaned down to kiss her, his churning emotions washed over Aileana. The connection between them waxed stronger since he'd taken her, no, since he'd awakened her, loved her, made her his. But what he was feeling—shock? Joy? The mix of emotions running through him confused her. It was almost too much to bear, knowing how she must hurt him to save her kin.

"Aileana," he vowed against her hair. "it matters no' who he is. Ye canna go into that camp. It isna safe. Ye are mine. Forever."

"And a day, aye," she whispered. If only that could be true, she thought as he attacked her defenses with his mouth. But no, she could not make love with Toran while Ranald suffered because of her. Nor could she let even a hint of the anguish that plagued her over what she was about to do leak through to him.

"Toran, please," she protested. "Let me rest."

"Aye, lass."

He left her after one more gentle kiss, after gazing at her as if she was the most precious thing in his world, after gently trailing his fingers down her cheek, then pulling her again into his embrace, the only place where she was warm and safe. Aileana stared at the door to her chamber after Toran closed it softly behind him and wondered if she would ever see him again.

****

Aileana waited until the clan settled down for the night. It was late, very late, when she ventured quietly from her chamber. The door closed silently, but the barely audible click of the latch stopped her. She breathed in and out, once, twice, three times, trying to slow the pounding of her heart. So far, she'd done nothing wrong. She simply needed something from the herbal to help her sleep after a trying day. That was all.

Only that wasn't all. From there, she would make her way down into the caves. If her luck held, she'd find a torch still burning that she could use to light her way. If not, and she didn't kill herself falling down the long flights of stairs in the dark or get lost on a side path that she didn't remember, she'd leave from the postern gate and be on her way to save Ranald. If all went well, she might be back with him before daylight. Toran would be furious both at what she'd risked, and at bringing Ranald back through the postern, but she didn't have any other choice. The guard on the main gate would raise an alarm if she returned that way, not that Ranald's sudden presence in the Aerie wouldn't cause alarm. Maybe she could hide him, at least until she could explain to Toran what she'd done.

There was little chance of everything going perfectly, she despaired as she crept down the main stairs into the Great Hall. She hadn't counted on anyone sleeping there, but several men were sprawled on pallets near the hearth, most snoring, loudly or softly. Their noise was good cover for any sound she might make as long as it didn't awaken one of them. Two hounds raised their heads to regard her briefly, startling her and giving her a bad moment until they put their heads back down and sighed. She supposed by now they recognized her as belonging here. Heart pounding again, she went carefully on her way down the long hall toward the kitchen, Senga's herbal, and the stairs she needed. There was no one to delay her progress as she took her first hesitant steps down to the storage caves and below.

The first stairs were easy despite the lack of illumination. She'd been down those to the area where Senga stored the bulk of her dried herbs many times. But below that, she'd only been once—the day she'd been brought down to heal Jamie. That trip down had been so hurried, she'd scarce noticed any details. And she'd swooned after she'd finished, so that Toran had carried her back up, and she'd seen nothing.

She kept one hand on the wall beside her as she carefully edged down. Finally, the blackness was pierced by a dimly guttering torch set into a bracket, and Aileana took it to light her way. The flickering flame quickly died to embers, but it provided enough illumination to allow her to see the next tread. Once she startled a sleeping ginger cat, a mouser, she surmised, slacking at its duty. It gave her a one-eyed glare and a twitch of its tail, then settled back to its nap as she passed.

It seemed to take hours, though she knew it couldn't have been more than minutes, before she reached the bottom step. The last faint glow from her torch chose that moment to die completely.

The darkness was absolute. Across the wide floor of this cavern waited the gap that led to the postern. It would be hard to find if she tried to cross the open floor. But if she kept one hand on the wall and went around, she'd come to it, she was sure. She didn't recall anything being stored here, but there had been so many people surrounding her as she worked on Jamie, that she couldn't be sure.

She smelled horses and heard their faint whickering from far away—another cave? Should she try to take one? No, that would make too much noise. Someone might hear and come to investigate what was disturbing them. She'd stick to her plan and go afoot. So she set the now useless torch on the ground then placed her hand on the chill rock beside her. She walked slowly and carefully, fearing the fall that could result from tripping over something in the dark.

She'd already passed several cracks no wider than a handspan when she finally came to the one she expected to find. She could smell fresh night air and feel a slight breeze as she reached it, but because of the way it angled, she could not see outside. Emboldened, she quickened her pace and turned into the corridor. But only three steps beyond, she found herself sprawled, half on the cold, rocky floor, and half on a large, warm body. Wide hands suddenly gripped her. As he stood, her captor pulled her to her feet.

Even in this deep blackness, she knew who now kept her from her mission. Toran! She'd know his scent anywhere, the feel of his big hands, his sheer size.

"I thought ye might try something like this," he began, without preamble, knowing full well whom he had captured. He'd expected her, lain in wait for her to arrive, that was plain. And though she could not see his face, she could sense anger coursing through him. "I told ye I could not let ye leave the Aerie," he said, gripping her shoulders and shaking her gently, like one would do to command the attention of a child. "Ye canna defy me, Aileana. No' in this."

"I must," she replied, struggling to escape his iron grip, and knowing it was futile. "I cannot leave Ranald to suffer an agonizing death at Colbridge's hands. You must let me go. I can heal him, bring him back with me."

"Aileana, ye canna ken that." He sighed. "If Ranald is injured as badly as he looks, healing him will use all of yer strength. If ye collapse, as ye did after healing Jamie, ye'll be at Colbridge's mercy. And even if ye do no' faint, if someone discovers ye, the result will be the same."

"Not if you come with me," she said, giving up struggling in Toran's arms as the idea suddenly occurred to her. "You can cut him down, keep watch while I heal him. If need be, you can carry me back."

"Ye and Ranald both? Ye heard what Colbridge said. He's crippled both of his legs now. He won't be fit to walk, much less run, if someone hears us."

"Then bring Donal, too. Or Kyle or Jamie, or all of them. I must not let Colbridge continue to torture Ranald. He'll kill him." Tears gathered in Aileana's eyes and slipped down her cheeks. "I must free him." She choked on a sob as she insisted, "Colbridge is doing this because of me."

Toran wrapped her in the comfort of his strong arms and wiped away her tears, but voice was resolute when he told her, "Nay, Aileana. I'm sorry. Truly I am, but it willna work. 'Tis no' yer fault. Colbridge's doing this because he's a crafty bastard. And because he thinks that if he can lure ye out, he can lure me and my men out, too. Even for yer brother, I canna allow it."

"We left the Aerie for the MacAnalen. It can be done."

"Nay, lass. We didna try to go right into Colbridge's camp, under his very nose, fer God's sake. And we had enough trouble with his patrols when they didna expect us. By now, they're looking for us even harder. It willna work."

Aileana realized he would not be swayed. Desperation seized her. If he would not be convinced to help her, then she could only do one thing. Now that they were married, she hated to use her Voice to compel him, but without it, she would not be able to get free of Toran and the Aerie to save Ranald. The risk was great. If he resisted, and if he realized what she was doing, he would gather his defenses and just might be able to prevent her. But she had to try. It was the only weapon she had left.

"Let me go," she commanded, and sighed in relief when his arms dropped from around her. Now what to do? She reached out in the darkness and took his hand as another complication occurred to her. She was a fool not to have thought of it before. *"Is there a gate at the end of this passage?"*

"Aye."

"And another guard?" A guard would add to her problems. She'd have to control both men at the same time. She hoped she could do it.

"Nay, I took his place. There was only me to await ye."

"Is the gate locked?"

"Aye." How could one syllable sound so satisfied?

"Do you have the key to unlock it?" she asked,

suddenly sick at heart. Why hadn't she thought of that sooner? If he did not have a key, they would have to go back upstairs to get it. And she'd have to count on her Voice to keep the one man who could withstand it under her control all the way up the long, dark steps.

She felt more than saw his nod, then heard him grunt his "Aye," as if he struggled against telling her.

"Give me the key," she demanded, eagerness lending more power to her Voice than she had ever used before. He used his free hand to pull it from wherever he had carried it and held it out to her.

She took it, nearly fainting with relief when he complied. *"Go upstairs to your chamber,"* she told him. *"Forget you have seen me. Lie down on your bed and go to sleep. And when you wake up in the morning, you won't remember that you saw me here or even that you came down here."* A wrenching sense of loss nearly undid her, but she stiffened her resolve, bending only to make a promise to Toran that she truly hoped she could keep. "I will return. I will. *Now go.*"

Aileana let go of Toran's arm and held her breath as he turned away. She listened to him walk across the cave and released a sigh of relief as he started up the stairs. Then his steps hesitated and her breath caught in her throat. She waited, hands clenched in front of her, trying to hear what she could not see in the blackness of the cave. Was he resisting her commands and coming back for her? "No," she murmured under her breath. "Go, go on. Leave me alone." The silence lasted for another moment, then the sound of his footsteps continued up the stairs.

Aileana strained to hear the noises he made as they faded away up into the darkness. Then she resolutely put Toran out of her mind and moved quickly down the twisting passage until she encountered the thick iron bars of the gate. She fumbled for the latch. The key turned easily, and the gate swung open on well-oiled hinges. Quickly, Aileana locked it behind her and secreted the key in a crack in the rock face where she could find it again. She congratulated herself on her presence of mind not to take the key with her into Colbridge's camp. If worse came to worse and she was captured, they would not find it on her. She might be forced to tell Colbridge about this way into the Aerie, but she would not make it easy for him to breach it.

Still in darkness, she followed the passage wall as it angled once more. Finally, a faint glimmer illuminated the last few steps. She reached the entrance and stepped out into the star-filled night.

Chapter Sixteen

Aileana was breathing hard and her heart was pounding by the time she finally reached the edge of the glen by Colbridge's camp. Her confrontation with Toran had taken precious time. Then it had taken her much longer than she'd expected to make her way around the tor, through the woods to the edge of the glen, and then on to the main part of the encampment where Ranald had been hung out like a slaughtered deer. Thankfully, she'd encountered none of Colbridge's guards. They would be alert for the sound of horses pounding out of the main gate of the Aerie on the way to attack the camp, not for a woman alone, on foot, in the deep of the night, so she'd been confident that she was safe from them unless she blundered right into a patrol.

But now she sensed daybreak was only a few hours away. She had to stay out of sight while getting Ranald well enough to move. And she had to do all of that much more quickly than she had planned before they could escape back to the Aerie, since Toran had delayed her. And she was cold, so cold. She hadn't dared carry a cloak when she left her chamber. It would have been impossible to explain why she wandered the halls of the keep with it.

She moved silently along the edge of the camp. But Ranald no longer hung from the trees where they'd seen him! Oh, no! Was he dead? Or had someone had sense enough to keep him alive by cutting him down and getting him out of the frigid night air? If they had, he must be in a tent nearby. Surely, they wouldn't have bothered to carry him far.

Carefully and ever so quietly, she avoided the glow of the banked fires and moved in the shadows to peer into the nearby tents.

The first one sat empty. She found Ranald in the second. A small brazier on the floor gave off as much smoke as light or heat, but it was enough to see him by, and Aileana almost wished that she could not. He shivered, despite the blanket pulled up to his chin, perhaps as much from pain as from the cold. He roused as she approached and touched his hair.

"Aileana," he groaned. "No. I'm dreaming. You can't be here." His gravelly voice told her he'd choked back screams as he'd been tortured.

"It's going to be all right," she said. "Lie quiet and let me Heal you."

"No. No…" He continued to moan as she pushed the blankets back from his chest and saw that he'd bled from scores of wounds. Some were mere nicks, but others were long slices. Choking back a sob at what had been done to him in her name, she touched him, and began to assess what else he'd suffered. Besides the wound to his good leg that Colbridge had boasted about, Ranald had been beaten. His ribs were broken, and he was bleeding inside. She wasn't sure what kept him alive.

"You must go," he gasped, pushing weakly at her hands as she began to heal the worst of the stab and slash wounds, reaching in to stop the bleeding inside his chest. "If you heal me, he'll just start over." He tried to push her hands away, but in his condition, he could not. "Let me die."

"No, I won't. And he won't touch you again," she whispered, frowning as she tried to work and talk to him at the same time. "You're coming with me."

Silence greeted her pronouncement, then he took a shuddering breath and spoke between gasps while she continued to heal him. "Aileana, be sensible...you'll be exhausted...we'll both be trapped. Save yourself. Go back...where you came from. You're not safe here."

"No, Ranald. He'll kill you. He's already come close."

"Aileana." Ranald grasped one of her arms. His voice sounded stronger. He was gaining strength as she healed his hurts and lent him energy. "I love you. I'd rather die than let Colbridge harm you."

"He won't Ranald, not again."

"He will. I won't let you sacrifice yourself for me. I want you to go."

"You won't let me sacrifice myself for you, but you'll sacrifice yourself for me? Is that it? You'll let Colbridge slice you to ribbons and beat you and stab you and think I'll walk away?"

Ranald had the grace to look abashed. "Yes. That's it exactly. You can escape. I cannot. Don't let him have both of us, Aileana. Please. Go."

"But he'll kill you. Slowly."

"It doesn't matter. As long as you live, my life doesn't matter."

"Yes it does," Aileana argued and put her hands back onto Ranald's belly. "The sooner you let me finish, the sooner we can leave."

She'd barely begun again when the tent flap was pulled aside and Colbridge entered, silhouetted briefly by the faint first glimmer of false dawn. Ranald groaned. Aileana froze in shock, then cried out as Colbridge grasped her arm and roughly pulled her away from her patient. She sprawled on the tent floor and cried out, "No! Please! Let me help him."

Colbridge merely laughed.

She scrambled to her knees and lunged for Ranald. Colbridge cuffed her aside. Ranald tried to sit up, tried to aid her, but Colbridge pulled his dirk, planted the tip in the skin over Ranald's breastbone and pushed him back down. Aileana wailed as a thin trickle of blood started from the new wound, and Colbridge turned back to her, dirk in hand.

"Witch! See what your defection has won you? You dared to aid my enemy. And you wonder that your lover suffers for your actions?"

For a brief moment, Aileana's blood chilled, thinking that he referred to Toran. But no, he thought she and Ranald...yes, he'd made the same accusation as he taunted them from the glen earlier today, no yesterday.

"My lover?" she challenged, more boldly than she intended, anger getting the best of her caution. She hadn't defected, she'd been taken! "Him?" She gestured at Ranald, and tried to put a look of contempt on her face instead of fear, hoping that Ranald would understand what she meant to do for him. "He's not my lover. He never has been."

"Then why are you here?" Colbridge demanded, frowning.

"Just because we are not lovers does not mean that

I cannot take pity on my assistant, when you treat him so brutally." Aileana stood, praying her voice carried more confidence than she felt capable of at this moment. "And for no reason," she spat, letting her anger show, then changed her tone to one of conciliation. Would Colbridge let her get close enough to touch him?

"I did not leave you. I was taken by the prisoners when they escaped your"—she put all the contempt she could muster into the word—"guards."

Aileana stood still, barely breathing. Any untoward move could easily get her killed. She knew Colbridge's temper. But her strategy seemed to be working. At least now he was focused on her, and not on Ranald.

"The men who were foolish enough to allow your escape have paid for their stupidity," Colbridge boasted. "The rest won't make the same mistake. Now, where are the men who brought you?"

"Brought me? No one brought me. I came alone."

She nearly flinched as Colbridge began to sputter, but she managed to keep her expression neutral. "You're telling me you came back to save this...cripple....that you escaped an unassailable fortress, crossed the glen, and snuck back into camp alone, without an escort, to save his worthless hide?"

"Aye," she said quietly, ignoring the twinge in her heart. She dared not lie, but she could not tell him how she'd gotten away. She carried knowledge about the Aerie that could aid Colbridge. This was the very thing that Donal had feared. And is that what Toran would think? That she had come willingly, left him and a life with his clan behind willingly? Risked their safety willingly? She almost shook her head, but held herself still by main force of will.

"And why should I believe this tale? Why would they let you go?"

Cold fear drenched Aileana. Colbridge's fury pulsed at her. He wanted to take that fury out on someone, and Ranald was an easy target. "No…I mean, aye, it's true. You can believe it." She put all the sincerity she could muster into answering his first question and ignoring the second.

"You did not leave willingly with the Lathan laird when he escaped my camp?" Colbridge demanded, and Aileana's fear turned to icy dread. No, he distrusted her, too.

"No, no. It wasn't like that. He grabbed me when his men cut him loose. I had no choice…"

"No choice, eh?" Colbridge began to walk around her, circling her, and Aileana tensed. Did she dare risk reaching out to touch him, to use her Voice? Could she command him in his enraged state? Then he stopped by Ranald and Aileana knew she'd missed her chance. She couldn't make a move toward him without risking that he would retaliate against the nearest target: her half-brother.

Colbridge, canny, stayed out of reach. Perhaps he feared that she would put him to sleep, as he knew she did to her patients after she healed them. Nay, she'd not put him to sleep. She'd stop his heart if she could for what he'd done to her brother. If only she'd listened to Ranald when they had the chance to stop his madman, to allow nature to take its course after he'd been wounded. But her heart had overruled her head and she'd let him live. She'd regret that for the rest of her life.

Please, don't do anything foolish, Ranald. She willed him to stillness. Stay calm, still, like the hare when it knows it cannot run. The slightest move could set Colbridge off. His attention remained on her. Ranald was safe for the moment, as long as he stayed still and quiet.

Then Colbridge surprised her. "No choice but to bewitch the Lathan laird," Colbridge hissed as he suddenly grabbed her braid and pulled her back against him. "So let's see if we can lure him out of his fortress as this one"—he smirked at Ranald—"lured you. A damsel in distress might just do the trick."

Desperate, she groped behind her for his hand, but encountered only the cloth of his sleeve as he shoved her ahead of him out of the tent. He shoved her again and she fell to her knees on the cold, hard ground. He stayed out of reach. Then he yelled for his guards to tie Ranald back up where he could be used to keep the Healer on her best behavior. The sight of Aileana's tears made him laugh, and she flinched. She should have listened to Toran. She'd failed. Ranald was still Colbridge's captive plaything. And now, so was she.

****

Toran awoke early, consumed with a sense of foreboding. Something hovered right on the edge of his memory, but try as he might to concentrate on it, whatever it was would not come to him. He threw the covers back and sat up. Confusion swept over him when he saw that he was dressed. In the Aerie, he always went to bed bare. Why the hell would he have gone to bed fully clothed? That made no sense. He wasn't that tired last night—or that drunk. In fact, he didn't remember drinking at all, or remember much else for that matter. What had happened to him? And why wasn't Aileana in his bed?

He went to stir the fire into life and threw on some more wood. He stared at the glow and watched the smoke rise into the chimney, a frown of concentration on his face as he tried to recall the events of last evening. He'd gone to get some answers from Aileana in her chambers where she rested after the shock of seeing what Colbridge had done to her assistant...assistant? The sense of dread that had woken him suddenly deepened. But in the end, despite his accusations, when she told him she loved him, he'd forgotten his questions, and simply held her. He'd been surprised, and happy. But later, he'd remembered her anguish over Ranald, and feared that Aileana might do something foolish. But...what? Had she? If so, why couldn't he remember?

There was only one thing to do: go talk to his wife. Perhaps she could explain why his memory was so unreliable. Despite the fact that Donal was now smitten with her, what if he'd been right about her all along, but Toran had been too entranced to see the truth? Perhaps she had abilities beyond her talent for healing the sick and injured, abilities that she hid until it served her purpose to use them.

Sudden traces of memory assailed him. Aileana defying Toran and leaving the Aerie for Colbridge's camp with some damn foolhardy idea of healing a man who appeared to be well on his way to hell already, and escaping with no one the wiser. Her brother? Was that real? His heart leapt to his throat, and he bolted from his chamber.

Toran's suspicions grew as he strode toward

Aileana's chamber. Scared and angry now, for her and at her, he yelled for Donal to attend him, not caring if he awakened the whole damn keep and Colbridge's army besides.

As he marched down the hallway, a few doors opened a crack and quickly closed as he passed. Apparently one look at his face and no one dared accost their laird in this temper. Wise of them, he thought.

He reached Aileana's chamber and slammed his fist against the door, popping it open. The sight that greeted him was the one he feared. Aileana was not there. Donal pounded up behind him, took in Toran's fierce look and the empty chamber and yelled for the men following him to scatter and search the Aerie.

Toran pounded his fist against the wall, whirled and strode back down the hall, Donal in tow.

"This doesna feel right," Donal muttered. "But perhaps she's in the kitchen, or the herb garden?" he offered to Toran's back.

Toran kept walking, his stride lengthening as he quit the tower and keep to cross the bailey. He wrenched open the gate to Senga's garden and looked inside. Misery and fury warred within him, and certain desperate knowledge. No one waited in the pale glow of starlight. The garden was empty.

If Colbridge had Aileana back, he'd have the upper hand, not that Toran wanted to bargain with him. Nay, what he did want, what he needed, was Aileana. Not for the reasons Colbridge wanted her. Aye, her healing skills had worked wonders for the clan. But there was more than concern for his people, or for her safety, at work here. She belonged to him, with him. He wanted her back in his arms. He wanted her touch, her warmth, her kiss, the way she wanted and needed him. It was ironic that at the moment he realized he'd married the woman he could love for the rest of his life, more deeply than he thought possible, he'd lost her. She'd left him. He was certain of it. He'd lost her to another man who probably loved her, too, or to a man who feared and used her. Either way, she was gone.

"She's no' here," he told Donal, who waited behind him. "And she willna be in the kitchen or the herbal or anywhere else in the Aerie."

"How in hell did she get out, then?" Donal asked, clearly frustrated. "The main gate's locked up tight, and she doesna ken the way down through the storage caves to the postern in the dark. That gate's locked, too. Did she climb down the tor, then? Or is she really a witch, to fly away on a bee?" Donal shook his head. "Nah, she's here, somewhere…and probably not aware of the commotion her absence has caused."

"Nay." Toran sighed. "She's gone to Ranald."

"What?"

"She's taken that bastard Colbridge's bait," he bit out, fists clenching. Toran's shoulders slumped and he turned to Donal, pain etched on his features. "I only hope she's healed Ranald and they're away, not caught by Colbridge's men. If they're caught, Colbridge will kill them both."

"Nay, Toran. Colbridge willna harm the Healer. He needs her."

"Aye, he does, but he's angry now," Toran spat. "He'll kill her if he catches her."

"But if she has gone back to save Ranald," Donal argued, "he'd have no reason to."

Toran shook his head, fear and doubt foremost in

his mind.

Kyle ran up and reported, "No one can find her. I sent men down into the storage caves, but..."

"Let them look, but they'll find naught but a few mice, I'll wager," Toran said, sucking in a harsh breath. "Make sure the postern's secure. Come daylight, we'll see what we can see in Colbridge's camp."

Kyle looked skyward. "Soon."

Toran looked up, surprised at the pale glow in the east. Was this miserable night over already? And a worse day just starting? "Come on, then," he said to Donal and headed for the guard tower stairs.

On the ramparts, the men were alert, on edge, aware that something was very wrong. Toran nodded to each as he passed, then stopped and peered out where he had the best view of Colbridge's encampment along the forest. The brightening sky did little to illuminate the ground below the trees, but the glow of the watch fires reflecting off of patches of snow and ice helped. Nothing moved. Yet. Worse, he could barely make out Ranald, hanging just as he had been yesterday. If Aileana had tried to reach him, she had failed.

Donal stood beside him, a solid, calming presence. He'd been Toran's second-in-command and chief advisor since the old laird had died and Toran had taken over the clan, three years gone. In the relatively peaceful years that Toran had spent as laird of Clan Lathan, Aileana had gone from apprentice healer, to captive, refugee, and Healer to Colbridge's traveling army. Their pasts could not be more dissimilar, yet Toran was drawn to her as to no other. He didn't understand it. He just knew he had to get her back.

Suddenly, Donal swore and pointed. Toran's

attention flew across the glen to the fireside Donal indicated. "There she is!"

Toran's heart plummeted while bile rose in his throat. Aileana marched between guards to Colbridge, who now stood in firelight, sideways to Toran's viewpoint. The better to display his captive, Toran thought, and ensure that Toran saw everything that happened. Toran clenched his teeth together in a futile effort to hold back an oath. "Nay..." he whispered between them.

"Ye ken what we must do," Donal muttered, clearly aggrieved. "She's been inside the Aerie. Colbridge's spy," he spat, "whether she meant to or nay."

Toran flinched at the description, hoping, praying it was not true. "Nay," Toran insisted. "She willna betray us."

"Likely she'll no' have a choice. She's seen inside our walls, and gotten out through them," Donal said between gritted teeth. "If she tells him about the postern, Colbridge's men will search for it around the base of the tor." He turned to face Toran, and along with anger at the apparent betrayal, Toran thought he recognized sadness in Donal's gruff features. "We must attack Colbridge's camp today, now."

Toran considered the options. Aileana looked frightened. Even from this distance, Toran imagined he could see the fear she tried to hide behind a frozen expression as she faced Colbridge. But Toran knew Donal spoke the truth. If Aileana told Colbridge, was forced to tell Colbridge, of the existence of another way up into the Aerie, Colbridge would not stop until he found it. While it could be defended, it would split

Toran's forces between the walls and the caves. The Aerie had never been taken, but Toran knew he must risk opening the gates if he was going to stop Colbridge, and save his bride.

"Get the men ready to ride."

****

Aileana dared not struggle as Colbridge pushed her ahead of him in the early morning sunlight. She'd had no chance to use her Voice on him. He hadn't allowed her to come close enough to touch him. After he'd shoved her out of the tent, he pulled his sword and told her to stand, then forced her to watch Ranald's agony as the guards hung him up like a side of meat.

When the guards brought her back to him, Colbridge marched her out onto the glen with the sword at her back. She knew her eyes had widened with fear, for herself, for Ranald, and for Toran. She tried to be calm, tried to think. If Toran came out after her, Colbridge would not hesitate to kill him. She did not doubt it. And there was no way she could stop either of them.

Colbridge stayed out of her reach, using his sword as a prod while making sure that it was visible at her back to the watchers on the Aerie's walls. Just out of range of Toran's archers, he ordered her to stop. Aileana could see Toran on the rampart, Donal at his side, both looking thunderous.

"Laird Lathan," Colbridge called, and Aileana winced at the volume of his voice near her ear.

"Aye," she heard Toran's deceptively calm response. She knew he would be anything but calm, looking at the scene Colbridge had set. Her at swordpoint. Ranald hung up as he had been yesterday.

"I want you to see what you've lost," Colbridge crowed. "The Healer has abandoned you. You were a fool, a weak, powerless fool, to trust her," Colbridge taunted. "She cared more for her lover here than she did for the comfort of your hospitality. Or so she tells me."

Aileana started, outraged at Colbridge's fabrication, yet knowing it was designed to enrage Toran. Would he remember what she'd told him last night, that Ranald was kin? She shook her head and stared at Toran, wide-eyed, trying to convince him without words that Colbridge lied. At her movement, Colbridge pushed the point of his sword more firmly against her back. The impulse set her off balance and she staggered forward. Colbridge merely followed, keeping his sword in place.

Toran's response tore at Aileana's heart. "I see that," was all he said, but it was enough to dash her hopes of ever winning his trust, his love again. If only she could get away from Colbridge. But she couldn't, not with his sword at her back, not here in full view of both camps. Despair swept through Aileana. Perhaps it would be best if Colbridge did kill her. If she fell back onto his sword and Toran saw that in her death, she had not betrayed him. Then Toran spoke again.

"But I also see ye holding a captive at sword point," he said, "so if I'm such a fool, why do ye think that's necessary?"

Aileana's breath caught in her throat as the march of her pulse increased. If Toran managed to taunt Colbridge sufficiently, he might kill her where she stood. But Toran's words gave her hope. If he remembered that she was not here with Colbridge by choice, he might yet recall what had happened, and might be willing to take her back. If she could just get free of Colbridge.

Instead, Colbridge yanked on her braid, forcing her to lift her head and expose her throat, then he moved the sword from her back to lay the blade against her neck. She could see part of it out of the corner of her eye. Blood smeared the cold metal. Ranald's blood, she was sure.

"I think you care enough about this witch to come out here and fight me for her," Colbridge growled and Aileana nearly fainted from fear—and hope.

"And if I don't?" Toran called back, seemingly unconcerned. But Aileana saw the narrowing of his eyes, and held her breath.

"Then she dies," Colbridge answered. He tugged on her braid. With the sword still in place at her throat, he began to back up and force Aileana with him, back toward his camp. She dared not try to touch him and use her Voice to force him to release her. There were too many watchers. She would have to wait for a better time. There was nothing she could do now but await Toran's decision.

"Come out, Laird Lathan," Colbridge called. "Let's settle this. Surrender. Or fight me—one on one. Save the girl, end the siege, or die trying and lose it all." With that he laughed and turned Aileana back toward his camp.

Chapter Seventeen

"Toran, nay, ye canna do that," Donal said, grabbing his arm and stopping him before he could descend the stairs and gather his weapons. "It willna be a fair fight, and ye ken it."

"Nay, it willna. But it doesna matter," Toran growled and gestured at the two crossing the glen toward the enemy camp. "Look at Colbridge dragging her around by her hair. Aileana is no' there because she pined to return to Colbridge and take up her duties saving his army." He shook off Donal's hand and pointed at the man bound and slumped between two trees. "She thought she was the only one who could save Ranald. He's her half brother," he explained as the memory surfaced, clean and sharp. "She had to try. But she failed. I intend to get her back. If I can save him, too, I will, but I will get her back."

"In the middle of Colbridge's entire army?" Donal scoffed. "Don't be daft, mon. Ye canna fight them all by yerself."

"I don't have to. Colbridge offered to fight me alone, Donal. Winner takes all. I'll kill him. And when I do, his 'army' will fall apart."

"Ye believe that, do ye?"

"Aye."

"Then ye are daft."

Toran slapped Donal on the arm and headed down

the stairs. "Come with me, then," he called back, as Donal stood watching him descend. "Pick an escort and come along. Ye can hold Colbridge's forces at bay while I finish him off."

Donal cursed under his breath, then clambered down the steps after Toran. "Ye're determined, I can see that."

"We have an invitation," Toran repeated, "Colbridge offered trial by combat. No interference by any of his—or any of ours. If he even comes close to abiding by the rules, I'll take him, easily. I'm younger, faster, and my reach is longer."

"And when he cheats?"

"Then it'll just take more time to kill him, that's all. The outcome is certain. He canna best me.

Toran pounded down the rest of the stairs, Donal still at his heels, and yelled for his weapons and a mount.

Donal likewise yelled for his gear and for five of the men to mount up. Then he grabbed Toran's arm again, and spun him around to face him. Donal's concern for him was plain for Toran to see.

"Lad, this is a bad idea. I feel it in my bones. He hasna gotten this far abiding by the rules of combat. He willna start now. There's too much at stake—for him and for us."

"That may be, but it's all we've got at the moment. He has Aileana. I must get her back. We can end this today, or sit here until spring comes again."

"And ye think seven of us can do that."

"Aye. I think one of us can do that. Me. I think Colbridge rules by fear, and once he is gone, his men will give up. Aileana opened this door for us, whether she meant to or no'. Let's use the opportunity she's risked her life to give us."

Donal snorted. "She didna risk a thing for us. She risked herself for that man Colbridge strung up. And what do you think that means, laddie?"

"It means that she cares about her brother. And about us. We're her family now, too."

"I hope ye're right," Donal said, pulling on a mail shirt and accepting his arms from one of his men, then swinging up onto the horse that had been led to him.

Brodric MacAnalen ran up. "What are ye doin'?"

"We're going to end this. Colbridge offered to fight me—just me. Send someone to Angus and let him know what's happening. He'll want to help break up that camp once Colbridge's dead."

"Aye," Brodric agreed. "I'll go."

Toran donned his fighting gear then leapt onto his Banner and spoke again to Donal as he leaned down to take his weapons from another man. "If ye doubt me, stay here."

"Nay, I'll niver do that," Donal spat, insulted. "Where ye fight, I fight. Recall what happened to ye the last time ye tried it without me." With that barb thrown, he kicked his mount toward the gate.

Toran smiled grimly, saluted Brodric, and gathered the other riders with a look. As the wide doors of the inner gate swung open, a shiver ran down his back. Was he right to risk his life in this way? Risk his clan? Risk Aileana? Nay, he couldna let doubts unman him now. He'd fought harder battles than this and prevailed.

The outer gates swung apart, leaving the Aerie open and vulnerable. He reminded himself that it had never been taken in battle or in siege. Nor would it fall this day. His responsibility was to his clan, to eliminate the threat. He'd kill Colbridge, then scour the ragtag army from the glen and chase them back to the Lowlands, if that's what it took. He could not let thoughts of Aileana distract him from his duty. The price of failure was too dear. As he passed through the gates, he heard the watch captain shout for them to be closed and secured. He followed Donal down the long trail off the tor and onto the glen, then spurred his mount and passed him.

****

Toran heard the other riders pounding after him as he raced toward the invaders' camp. He counted heartbeats as he rode headlong across the glen. Too many. Too much time for Colbridge to ready an ambush. As Toran approached, he never took his eye off of his enemy. Colbridge stood in front, bloodied sword in hand, watching Toran's group arrive.

Toran reined Banner in well out of his enemy's reach and leapt to the ground, his sword swinging in a great arc in front of him, wrist supple, arm strong.

"Release them, Colbridge," he ordered as he strode forward.

Aileana stood off to the side near a crackling fire, struggling between her two captors. She managed to give one a hard kick in the knee, forcing him to dance away from her. Good lass. The man held on to her arm, but just barely, as Aileana nearly twisted out of his grasp. The other eyed her warily and kept as far from her as his grip would allow.

"Them?" Colbridge taunted. "You demand not just the girl but the cripple, too?"

Ranald still hung by his arms, conscious, Toran

saw, and glaring at Colbridge. Rivulets of blood from fresh cuts mixed with sweat and streaked over the large bruises that covered his torso and face. Toran wondered that he was still alive. Aileana must have stolen a few minutes with him before they were caught. But at the rate he was bleeding, he wouldn't last long.

Colbridge laughed and swung his blade at Toran's neck. Toran ducked and thrust his own blade up to parry. As the two squared off, a large circle formed around them, some of Colbridge's men, including those holding Aileana, on one side, Toran's men on the other. The bonfire separated the two groups on one side, a gap on the other.

Toran circled to the left, his blade flashing in the early morning light. Colbridge kept his sword in front of him, watching Toran closely. Then he lunged. Toran raised his blade to parry, and pushed Colbridge backward as their blades slid along each other until the hilts locked together. They were face to face, breath to breath. Toran swung his empty fist and knocked Colbridge sideways, breaking their swords apart. He swung, but his target rolled out of danger.

"Aye, the lass and her assistant, both," Toran kept moving, giving Colbridge little time to regain his feet, forcing him to twist and turn to defend against him. Toran's blade never wavered. Neither did Colbridge's.

"Nay, I won't release them," Colbridge answered. "They're mine, to do with as I wish. Spoils of war, aye?"

Toran grimaced, hearing his own words thrown back at him. "Not after ye're dead," he challenged.

"I'm not the one who'll die here today," Colbridge snarled confidently as he pulled a dirk from his belt with his left hand. It was a move calculated to intimidate his opponent, but thanks to Donal's training, Toran remained unimpressed.

So, Toran thought, *we'll do this the hard way.* But easy or hard, Colbridge would not see the sun set.

Now facing Toran with two blades, Colbridge leapt forward and slashed, forcing Toran to duck sideways and step back or risk being sliced in his sword arm.

Toran parried and thrust between Colbridge's blades while reaching for the dirk at his own belt. Two could indeed play this game. They would see whose strength failed first. Toran was gratified by a fleeting look of consternation on his opponent's face, quickly controlled. Colbridge clearly did not expect to face an adversary who could fight one-handed with a longsword. He had to be concerned that his younger, stronger opponent would outlast him.

Colbridge danced back and Toran pressed forward, forcing him off his balance. Just as Toran thought Colbridge might fall, he twisted and leapt to the side, then squared off again against Toran's blades.

"Well played," Colbridge snarled, then laughed. "But not well enough." He thrust, feinting with his claymore as he turned to bring his dirk in close. He sliced at Toran's face with it. Toran blocked him with his dirk, then swung hard with his claymore and connected, but with the flat of its blade, knocking Colbridge back instead of cutting him in half. *That blow should have at least knocked the wind out of him, if it hadn't cracked some ribs,* Toran thought. Colbridge laughed, but not nearly as heartily as before, and made space between them, breathing hard.

As they fought, they moved in an outward spiral.

Toran realized that Colbridge was trying to maneuver him so that his back would be to Colbridge's men by the time they reached the outer edge of the circle. Aye. Donal had said it. Colbridge would not fight fair. If he managed to back Toran into his men, one of them could easily run Toran through while he fought their leader.

He risked a glance at Donal, saw his eyes narrow on Colbridge, then sweep quickly across the men arrayed on the other side of the circle, and Toran knew he was gauging the effectiveness of Colbridge's strategy. Aye, Donal had seen through it, too, but would wait for Toran to signal before entering the fray. Nay. One of them would fight fair, Toran vowed. Instead of continuing to dance to Colbridge's tune, Toran feinted and reversed course, wrecking the pattern and forcing Colbridge to back up.

Toran fought on, knowing that to lose this fight was to lose everything he held dear. His life would be the least of it. His clan would fall to Colbridge's army, the Aerie would become a stronghold for the invader, and Aileana…nay, he had to forget her for now. Focus on the man who challenged him.

Suddenly, Colbridge stumbled, and Toran saw his chance. He moved in closer to his panting opponent and thrust toward Colbridge's chest. But Colbridge rolled out of the way, came up swinging, and knocked Toran's sword out of his hand. Left with only his dirk against both of Colbridge's weapons, Toran knew he was in trouble.

****

Alieana gasped as Colbridge knocked Toran's sword from his hand. It ended up several feet away after tumbling hilt over point, but Toran never took his gaze off of Colbridge's. He watched, Aileana reasoned, for any sign that might give away his opponent's next move. But with only his dirk against the longer blade of Colbridge's sword, it would be difficult to defend against Colbridge's attack, even if he saw it coming.

Aileana feared for Toran's life. He could not defend against the longer blade with only a short dirk. Colbridge kept thrusting with his longsword, forcing Toran to back up toward the bonfire, getting between Toran and his weapon on the ground. Toran feinted to the side, but Colbridge countered with a sweep of his blade, blocking Toran from getting around him. Toran was running out of room to move. He had to be getting singed by the heat of the blaze at his back and Colbridge was effectively keeping him from retrieving his sword. The time had come to use her talents.

But would it work? She needed to control both of the men holding her. And she'd never done this with more than one person at a time.

Still held between two of Colbridge's men, Aileana used their grip on her arms to link to one, then the other. Quietly, but with the power of her Voice, she ordered them to release her, not knowing if her Talent would affect them both or fail to affect either one. When they let go of her, Aileana wanted to cheer.

Colbridge had succeeded forcing Toran closer to his men, but rather than one of them running Toran through, as Aileana suspected he had planned, she had a surprise for him. She stepped close behind the circle of men surrounding the fighters and touched one of her former captors. Before he could react, she ordered him to draw his sword and toss it to Toran, then remain still.

The man complied, pulling his blade out too slowly

for Aileana's fractured patience, but then tossing it quickly at Toran's feet. Colbridge's shock at the apparent defection slowed him down and gave Toran time to duck toward the blade, but not to retrieve it. Instead of being able to come up swinging Toran had to scramble to keep moving sideways, away from the fire and from Colbridge's weapons. This took him farther around the circle, away from Aileana. So she ran, and moved ahead of the path Toran was on, to grip the hand of another of Colbridge's men.

She ordered him to do the same: pull his weapon and toss it to Toran and not interfere. When he did, Colbridge stopped, shocked at the second defection. Aileana moved farther on, careful to stay behind the circle of onlookers so she would be invisible to Colbridge, and had a third man throw his sword onto the ground. Toran had a time to take advantage of Colbridge's shock to pick up the second blade, then back up, tuck his dirk back into his belt, and pick up the third sword.

Aileana released the breath she'd been holding. She'd been fearful that Colbridge would take advantage of Toran's attempt to retrieve one of the blades. Or would be able to force him away from both of them, so that Toran had to continue to fight him with only his dirk. But Toran had succeeded in using the chance Colbridge's men had unwittingly given him and rearmed. Colbridge stared for another second at the men around him whom he thought supported him, then shook himself and faced Toran again. But the sight of Toran now holding two swords clearly gave Colbridge pause. Toran, for that matter, appeared a little nonplussed by the defections that aided him, but he kept his gaze on Colbridge, giving the man a fair chance to resume the fight.

With Toran rearmed—doubly armed—with his borrowed broadswords, Aileana was satisfied she was free to tend to Ranald. She pushed her way through a few of Colbridge's men, none of whom tried to restrain her, and went to Ranald, where he hung, now barely conscious, still bleeding. Frantic, she turned to some of the nearby men and begged them to cut Ranald down. No one moved, so Aileana grabbed the nearest and used her Voice to order him to release Ranald.

Ranald groaned as he was let down. "Leave me, Aileana. Let me die."

"No, Ranald. I won't do that. I can heal you."

"No, you can't. They'll stop you. Then they'll kill you, too."

"No. The Lathan laird, my husband, is fighting Colbridge. Toran will win. Then you'll be free to go. All of Colbridge's men will be free."

Ranald managed to shake his head. "Aileana, if they're still fighting, why are you here? Go to the Lathan. He may need you. If he can't defeat Colbridge, we'll all die."

"I must stay with you."

"No, you must go to your husband. Come back to me after he's won."

Aileana nodded, tears blurring her vision. Ranald was near death, yet he ordered her away. How could she leave him? And yet, he was right. If Toran needed her help to defeat Colbridge, then that was where she must be.

"I'll be back soon," she told Ranald, and gripped his hand. He tried to pull it away, as if he feared she would take time to heal the worst of his injuries, but she contented herself with squeezing his hand, then gained her feet. One of Colbridge's warriors who had watched her conversation with Ranald, was nearby. She touched his hand and told him to guard Ranald, and to let no one else harm him. He nodded and took up position next to the injured man.

With Ranald being watched, she ran back to the circle of men bordering the field where Colbridge and Toran fought. They were still at it. Neither one appeared to have inflicted any major injuries on his opponent. But both were moving more slowly, reacting less quickly, breathing harder. And both still looked fiercely determined. Aileana's breath caught with each clang of their swords. How Toran wielded two broadswords was more than she could imagine. But wield them, he did. If his show of strength was meant to intimidate Colbridge, it was working. The older man looked wary, an expression she had never seen him wear before.

Aileana glanced back in Ranald's direction, still torn between her need to support Toran and her need to heal Ranald. If only she could do both at the same time.

One of Toran's men shouted his name, and Aileana turned back in time to see Toran stumble to his knees, over the first blade that he'd been unable to pick up. No! Was her help going to get Toran killed? Aileana's heart leapt into her throat, choking back the cry that would have ripped her in two as she reached toward her husband. Colbridge rushed forward, dirk raised to strike, but Toran managed to raise one of his blades in defense.

Colbridge reached past Toran's blades to swipe at

his neck. Toran leaned away as Colbridge's momentum carried him to the ground on his belly. He rolled to his back and lifted his blade. But it was too little, too late. Toran ran him through the heart, pinning him to the turf with the blade of the sword borrowed from one of his own men. The fight was over.

Stunned silence greeted the end of the battle as Toran stood and pulled his weapon free, wiped the blood onto Colbridge's leathers, and turned to face Colbridge's men. None moved. Toran waited, and Aileana held her breath. She knew he was expecting a charge. Donal approached Toran, his men fanning out behind him, eyes on Colbridge's men, expressions puzzled. A few of the invaders stepped hesitantly forward, but the men Aileana had commanded remained in place and their stillness stopped the others.

Toran stepped forward, panting. He looked right and left, taking in all of the stunned faces lining the circle. Then he straightened and raised his voice. "Men," he called, "the fight is over. Colbridge is dead, and his army with him. Drop yer weapons, now, and ye can go free."

At that announcement, a few swords fell to the ground. Then more. Then the clatter became deafening for a moment. Then silence reigned again.

Aileana began breathing again. It was over.

Nodding, Toran continued speaking. "Ye may return home in peace. Anyone who has no home to return to, anyone who wishes to stay, is welcome to settle here, become part of one of the clans in this area, but only if ye are willing to live in peace. Colbridge's conquest stops here."

Chapter Eighteen

Aileana fought through the crowd, the stunned faces of Colbridge's men barely registering as she ran for Ranald. She could not linger to see how the men reacted to the demise of their leader. She cared now for only two things: Toran's safety, and Ranald's welfare. Toran's wounds were minor and did not need her care. He had Donal and the others at his back should more fighting break out. And without a doubt, the contest had been watched with great interest from the walls of the Aerie and more of Toran's men were already on their way to help deal with the dissolution of the invading army.

No, Toran did not need her. But Ranald did.

"Stand aside," she cried as she shoved past men twice her size. "Let me by!"

It must have been an indication of their stunned reaction to their new circumstances that none stood in her way. No one tried to grab her or grope her as she passed. The fight seemed to have gone out of them. There were no sounds of conflict behind her—no clash of blades, no grunts of effort, and no screams of pain. Eerie silence smothered the camp. There only compliance with her frantic demands, dazed expressions, until finally voices broke the stillness here and there. Murmurs built, gaining strength, then a few cheers erupted. Aileana ignored them all. She'd take time to sort it out after she took care of her brother.

Ranald lay where she'd left him. The guard she'd posted still stood silently over him, frowning at anyone, including Aileana, who ventured too near to his charge. But she knew he would not interfere with her.

She dropped to her knees. Ranald lay deathly still on the cold, hard ground. She placed her hands on his chest. His breathing was shallow, and she could barely sense his heartbeat. A chill skittered through her.

Ranald had very little time. Death hovered so near that she feared attempting to heal him. The risk she contemplated exceeded any she'd taken so far. And she didn't know where to start. Damn him for forcing her away when she could have helped him! Stymied, she fought to find calm amidst her anger and despair at his foolishness and her poor judgement. She had sensed how badly he was injured. She should not have left his side!

The noise of the camp, the rumble of male voices, the brightening daylight, all faded away as she reached into Ranald's body to assess his most urgent needs. So much blood spilled where there should be none that his organs were bathed in it. His lungs were filling with it, and the fluid in his chest kept his heart from beating fully. That was a blessing in disguise, because with each beat, his internal wounds allowed even more of his life's blood to seep into his body where it didn't belong, and where it was doing harm.

Frantic now, she tried to heal the damaged organs that were leaking the most blood. She heard him groan and softly sigh, "No." But she kept on knitting tissue, draining fluids, trying to give his heart room to beat and his lungs space to breathe.

Her head was spinning, and she knew she could not continue at this pace, or even continue at all, much longer. But she still had so much to do. Ranald still lay dying, and what she had repaired so far was not enough to save him. She was making many things worse before she could make them better. Tears ran down her cheeks as she worked.

She dared not impose the healing sleep on him; she feared it would make him too quiet in his body and his spirit would give up and leave him. He still fought her, but he'd ceased moaning "no" as his condition worsened. Instead, his fingers twitched, or his head fell slowly to one side, then the other, with each touch of her fingers. If he could not speak, he still tried to make his wishes known. But she would not let him quit. She could not let him die.

"Toran won," she whispered, fighting her growing exhaustion, fighting to make him want to live. "Colbridge is dead. We're free."

Ranald didn't respond. There was no movement left in him, save for his shallow breathing and faint heartbeat.

"Do you hear me, Ranald? You're free. You can go where ever you wish." Aileana's view of Ranald grew spotted and grayed as she swayed above him. So much blood…too much…

Rough hands pulled her up, breaking her contact with Ranald.

"No!" she shouted, and flew into frenzy, fighting with the last dregs of her strength to return to her brother. But the hands that held her would not let her go, no matter how she fought. Recognition penetrated her panic. Toran. Toran held her. She knew his strength, his scent, his arms. His voice. It came to her finally that he was murmuring to her.

"Nay, Aileana. Ranald is gone. Ye did the best ye could. He's gone, Aileana. It's over."

"No!" she wailed. "Put me down. He still lives...I can save him."

"Nay, lass, ye canna. He breathes nay more."

Aileana fought to free herself, but Toran's grip held her up like an iron band away from the life she was trying to save.

"No, no, no. He lives! Let me go to him."

"Aileana, I canna. Ye'll kill yerself trying to bring back a dead man. He's gone. Colbridge killed him. There's nothing ye can do for him now."

Aileana stilled in Toran's arms and took a deep breath of the chill morning air, trying to clear the fog in her head and regain some vigor. Fighting Toran was sapping the last of her strength. Her nose filled with the sharp scent of Toran's sweat, the blood on her hands from Ranald, and the pitch of the nearby pines. None of them did much to revive her. When this was over, she knew she'd pay a price in her own recovery. It would be long and difficult, but she could not let Ranald go without a fight.

She knew she was too weak to be able to summon her Voice. She could not order Toran to release her. But if she feigned acceptance, perhaps he'd let her go. So she sighed and put her head on his shoulder. Toran eased his grip and held her gently, rubbing her back rather than restraining her.

And she bolted from his grasp and fell across Ranald. Sensing, touching, there a beat of his heart, a small movement of his chest. She tried to work faster, harder, deeper, her senses open wide, her Talent surging into his still body. But her strength was leaving her…too soon. Her Healing was not working! And just as quickly as she started, Toran's hands gripped her arms and pulled her up before she could pour all of herself into saving Ranald.

"Let him go, lass," Toran whispered as she all but swooned in his arms, tears running down her face in hopeless, angry torrents. "Ye did all ye could. He was too far gone. He wouldna want ye to take harm trying to save him." Toran's exhaustion made his voice gruff, yet he held Aileana in his arms as if he would never let her go.

Indeed, he would not. When Donal tried to take her, Toran only grasped her more tightly to his chest. "Leave her be," he told Donal sharply. "See to dismantling this camp. Provision any of the men who want to head south, and find places for the rest. I'll take Aileana back to the Aerie where she can recover."

****

"No!" The strength of Aileana's shout startled Toran into releasing her. She backed away from him, pale and shaking but eyes blazing. "No, I will not go with you. You killed him…I could have saved him."

"Nay, lass."

"Aye," she snarled, backing up, her gaze darting to Ranald as she moved, looking crazed. "You pulled me from him when I could have helped him. You killed him."

Toran stared, unmoving. This helpless rage revealed a facet of Aileana he had never seen before. He wasn't sure what to say, what to do, to calm her. Where had she found the strength for this sudden fury?

A moment ago, she had been all but limp in his arms. Now she seemed intent on blaming him for the evil that Colbridge had done. Her eyes were wild. Blood, Ranald's blood, streaked her dress and the hands she held up to ward him off.

"Lass," he cajoled, "have done. 'Tis over and ye need to go home to the Aerie and rest."

"Home? To the Aerie?"

"Aye, lass. I'll care for ye there. No' here in this rough camp."

"This rough camp...is my home. It has been for two years." She was shaking her head and backing away from him even while she shivered from cold and exhaustion. Toran took a step toward her.

"Stop!" she cried and backed up a few more paces. "Do not follow me."

"Lass," he began, but she shook her head again. Donal gripped his arm then.

"Let her be, Lathan," Donal advised quietly. "The lass is out of her mind over her kin."

"Nay," Toran answered, not daring to look away from Aileana. She'd stopped backing up and stood, shaking, staring at him with a wounded expression that nearly ripped his heart from his chest. "She's worn to the bone and doesna ken what she's doing or saying."

"I can hear you," Aileana spat with more anger than he thought her capable of, "and I know exactly what I'm doing and saying."

"Then ye ken I speak sense," Toran told her, signaling Donal to move away. "What ye tried to do was brave, lass, but it would have killed ye. I could no' allow that."

"Allow?" Her back suddenly straightened and her

frown grew more fierce. Toran had the feeling he was going to regret using that word. But he had spoken the truth and he had done what was needful to save her life.

"I couldna allow ye to sacrifice yerself, Aileana. I need ye. The clan needs ye."

"And Ranald needed me," she snarled, marching up to stand toe-to-toe with him, fury plain in the grim lines of her face even as her body shook with her anger and fatigue. "But you didn't trust me. Or you believed Colbridge's lies and thought that I was intent on saving a man I loved."

"Nay, Aileana…"

"Yes, you did. You knew we were never lovers…" her voice faltered and she swallowed. Toran was certain images of their lovemaking were flashing before her eyes, and their handfasting. "But he loved me. He was the last of my kin. I cared…enough to want to help him. No more than that. But it would have been enough."

Tears started afresh down her cheeks. It was all Toran could do not to lift his fingers and wipe the wetness from her skin, but he kenned that she would bat his hands away, which would be bad enough, or run from him, which would be worse. "And for that, you kept me from him. You let him die." Her words fell like stones at his feet. Her recriminations clawed at him. She believed them, that jealousy had guided his actions, not concern for her welfare.

"Aileana, I love ye, and ye love me. I couldna let ye die along with him, no' when I could prevent it. It is my place to protect ye."

"No," she said, backing away from him again. Toran wanted to reach out, but her cold expression stopped his hand. "That won't be a problem for you any longer."

Ice suddenly slid down Toran's back, from his neck to his buttocks. "What do ye mean, lass?"

"You made a promise to me."

"A promise?" Panic surged like beating wings in his belly. He knew the promise she meant. One he'd never wanted to make. One he damned himself now for ever uttering.

"You promised me that once Colbridge was dead, or gone, I could leave."

"If ye truly wished to…"

"Yes. And I do. I wish to leave. I'll go south with the men. Back to my village. Maybe some of the people I knew are still there. They'll take me in…"

"Lass," Toran choked, and couldn't believe his voice could break on a single word. But it had, and it had not affected Aileana at all. She still stared at him, determination replacing the fury that had inhabited her features only moments before. "Ye canna."

"Can't I? What? You won't allow it? After you promised? You'll hold me prisoner, then, while you let the rest of these men, who injured or killed some of yours—you'll let them leave. And force me to stay? What? As your healer? As your slave? What will it be, Toran?"

"Nay," Toran acknowleged, feeling like the only word left to him to utter was nay. Nay, he couldn't believe what she was saying to him. Nay, he couldn't let her leave. He loved her and needed her by his side. "Nay," he repeated and sighed. "I willna force ye."

"No, you can't. You may be a big, bad warrior, Laird Lathan, but you made me a promise. You can't go back on your word in front of all these men," she said, her hands sweeping in a wide gesture to encompass the camp and the men milling around in it, "or they won't trust your word to them, will they? You want them to leave peacefully, don't you? You must let me leave peacefully, too."

"I dinna wish to force ye, Aileana. I wish for ye to stay with me. Ye made a promise, too, Aileana. We both did. Have ye forgotten so soon?"

"No, Toran. I haven't. But I cannot stay. You still don't trust my judgement, my Talent. You don't trust me."

"Please…Aileana…get some rest. Dinna leave. At least dinna leave without talking to me again."

"No. I will not speak to you again. I cannot forgive what you did here today. I cannot."

With that, she turned on her heel and started to walk away from him into the camp.

Toran stood, helpless to restrain her, without the words to call her back. Without the words to gain her forgiveness. Without the words to convince her that his actions had been for her benefit, not because of some petty jealousy or wounded pride. She said she could not forgive him. She was walking away from him, her shoulders straight, her braid a dark line down her back, her bloody fists clenched.

Then she disappeared into the chaos of the camp. He was alone, the only woman who cared about him gone from his life in pain and heartbreak and tears…just like his mother, and his childhood love, Fia. Now Aileana. Was he destined to be alone? Spurned or abandoned by the women who should have loved him? Toran's gaze swept the camp, but he barely noted the activity taking place, the Lathan clansmen who had come from the Aerie, and the MacAnalens who were guesting with them, except as movement and chaos. He couldn't focus on any single part of it, or any one person.

He felt isolated and dazed. Donal and the rest of his men had left him to deal with Aileana while they took care of the camp. He was vulnerable to any of Colbridge's men who might still hold a grudge. But he could not move, could not think.

He could only stand there, lost in the memory of when she'd told him that she loved him. She'd meant it, he was certain she had. How could she walk away from him after that? After all they'd shared? All they'd promised to each other? How could she leave the comfort and security of the Aerie, and a life with a man who loved her. For this rough camp? Or worse, for the dangers of the trail and the slim possibility of finding anything like the home she'd been taken from two years before?

Toran grimaced at the moisture gathering in his eyes.

Donal must have been right: she was spent, and out of her mind. So was he. She needed rest and food and drink, just as she had after healing Jamie. Perhaps even more than she had then. She needed care and comfort, not this crazy path she planned to take. She needed to come home to the Aerie, where he could care for her, love her, live his life with her.

But nay, she could not forgive him. Toran shook his head and blinked away the tears. She must. She was his wife. He would find her, cajole her, convince her. He could not live without her. He would not let her leave him, not like this.

****

Aileana kept her gaze straight ahead as she walked away from Toran. She dared look neither right nor left or she might turn back to look at him. And if she did, she'd be lost. All her anger, all her grief, would be wasted if she ran back to him. No, she must leave him. He did not trust her Talent, and she could not trust him to let her use it as she needed. Because of him, a good man, the last of her kin, and the closest thing she had to a friend in the last two years lay dead.

She passed through the camp like a ghost. No one seemed to notice her. Everyone was intent on their own business, gathering their belongings, packing up their meager provisions for the long march southward, finding traveling companions. The army was quickly breaking up into groups of three or four, the better to move unnoticed, she supposed, and less likely to look like the army that had passed through the area not long ago with such devastating results.

Colbridge was dead. There was nothing to hold them together. And nothing to hold her, either. She had loved Toran, handfasted with him, but without trust, she could not stay. Breaking her promise to him stung. She'd given her word, said she loved him. And she did. But he had lied when he said he loved her. He could not—not and treat her this way. Kill her brother, deny her control over her own Talent. No. He wanted to control her for his clan, that was all. And that was over.

The Healer's tent still stood. Of course it did. Colbridge would have had no reason to take it down. He intended to get her back. She passed by, knowing there was nothing within she needed.

Her sleeping tent was also still in place. That

surprised her. She thought her things would have been pilfered by now. She ducked into the entrance and gazed about her. Her pallet, her brush, her clothes, her few possessions lay where she'd left them. Perhaps Ranald had done her this service. Or Colbridge had threatened anyone who thought to disturb her things. Either way, she had little to gather, and if she was to find trustworthy traveling companions, little time in which to do it.

She bent to work, finding a rag and some water to clean Ranald's blood from her hands. Then she tucked her spare clothes into the sack that served as her pillow. It didn't take long. She donned her travel cloak and looked around. She despaired of leaving the pallet and tent behind, but she could not carry them, and since most of the horses had been stolen or run off during the raid that had freed Toran and the MacAnalens, like most of the others, she'd be traveling on foot.

She shouldered the sack and left the tent without a backward glance. A crowd had gathered around the cook fire, and she could see Cook and a few others dividing up what little food remained. She was surprised that no one was fighting over the scraps, but the small bundles were handed out without comment or difficulty. After each man received one, he moved aside. Aileana joined the queue and prayed that there would be something left when she got to the head of the line.

She hadn't been waiting long when she saw Cook notice her and start toward her. "Healer, take these," Cook told her, pressing several packages into her hands. "You cared well for me. Now I can return the favor. And there's more coming from that keep on the hill.

Godspeed."

"I…thank you, Cook," Aileana stuttered. "What about you?"

"Me? I'm staying here. There's nothing left for me in the Lowlands, and a keep like that," she said as she gestured toward the Aerie sitting high and proud on its tor, "can always use another cook in the kitchen." Cook squeezed her hand, then went back to her station.

Aileana glanced around her. No one seemed to object to her special treatment, so she stepped quietly out of line and tucked the food into her sack. She'd eat some of it as soon as she found someone to travel with. God, she was tired. She desperately needed food and drink and rest, not to set off on a long trail. She scanned the crowd for familiar faces but saw no one she recognized. She had to find someone she could trust. She dared not risk the trip alone, but feared that going with some of the rough soldiers could be even more dangerous, unless she could find someone that she had healed.

Just then she spotted one of the other healers who had taken care of the less seriously injured. She gave a sigh of relief as she started toward him. He stood with three others. She couldn't believe her luck.

"Healer," they greeted her.

"Are you leaving soon?" she asked without hesitation. "I seek companions for the trip south."

Galen, the eldest of the four, nodded. "We are, Healer, and would welcome your company as we go."

Exultation filled Aileana, and despite her weariness, she told him, "I am ready."

"As are we," Galen responded with a bow and gestured for her to preceed him. "Shall we, then?"

She nodded. As she started walking, the others fell in around her. No one took her arm, no one touched her, but they made it clear that anyone trying to get to her as they left the camp would have to go through them. Relief washed through Aileana, and brought with it the return of the fatigue that had swamped her when she'd lost Ranald. A tear slipped from her eye and left a damp trail down her cheek. She wished she had a chance to go back and say goodbye to him, but to turn around would mean losing her escort, and it would put her face to face with Toran. She could not bear to see the hurt in his eyes again. No, she'd chosen her path. Now she would walk it.

Chapter Nineteen

Aileana sat on a log next to the fire and pulled her cloak more closely around her shoulders. She could get warm on the front facing the fire, but her back still felt chilled, despite the heavy travel cloak.

She longed also for the warmth of Toran's arms around her, but she knew she was no more likely to feel that comfort again than she was to find herself magically transported to the luxurious depths of the bedcovers in her chamber in his fortress...the cozy chamber that she'd left behind the night she stole from the Aerie. That action had set her on this path, and she wondered if she had to do it all over again, what she would do. She had failed to save Ranald. In her despair, she had blamed Toran and run from him. But was he really to blame?

Tiny snowflakes drifted lazily down from the leaden sky. And her feet hurt. She didn't know how far they'd walked these past few days, but she knew that without some rest and warmth, she might not make it much further.

Not that her companions were any better off. They had carried what they could of warm clothes and provisions, but they, too, were tired and footsore. And hungry. The food that Cook had provided was long gone, and their skills as hunters were evidently vastly less accomplished than their skills as healers. This time of year, brambles yielded a few berries frozen on their stems that the birds had yet to find, but any wild apples had long since fallen or been nibbled away by the canny wildlife hereabouts.

Aileana was becoming convinced that they were lost.

Though she thought they tended generally southward, no one could keep to a straight course on the winding mountain paths. Heavy cloud cover hid the sun and made daylight flat, cold, and unhelpful. For all she knew, they could be circling back to Toran's glen, or miss it completely and wind their way further into the mountains. They had not found anything resembling a village, or even a simple croft, to shelter them and provide directions. Not even the remains of the MacAnalen village that Colbridge had razed. These Highland hills went on and on, green and brown, then white and sere with the dusting of snow that carried little moisture. The burns, as they called the streams here, ran cold and sluggish, some coated with a thin glaze of ice that melted away if any sunlight managed to find them.

On the trip, she had learned more about her traveling companions than she had in two years of traveling with the army. She had known that Galen was the most experienced healer among them. Edward was the next eldest. Paul and Clarence had been apprenticed to Edward when they were caught up in Colbridge's rampage through their village.

Now she had found out that Galen was stern and that Edward was only a few years past her own age and handsome enough if she cared to look, which she did not. No man could compare with Toran. The apprentices were younger, but wise beyond their years after experiencing the aftermath of Colbridge's battles. They all kept a polite distance from her while lending what support they could, except Edward, who had begun giving her long looks. She feared what that meant. Oh, she could put him off with her Voice, but if he was contemplating forcing her, then he surely thought they were doomed, and she was his last chance to know his release in a woman's body.

Aileana shivered and leaned closer to the fire. Already the apprentices had resorted to bedding down together for warmth. She expected she would receive a similar invitation soon from Edward. Or even Galen. If she was cold enough, she might break down and agree to it, even though she knew where it might lead.

She held her hands out to the fire and watched the light flicker over her ruddy and chapped fingers; her fingernails nearly blue with cold. It was dusk; the night stretched long ahead.

Suddenly Edward entered the circle of firelight, two mottled white hares clutched by the ears in his fist.

"Supper," he announced, pulling a knife and beginning to skin one of them. "Clarence, find some sticks. We'll roast these over the fire."

The young apprentice jumped up and began searching nearby, stooping to collect suitable deadfall for skewering their meal. Any stick that met their needs, he handed off to Paul, who stripped it and whittled a sharp point on one end with his knife. Soon, Edward finished his bloody work skinning, cleaning and halving their dinner. He punched the sticks through the meaty portions and handed one to each of them to hold over the fire, then cleaned the blood and gore from his hands with a clump of snow.

The scent of roasting meat soon wafted into Aileana's nose and made her mouth water. The hiss and pop of melting fat falling into the fire warmed her as much as the flames.

"How did you catch them?" she asked.

"Carefully," Edward replied sagely and winked at her. Then he reached into a pocket with his free hand and pulled forth a sling and several small stones.

"These two are the first I've seen or we would have eaten better before now."

"I'm glad you saw these, and were so careful with your throwing stones." She turned the rabbit haunch over to cook the other side. "Thank you."

"Indeed," Galen seconded. "Well done."

"You're all welcome," Edward answered. "Perhaps there will be more tomorrow, or a small deer."

"Might as well wish for a village to shelter us," Clarence muttered, "or the Regent's coach to carry us home."

"Or a horse or two," Paul said, continuing the wishful game Edward had unwittingly started, "to carry us farther and faster than we can go afoot."

"No use tormenting yourselves wishing for that which does not exist," Galen pronounced, effectively putting an end to conversation.

Aileana sighed and pulled her dinner away from the fire to test its readiness, then put it back to the flames again. Finally, the meat was cooked to her satisfaction and despite Galen's dour pronouncement, hot food gave her heart, warming her from the inside out. Far from replete, but no longer empty and cold, Aileana settled back and let her eyes drift closed to the sound of the men's conversation.

****

Toran cursed as he followed the trail. And cursed again, and again. Light snow had been falling all day. Darkness was upon him and still he kept on. Banner kept on, unflagging despite the miles he'd carried his master. Toran patted the big horse's neck, then cursed again. Why had he let Aileana go when he had her close to hand? He'd meant to talk to her, and even to carry her back to the Aerie against her will, if that is what it took to make her realize that was where she wanted to be, not wandering the Highlands on the threshold of winter with a band of refugees.

Instead, he'd lost his reason. Before he'd thought of the right words to say to her, she'd disappeared. And before he'd set out to search the camp for her, Kyle had found him. He'd carried an urgent summons from Donal. Some of Angus's men were intent on taking revenge on some of Colbridge's, and the laird was needed to remind them all of the truce he had declared before blood was shed. Or before Donal took matters into his own hands and silenced the lot of them. One thing led to another, and by the time he got free of the demands on his time, Aileana had left the camp—with the other healers, to his relief. He hoped she would be safe with them, at least until he caught up with her.

No one had been certain exactly which way they'd gone, just southward. Toran had packed enough provisions on Banner to last a few days and set out after them. He'd found several groups of Colbridge's men along the way, but none included Aileana. The longer he searched, the more he worried that she'd been attacked by her fellow travelers and left for dead. If that was the case, he might never find her.

He wished that he'd brought several men with him to expand the search. But where Aileana was concerned, he had no sense, and he'd taken off after her alone.

He contemplated stopping for the night just as a chill wind brought the faint scent of a fire and roasting meat. Where? He turned Banner upwind and rode slowly and silently. Finally through the trees he spotted the glow of a small campfire. He dismounted and led Banner a little closer, then left him in a clump of trees and approached the camp on foot.

One man sat tossing twigs and bits of wood into the fire, as he stared at the ground nearby. Toran studied the other four stretched out near the meager warmth, but they were too bundled up to see if one of them was the woman he sought. Toran decided to stay hidden and watch for a while. Something didn't feel right, but he didn't know what was causing that prickling in the hair at the back of his neck. Then the man at the fire stood and moved to the bundled-up figure closest to him. He knelt and pulled back the cloak covering the still form then lay down and pulled the cloak over both of them. When he started stroking and nuzzling his companion, Toran's hackles went up, but he stayed in place. When Aileana sat up suddenly and pushed the man who'd joined her away, Toran bit back an oath.

"Edward!" Toran heard her muffled cry. "What are you doing?"

"Claiming my reward," the man answered her, grabbing her hair and crushing her mouth under his own.

Toran could stand it no longer. He stepped forward to intervene, but stopped when he saw Aileana duck away from Edward's assault, grab his face with one hand and speak softly but sharply.

"Get away from me, Edward, and never touch me again!"

Toran's skin broke out in goosebumps. He froze where he stood, watching Aileana work her will on the bigger, stronger man. Edward's face took on a blankness that Toran recognized. He recalled wearing that slack expression on his face a time or two. The power of her order shimmered in the air around her. A ripple of chill ran down Toran's back. Oh, aye, he kenned this trick of hers. And now he kenned how she'd kept herself untouched both with Colbridge's army, and with Toran. And how she'd escaped the Aerie to go to Ranald. She'd used this power of hers to compel men to obey her. She'd used it on him—more than once, of that he had no doubt. Donal had been right to fear her Talents. Healing was not all she could do. There was more to his wife than it seemed. Much more.

Toran slipped back into the shadows and watched as Edward stood and moved back to his seat by the fire. He looked puzzled, and the glance he sent Aileana's way as she resettled herself for sleep was deeply troubled and confused.

Aileana, on the other hand, looked supremely calm and confident as she muttered, "No rabbit is worth this." Toran recognized that expression on her face as well. No wonder she had shown little fear in the camp, or even when Toran kidnapped her. Why had she allowed him to take her? She could have stopped him at any time. She could have ordered him to let her go and returned to the camp. Had she then truly wanted to get away from Colbridge's army?

Edward was back to tossing twigs into the fire. A sly smile lifted the corner of Toran's mouth. He suspected that Edward had no idea what had just happened, or even that he had tried to claim his "reward" from Aileana and been easily repulsed.

Having seen her powers at work, Toran realized that not only had Donal been right to suspect her, but Toran now had a decision to make. Should he bring her back to the Aerie? Or let her go on her way? He might be risking his clan, his home, everything he had fought Colbridge to save. But he would be risking Aileana, too. He loved her and had fought Colbridge to save her.

Should he wake her now, and carry her home with him? Or, now that he'd found her, should he follow for another day and see what other talents she displayed? He had never been more torn by a decision he had to make. But now that he understood more of her powers, his feelings for her were tempered with caution. He tried to focus on the good she had done, the men she had saved. But Donal's admonitions were also in his thoughts. Bringing her home right now was too great a risk, he decided. He'd stay close by to make sure she came to no harm, and to make sure she harmed no one else. Could he leave her if she showed she had more dangerous talents? Toran wanted to cry out his frustration. Instead, he went back to Banner and settled down for the night.

****

The snow had stopped during the night. They'd set out at first light, the warm meat of their dinner a fond memory in Aileana's belly, and with nothing to replace it. But their path seemed to trend more downhill than up, so Aileana allowed herself to hope they might be headed in the right direction after all, coming down out of the mountains. Her only regret was that she was leaving Toran and the life they might have had together farther and farther behind.

She missed Toran. As much as she hated to admit it, even to herself, she knew he had been right about Ranald. He'd been trying to protect her, to save her life when she was too distraught to care about her own safety. He'd been gentle with her in his anger, comforting to her even in his fear for her life. And had acted nobly against his own wishes when she'd demanded that he honor his first promise to her. She'd never forget the stricken look on his face as she turned away from him. She could sense his inner battle as she walked away. There was no mistaking how much he wanted to come after her, how he'd fought to allow her the freedom she demanded—the freedom he'd promised, even as she broke her promise to him.

But if she returned to him of her own free will, she was still free, was she not?

They were days away from the glen below the Aerie. If she turned back now, could she find it? Would she recognize any of the paths they'd taken? There had been trees and more trees. And occasionally wolves howling in the night. She'd be alone—truly alone. No food. No shelter. She'd be completely vulnerable to any storm, any predator, four-legged or two. But was that any worse than the danger she knew she faced if she continued on with these men?

Aileana slowed her pace while she debated,

allowing the other four to get well ahead of her. It was risky either way. She had only herself to blame for being here and for letting her anger and despair drive her away. Her fault for not listening to the man who loved her.

But would Toran welcome her back? That thought stopped her in her tracks. What if he would not? Or could not? His pride had to be wounded. The woman he'd wanted had turned her back on him in his moment of triumph. He'd bested Colbridge and broken up the army bent on destroying his clan and home. Would he lose the respect of his people if he took her back? She'd treated him worse than Coira ever had. She'd lied to him, then she'd told him she hated him and walked away from him. She'd broken the vow she'd made at their handfasting. She wouldn't blame him for barring the Aerie's gates against her.

No, he wouldn't welcome her back.

She started walking again, head down, wrapped in misery. She might as well take her chances with the four ahead of her. She'd had a chance at a home, at a man who loved her, at a family, and she'd thrown it all away.

The only path left to her went southward. Perhaps there she could find someone who would accept her as she was. Talented. Flawed. Heartbroken.

"Aileana!"

The voice barely penetrated the veil of misery she'd drawn around herself.

"Where are you going? This way!"

That made her look up. With a start, she realized that Galen was calling from behind her. Somehow she had turned around and was retracing her steps back to the Aerie.

"Aileana!"

Slowly, she looked around her. The sun rising over the shoulder of a mountain spilled a bright gold arrow across the snowy landscape, pointing back the way she had come. She was no seer and really didn't believe in signs, but this was too compelling to ignore.

Turning to face her traveling companions, who were now far below her, well down the path, she waved. "Go on without me. I've decided to go back. I left something there that I can't live without."

Galen started in her direction and she waved him off. "Go on. I'll be fine."

"You'll be alone. You won't survive it."

"Yes, I will. Safe journey, Galen." The other three were staring at her as if she'd lost her mind. Perhaps she had. Or perhaps she'd finally found it for the first time since Ranald's death. With a wave, she turned on her heel and started back up the path, a smile on her face for the first time in days.

Chapter Twenty

Toran couldn't believe what his eyes beheld. Aileana had turned around. She'd bidden goodbye to her fellow healers and started back up the path she'd just trodden. She was headed home! To the Aerie. To him...or where she thought he was. And her expression, remorse and stoic stillness, had been replaced by a smile that refused to leave her. She was alone in a strange place, her only kin dead, the man she loved far ahead of her for all she knew, and all hope of the home she might have had there lost. And yet, she looked happy with her decision. She'd told Galen that's she'd left something behind that she couldn't live without.

Him? Toran swore he would pray forever to any deities who could make that wish come true.

He flicked the reins. Banner carried him out of the cover of the trees. Toran had been following Aileana at a distance since they started down the trail this morning, but now that she'd turned back, he was ahead of her.

If she looked up the hill—when she looked up— she would see him. How would she react? With joy? Relief? Or anger? He forced himself to sit quietly in the saddle and wait for her notice. He wouldn't startle her by riding to her and sweeping her up into his arms, though he longed to do just that.

No, he had to let her come to him. That was the

only way he'd be sure that the woman who had walked away from him really did want to walk back into his arms.

He'd deal with her unexpected abilities another time. His Aileana would not harm him. He kenned that as clearly as he kenned that his heart was beginning to pound its way out of his chest as he watched her, waiting for her to see him. After he'd given it more consideration last night, he'd realized that the compulsions she'd laid on him had always been for her protection, or to save another person. She had never betrayed him or his clan. Perhaps Donal had been right to be cautious, but not to dismiss her out of hand.

Toran would bring her home, if she still wanted a home with him.

It was what he wanted, almost more than he could stand...to have her with him day and night, for the rest of his life. Almost, he flicked Banner's reins to start forward. Almost, he called out to her. But no. He held his peace, forcing himself to trust her, to allow her to decide her fate, and his.

What if she turned away from him? That was unthinkable. He could not let her leave him again. He would convince her, somehow. His words would not fail him today.

At that moment, Aileana saw him. There was no mistaking her surprise. She froze mid-step and stared for the space of several heartbeats. Her smile fled her face, replaced by a frown of doubt, even fear. Toran's heart sank to see her turmoil written on her face. Then she took a step, and another. Not back toward her traveling companions. Not off into the woods. Toward him. Step by deliberate step. Her gaze never left him.

Her eyes blazed in her face. Ah, angry then. He could deal with that.

"Have you been following me all this time?" she shouted.

"Nay. I only just found ye…"

"You haven't been riding in comfort while I walk my feet off, wondering where the next bit of food is going to come from?"

"I would never do that to ye, Aileana."

"Then why are you here?"

"I've been searching for ye since ye left the camp. I'm here to bring ye home, lass."

At that, a glimmer of tears shone in her eyes. "Have you?"

"Ye ken I never wanted ye to go."

"Aye."

"Ye ken I am a determined man."

"Oh! Aye."

"Ye ken that I want ye and love ye, wife, do ye no'?"

That brought the smile back to her face and Toran's heart lifted along with the corners of her sweet mouth.

"There's never been a doubt in my mind."

Toran dropped the reins and leaned over Banner's neck. "Then why did ye go?"

Aileana pursed her lips, then shrugged. "I was upset. I was wrong. I should never have left."

"Ye were wrong?"

"Aye. And you were right. Is that what you want to hear? Is that why you're making me stand here instead of pulling me up onto that great big horse and carrying me home?"

"Nay, lass. I only wish to be sure that's what ye want."

"I do, Toran."

He reached down for her hand and pulled her easily in front of him, wrapping his arms around her and holding her as tightly as he could without crushing the breath from her chest. "So do I, Aileana. So do I."

Toran picked up the reins and turned Banner around. "We've a day's hard ride ahead of us," he told her, "but nightfall will see us inside the walls of the Aerie. Safe and warm."

"And fed?"

"Aye. And loved."

"That's good then," Aileana said and relaxed into his embrace. Toran kicked Banner into a gallop. With any luck, they'd beat the sunset home.

****

Shouts went up as the guards on the Aerie's main gate spotted the Lathan riding up the ridge. Toran was glad to see the gates of home. It had been a long ride. Aileana slept in his arms for most of it, and whenever she awoke, she had little to say. He supposed she was exhausted from her journey. They'd stopped several times for necessities and to finish the last of his trail food, which allowed Banner some respite. Aileana had bestirred herself enough to stroke the big warhorse's nose, a liberty that Banner usually allowed only Toran, then she'd withdrawn back into herself. At the shouting, she woke from the latest doze, which had lasted for several hours, and straightened up within the circle of Toran's arms.

"We're home, lass. Time to get some food into ye."

"Food?" Aileana's sleepily mumbled response

sounded hopeful. Toran had to grin.

"Aye. All ye want. Then a bath, then back to bed with ye. The last few days have been hard for both of us."

"Harder for me," Aileana muttered, clearly miffed. "I had to walk."

"And whose fault was that?" Toran couldn't resist taunting. Aileana was saved from responding by the din that rose within the gates.

With a nod to the men holding wide the heavy oaken doors, they passed through and kept going until they reached the inner bailey. Stable boys ran to take Banner's lead. Toran spotted Jamie among those waiting for them, and gestured him over.

"Take Aileana," Toran told him. "Her feet are sore. And I want Senga take a look at her."

"Aye," Jamie answered with a wink at Aileana as Toran handed her into his arms.

"You're looking well," she told Jamie.

"Better, now that ye're returned, Healer," Jamie told her with a smile. "Come, let's get ye inside."

"Wait! Just hold on, ye two." Senga's command pierced the babble of voices greeting Toran as he dismounted. Her slight frame was headed straight for him and he had the whimsical thought, just for a moment, that she would knock him over, so great was her haste. Then she stopped in front of him, hands on hips, glaring up.

"Greetings, Healer."

"Greetings, my left foot. 'Tis about time ye brought her home," she scolded. Toran only raised an eyebrow in response. Then she turned on Jamie. "Set her down. Ailith near to cut off a finger in the kitchen when the news came that ye were on the path to the gates. I need Aileana's help. I wrapped the wound, but I don't know if I can stand the weepin' and the wailin' for much longer."

"I'd better help her," Aileana said, nudging Jamie's shoulder.

Without a word, he set her down. Once she'd gotten her feet firmly under her, Toran took her hand.

"Are ye able to do this?" he asked before she could walk away with Senga.

"Aye. It doesn't sound like much. I won't be long."

"I'll wait for ye in the Great Hall."

"With food and drink."

"Aye, all ye want."

With a smile, Aileana turned to go. But Senga wasn't quite done with Toran, it seemed. "How could ye let her leave, Laird?"

Toran only sighed. "I had to keep my word. She forced me into it."

"Hmmph," was all Senga said as she took Aileana's arm and led her into the keep. Toran heard her scolding Aileana as they left. "What did he mean, ye forced him into it? What a ridiculous notion! No one can force that great lunk to do anything he doesna wish to."

"It doesna matter how young or how old a woman is," Jamie said, a wide grin lighting his face as he watched them walk away, "they're all the same."

"Ach…let me think on that awhile. In the meantime, something to drink by the fire will do until Aileana joins us for a meal. And ye can fill me in on the latest developments."

"As to that," Jamie said as the entered the Great

Hall, "we've kept a lid on tempers, but it's been a challenge at times. I'll get some ale and join ye at the hearth."

Toran shrugged out of his travel cloak and laid it on the bench. Ah, warmth. He knew how Angus had felt that morning he'd made a run for the gate with a plea for Aileana's help. At least Toran had the benefit of Aileana's warmth snuggled against him all day. He shook his head and held his hands out toward the flames. He watched their flickering dance as he pondered. After the long search for Aileana, all the fears for her safety and the doubts about her feelings for him, it was sweeter than ever to be back home, by his hearth, in the company of kin and friends. Having her home with him, safe and well, wanting to be here with him...aye, that was the sweetest of all.

He had a sudden, overpowering urge to go to her and fold her in his arms. But nay, Senga needed her; Ailith needed her. He could wait until she finished with her magic to hold her again and care for her needs in all the ways he wished to. She must have food first, he reminded himself with a mirthless smile as he lowered himself into his usual chair. Then a bath and sleep. Then...perhaps then she would be ready for the closer welcome that he was eager to offer his handfasted bride.

Jamie returned from fetching their ale and handed him a cup.

"'Tis good to see ye back, Laird," Jamie said after they both had a taste.

A sigh of appreciation escaped Toran. "'Tis good to be home," he answered simply. After another sip, he nodded. "Tell me, then, what the challenges have been while I've been scouring the countryside for our wandering Healer."

"We've taken in the sick and the injured from the invaders' camp, over the objections of some of the MacAnalens who still need Senga's care. We've had to separate them, which means she's had to go back and forth between them. She's complained about the arrangement, but we both know it's better than having them at each other's throats. And even she admits they'll all get better faster if they dinna fash about having an enemy so close by. Now that Aileana's back, perhaps she can speed up the process. Senga will be happy to see the last of the lot of them."

"Is Angus one of them?"

"Nay. He's a good lad, that one, and a good laird, even if only in name. He's taken his able-bodied back to their village and begun the rebuilding. Some of ours and some of Colbridge's men volunteered to join him and lend their skills. I havena seen it for myself, but they're said to be making good progress. If the weather doesna turn bad, the lasses and the bairns should be able to return to their men and new homes in a few more weeks."

"That's good then."

"Aye. After they brought their sick and injured here, they took care of their dead, and refused any help in the doing of it. Angus wants the clan back together in their village to do a proper mourning before they hold a council to decide on the next laird. But I've no doubt he'll be chosen as soon as that's done."

"Where is Donal?"

"Still at the camp. It's taking more time to sort out the rest of Colbridge's men than we thought. We're finding places for those who want to join with us. But some don't want to stay, and they also don't want to make the trek south until spring. They've been more of a pain in the arse than the rest."

"Aye. Knowing they're bound to leave, we canna bring them into the Aerie if they aren't willing to join with us. 'Tis a matter of trust."

"And the MacAnalens' hospitality won't extend so far as to take them in for the rest of the winter, with good reason. After burying their dead, the MacAnalens would sooner see Colbridge's men freeze than offer them a warm pallet. Kyle is helping Donal sort it out, but they think we're going to have to build a temporary village to shelter them until the cold breaks."

Toran nodded and Jamie lapsed into silence. The rest of the news, good or bad, would wait.

Where was Aileana? Was Ailith's care taking so long? Or had the strain been too great for Aileana's exhausted state? Had she collapsed again? Nay, Senga woulda sent word.

More likely, she had finished her work and Senga was taking care of her before she allowed Aileana out of her sight. With a sigh, Toran stood.

"I'm going to check on Aileana's progress in the kitchen."

Jamie laughed. "Aye, ye'll likely have to pry the lass away from there, from the way she sounded when ye arrived. I gather she wasna eating well while she wandered from us."

Jamie's chuckles followed Toran down the hall to the kitchen. The sight that greeted him as he entered it nearly had him laughing, too, but instead, he schooled his face into a stern expression.

Senga stood over Aileana, looking fiercely determined. Aileana, catching sight of him, blanched and put the bread she was about to take a bite from down into the bowl of stew steaming fragrantly in front of her. Her guilty reaction had amused him. She had promised to eat with him in the Great Hall after all was said and done in here. But her obvious exhaustion stopped him. Senga noticed him then, marched over to stand toe-to-toe with him and direct her glare upward.

"Dinna be giving her that look, Laird. The lass has been hard used and needs food and rest. She hasna the strength to wait on ye."

"Healer Senga, I ken it." Toran offered his old healer the appropriate respect and saw her tension ease. "How is Ailith?"

"Well enough, now, Laird," Senga said after taking a step back. "Thanks be to Aileana, who used her last of her strength in the care of another."

"Nay, Senga," Aileana said then. "I'm fine, truly. Just a bit tired. Nothing a wee more sleep won't cure."

"A wee sleep, my bonny lass, willna do it," Senga replied, rounding on her. "Ye'll get a good night's rest tonight, in yer own bed, alone." She uttered the last word with a glare at Toran. "We'll feed ye up tomorrow and see how ye fare then. Now eat that stew before ye fall into it."

Aileana obediently picked up the bread she dropped and took a bite where the meaty broth had soaked into it. Toran's mouth watered at the sight and the scents, longing for Aileana set aside as hunger overtook him.

"Do ye think ye could find a bowl for me, too? I can eat here just as well as in the Hall."

Senga smiled at that. "Sit, Toran. I'll see ye fed." She stepped away to direct the cook's helper.

Toran sat across from Aileana, who paused in her chewing to raise an eyebrow at him.

"Eat, child," Senga's command rang across the kitchen and Aileana smiled and started chewing again.

"How are ye, lass? Truly?" Toran asked, reaching out to touch her hand where it rested on the table.

"Leave her be, Toran," Senga ordered, arriving with a steaming bowl of stew and a hunk of bread for him. "I suppose ye left yer ale in the Hall." At his nod, she turned and looked over her shoulder. "Callie, ale for the laird, if ye please." Then she looked back at her two charges, who were watching her with interest. "Well? Go to it, or I'll toss it to the hounds."

At that, both Toran and Aileana laughed, then bent to their supper.

****

Spring had come and gone and autumn waited, not far off. Aileana admired the late summer thistles in full bloom outside the window of their chamber. The Laird's chamber. Now Toran's and hers. Even now, it was hard to believe all that had happened to bring her here. Not so long ago, and yet so much had changed, and for the better.

The news had come that a priest would reach them in a few days. Perfect timing, so Toran had said. Even though their handfasting legitimated their offspring under clan custom and Scottish law, it would be better if the birth occurred after their joining in the eyes of the kirk. Their babe was due in a month, and Toran would not have it hidden under Aileana's wedding attire during the ceremony as if she still carried it, and then brought forth from beneath her skirts after the marriage vows were blessed, only then to be a legitimate heir in the kirk's reckoning.

So great was his impatience to claim her fully and formally as his lady that he planned for them to be married before the priest in the Aerie's small chapel on the very day that the Father arrived. And so Toran had posted the banns on the chapel door the last three Sundays. He told her he did not expect anyone to object, of course, not within their laird's hearing or that of anyone who would have related the dissent to him.

Since Aileana's generous treatment of her attacker, Coira, they had heard no further murmurs among the clan against her. Even Donal had become her devoted champion after helping to save her life in that confrontation, and having heard every word Aileana uttered granting grace to the poor woman who'd harmed her. But Toran was determined to take no chances. Toran had sent Coira back to her clan. Marriage in the kirk would silence any lingering doubts that any in the clan might harbor about Aileana having any ties to witchcraft.

In the meantime, everyone cosseted her, catering to her every whim. Chairs were pulled out for her and cushions placed before she could even think to take a seat. Instead of the regular meals habitual in the clan, anything she wished for was brought to her as quickly as it could be prepared.

Toran had wondered aloud how she would adjust once the bairn was born and all the special treatment was no longer necessary—not that it was now. But his people seemed to delight in caring for their lady, whom they had distrusted and in some cases, scorned, during her first weeks with the clan. They seemed determined to atone for their behavior, and Aileana allowed it with good grace, even when she told Toran privately that she longed for some peace and quiet and time to herself.

"Ye canna shut yerself in our chambers, lass," he told her now, as he had more than once. "The clan needs to see ye, and ye need to be among them. Never fear, once the bairn arrives, they'll settle down, and all their devotion will turn to the wean. Ye'll hardly gain any notice after that, I'll wager."

"Until I increase again?"

"Possibly."

"'Tis enough to make this babe an only child," Aileana said wearily.

"Nay, lass, never say that. We'll have many strong lads, aye, and lasses as beautiful as their mother."

"I know, Toran. I do. I'm just a bit overwhelmed by all the attention."

"Enjoy it while it lasts, then. We're a small clan, ye ken. The more bairns, the better, aye?"

"We'll talk about that in another month, my laird."

"At the verra least, there'll be more to enjoy in the getting of them, would ye no' agree?"

Aileana couldn't help but smile as her big, handsome husband did his best to cajole her. Truly, he spoiled her, as did the rest of the clan. Once they said their wedding vows before the priest, she would have a gracious plenty to confess…gluttony being the least of her sins since meeting Toran. It seemed as though everyone in the clan conspired never to let her go hungry again.

She consoled herself that she was eating for four. Her Talent would not be mistaken. And that bit of news she'd kept to herself, though she thought Senga suspected. And Elspie, who was remaining uncharacteristically silent on the subject. Aileana would have to tell Senga the truth when the time came so that she would know how many babies she had to catch, but she could be relied upon to keep her silence until all was done.

"Aye, love. Your sword will see plenty of use soon enough."

Toran's laughter gave her all the reward she needed.

So, her husband wanted many children for the clan? They'd gotten and good start, and wouldn't he be pleased when not one, nor two, but three babes made their appearance. She allowed herself a small, secret smile. She carried a lass and two brothers who would help their da protect his beautiful daughter and who would carry on the future of the clan. Toran would be pleased. And if the lass was a Healer like her mother, Aileana would be most pleased of all.

"Speaking of swords," he said when he'd caught his breath, "I do have one question about that day." A smile quirked up one corner of his mouth. "Events turned in my favor just as I needed them to. Swords started landing at my feet after Colbridge managed to knock mine from my hand. I think the defections undid him as much as the actual fight. Are ye going to confess how ye accomplished that?"

"Carefully, my love. With a touch," she said, lifting her fingertips to his lips, "and a few words. I moved quietly behind them while you fought, so that no one realized what I was doing until it was done."

"Ah, much as ye did to dissuade yer traveling

companion that night I found ye."

"You saw that?"

"Aye, and felt some kinship with the dazed expression the man wore after ye were done with him. Ye tried that trick on me more than once, I think."

Aileana blushed. "Aye, Toran, but only out of necessity."

"Such as the necessity of leaving the Aerie on a fool's errand?" Toran raised one eyebrow.

"I don't know how you do that, but I hope our...child inherits that adorable quirk of expression."

"Adorable, am I?

"You have your moments, my love."

She lowered her gaze from her beloved husband's face, and then looked back, suddenly sad to remember that day.

Toran reached for her. He knew she still grieved for Ranald.

"Yer brother is gone, Aileana, and ye must mourn him. But yer life is here now, with me, with the clan," Toran said, and put his big hand on her swollen belly, "and with our family. Colbridge's death ended that part of your life, forever."

Aileana nodded, and smiled up at her husband. "I am where I wish to be, and will be, always."

"And did ye also speak to the child that Coira threatened?"

"Aye, but softly, very softly."

"That's a useful talent, my love," Toran responded, "but never, ever, think to use it on me again. However," he continued, "when our child arrives...all of our children," he said and paused, grinning an evil smirk and quirking that eyebrow.

She gasped. "Who told?"

"Who do ye think?"

"Elspie, of course."

"Aye. So, when the bairns are of an age to need their mother's guidance," Toran continued with a canny grin, "ye have the laird's permission to use that talent at will. On them."

A word about the author...

Willa Blair lives with her own romantic hero, her wonderful husband, and a calico cat who, after walking on her keyboard, sits on her desk and demands that she write "Meorw, meorw, more."

Her stories are set in the Highlands of Scotland, home to some of her ancestors, in the difficult years after the 1513 Battle of Flodden Field. She explores the lives of her brave heroes and talented heroines as they fight to find and love each other, and to save their clans.

Thank you for purchasing
this publication of The Wild Rose Press, Inc.
For other wonderful stories of romance,
please visit our on-line bookstore at
www.thewildrosepress.com.

For questions or more information
contact us at
info@thewildrosepress.com.

The Wild Rose Press, Inc.
www.thewildrosepress.com

To visit with authors of
The Wild Rose Press, Inc.
join our yahoo loop at
http://groups.yahoo.com/group/thewildrosepress/